SUE FORTIN

Death at Applewick Schoolhouse

An Applewick Village Mystery Book

Copyright © 2022 by Sue Fortin

All rights reserved. No part of this publication may be reproduced, stored or transmitted in any form or by any means, electronic, mechanical, photocopying, recording, scanning, or otherwise without written permission from the publisher. It is illegal to copy this book, post it to a website, or distribute it by any other means without permission.

This novel is entirely a work of fiction. The names, characters and incidents portrayed in it are the work of the author's imagination. Any resemblance to actual persons, living or dead, events or localities is entirely coincidental.

Sue Fortin asserts the moral right to be identified as the author of this work.

Sue Fortin has no responsibility for the persistence or accuracy of URLs for external or third-party Internet Websites referred to in this publication and does not guarantee that any content on such Websites is, or will remain, accurate or appropriate.

First edition

ISBN: 9798842884131

This book was professionally typeset on Reedsy. Find out more at reedsy.com

Contents

Chapter 1	1
Chapter 2	3
Chapter 3	14
Chapter 4	26
Chapter 5	40
Chapter 6	53
Chapter 7	65
Chapter 8	75
Chapter 9	84
Chapter 10	91
Chapter 11	100
Chapter 12	109
Chapter 13	119
Chapter 14	129
Chapter 15	140
Chapter 16	149
Chapter 17	161
Chapter 18	170
Chapter 19	178
Chapter 20	186
Chapter 21	196
Chapter 22	206
Chapter 23	218
Chapter 24	225

Chapter 25	233
Chapter 26	244
Chapter 27	250
Chapter 28	259
Chapter 29	271
Acknowledgements	275
About the Author	277

Chapter 1

MAX

A Bump in the Night

Sitting at his desk in the study of the two-bedroom cottage that adjoined the old part of Applewick's village school, Max Bartholomew poured himself a Scotch and gulped it down in one. He looked at the clock on the mantelpiece over on the adjacent wall. It was nearly ten o'clock and he really should think about going to bed. It had been one of those days, with parent complaints, disruptive pupils and disgruntled staff.

He was already counting down the days on the calendar until half-term break at the end of May. Only a few weeks to go. Today he'd had to employ his tactic of fighting fire with fire on several occasions. In fact, the last few months had been pretty full-on, both at school and in his personal life.

He picked up the wad of twenty-pound notes that he had just been counting out and took it over to the bureau, where he slipped it into place alongside the other stacks of notes. He stroked his hand across the bundles, pleased not just with the amount in monetary terms but also with the gratifying repeat pattern of the Queen's face gazing back at him. With a nod of satisfaction he closed the drawer, then poured himself another drink as he thought of the scenario he was now faced with.

A crashing noise from the kitchen put a stop to his ruminations.

'What the hell?' It sounded like a cup breaking on the tiled kitchen floor. He frowned to himself, wondering if he'd left the window open and a gust of wind had blown something over. Highly improbable. He was just about to stride across the room when, from across the hallway, he heard the unmistakable sound of the kitchen door squeaking as it opened.

Max froze and listened intently. Call it sixth sense, but he knew he wasn't alone in the house. He could feel a real danger, which set his usually unflappable self on edge. He looked back at the fireplace and, hanging proudly to its side, the cricket bat he'd won at university for Batsman of the Year. He lifted the bat from its hook on the wall and crept towards the study door. The light in the hall was on so he dimmed the study light to give himself the advantage of seeing without being seen. His hand gripped the brass handle of the door and, in one swift movement, he yanked it open and raised the bat to shoulder height, ready to defend or attack.

Chapter 2

ESME

Trouble Afoot

Esme Fairfax-Murphy checked the kitchen clock and went out to the hallway to call up the stairs to her two children. 'Amelia! Dylan! Time to go. Make sure you've brushed your teeth properly!'

'As if they'd dare do otherwise,' said her husband, Conor, as she came back into the kitchen. He took a last slurp of his coffee and poured the remainder down the sink, then winked at Esme and gave her a peck on the cheek. 'Got to dash. We've the new DCI starting today. Don't want to make a bad impression.'

'Oh yes, good luck. Do you need to take an apple in for him?'

Conor shrugged on his jacket and straightened his tie. 'Ha-ha, very funny.'

Esme followed him down the hall and waved from the doorstep, as she always did, feeling a swell of pride for Conor. He'd worked damned hard to get into CID and, after a departmental reshuffle following the retirement of their DCI, had just been promoted to Detective Sergeant.

The thundering of feet as her ten-year-old twins hurtled down the stairs broke her thoughts. Turning back through the door, Esme reached for her keys and briefcase on the console table in the hallway. She checked her watch and was pleased to see that her children were exactly on time.

Esme readily admitted she was a creature of habit and liked to be organised. She put it down to being the eldest of three girls – and while her parents had worked hard expanding the family business, she'd been tasked with keeping her sisters, Bella and Isla, in check. She may be in her mid-thirties now, but somehow that mothering element had stayed with her. Indeed, it was so engrained in her nature that she doubted she'd ever stop being chief organiser of her sisters – or chief fusser, as Bella often dubbed her.

With Dylan and Amelia in the car, Esme pulled out of the driveway and headed into the village towards the local primary school. It wasn't so far away that they couldn't walk, but she needed the car today as she was visiting a gentleman in the neighbouring village of Applemere to discuss his funeral plan. Esme worked alongside her father at the family-owned funeral parlour, having joined the business straight out of school.

As she rounded the corner into Hook Lane she was greeted by the sight of several police cars and a van outside the schoolhouse. A uniformed officer stepped off the kerb and held his hand out for her to stop.

'I'm sorry, madam,' he began, then hesitated as he recognised her. 'Mrs Murphy.' In a nod to her father and the fact he'd not had any sons to carry on the family name, Esme had doubled up with her surname when she married. Conor hadn't, so it wasn't unusual for people to address Esme simply as Mrs

Murphy and she wasn't precious enough about it to correct anyone.

'Hello, Owen,' she replied, grateful she had a knack for names and had remembered Conor introducing the young officer to her at the recent Easter fête. Owen was hoping to get into CID, she recalled, but she assumed he hadn't quite made it yet. 'What's going on?'

'I'm afraid I can't say right now. We're just directing traffic away from the main entrance and asking all parents to park by the green and walk in.'

Esme looked over at where the police tape was strung across the gateway to the flint schoolhouse.

'Has there been a break-in?' chirped Amelia from the back seat.

'Or a murder?' added Dylan eagerly.

Esme had been a detective's wife for long enough to know when to ask questions and when not to. This occasion fell into the latter category, but as she took in the grave expression on Owen's face and the level of response to the incident, she knew something serious had happened. 'I do hope Mr Bartholomew is OK.'

The PC looked at the two children and back at Esme. 'So, if you wouldn't mind parking down by the green and walking back up, that would be much appreciated.'

Esme shot another glance towards the pathway of the schoolhouse and when she saw someone in a white coverall cross the hallway, she knew it must be bad news indeed. Slipping the car into gear and driving away, she really did have an uneasy feeling about it all.

Her fears weren't allayed when she dropped the children off. A group of mothers, most of whom she knew, were huddled together talking in hushed tones accompanied by rather concerned looks. Esme went over to them and, spotting her sister's friend Suzanne, nestled herself into the throng.

'What's happening? Does anyone know?' she asked.

'No one's saying anything,' replied Suzanne, adjusting the rolled-up yoga mat under her arm, 'but Mrs Bonham looked white as a sheet when she came out to ring the bell. Did you see her?'

'Only briefly. We ended up being a bit late from having to park down the road,' said Esme. Mrs Bonham was the school secretary and it was unusual for her to come out into the playground. 'Has anyone seen Mr Bartholomew?'

The mums shook their heads. 'We haven't seen any of the teachers at all,' said Suzanne. 'Mrs Bonham sent the kids in class by class.'

That wasn't quite as big a task as it sounded given that the village school comprised six classes in total but, even so, Esme understood the significance of it. 'Well, I hope he's all right. I've got to get to work but keep me posted if you hear anything.'

'You'll probably know before us,' called Suzanne over her shoulder as Esme headed out of the playground. The serious tone and grim expression on Suzanne's face told Esme she wasn't joking. Gosh, she hoped she wouldn't be the first to find out.

'Oh, Esme! What on earth's going on?' It was Bella, the middle Fairfax sister, some eight years Esme's junior. Bella was herding her young son, Jacob, in towards his reception class while at the same time grappling with her abundance of dark curls as she tamed them into a ponytail. 'Is Conor here?'

'I doubt it, he's only just set off for work,' replied Esme, ruffling her nephew's hair and then smoothing it back down.

CHAPTER 2

There was no need to comment about Bella being on the wrong side of nine o'clock – her sister hadn't inherited Esme's timekeeping skills and, in fact, was the complete opposite of Esme in how she organised and lived her life.

'Oh, wait. Speak of the devil. Isn't that Conor's car?'

Esme looked up the road and, sure enough, her husband's black BMW was pulling up outside the schoolhouse. He unfolded his six-foot frame from the car and greeted Owen with a nod. Esme couldn't help thinking how handsome Conor looked in his dark suit, his broad rugby-player's shoulders filling out the jacket. He turned his head and met her gaze, but there was no smile or wave of acknowledgement before he strode through the gate and up the path.

'That doesn't bode well,' said Esme. 'They wouldn't call Conor out if it was a burglary. Something serious has happened.'

'Bloody hell,' muttered Bella, having now deposited her son in his class. 'It must be Max. God, I hope he's OK.'

Esme raised her eyebrows. 'Max, is it? Not Mr Bartholomew?'

Bella rolled her eyes and tutted at her sister. 'You're not the only one who gets to call him by his first name.'

'That's because I worked with him on the fund raiser for the new school gym last year.'

'And I'm on the PTA, remember. It's all very informal when we have our meetings. Keeps us on an equal footing with the staff.'

'How very liberal.' Esme laughed. 'Look, sweetie, I've got to go. I'm late as it is.'

'Me too.' Bella gave her sister a brief hug. 'I'll speak to you later. And do let me know if Max is OK, won't you?'

A few minutes later Esme pulled into the car park of the

former Wesleyan chapel where her father had operated his funeral-directing business for the last twenty years. The gravel crunched under her tyres as she manoeuvred the car into her parking bay, denoted by a granite plinth with her name engraved in off-white letters. To her left, Frank Fairfax's unoccupied bay was marked by an identical plinth with his name on. Esme was surprised her father wasn't there yet as he usually arrived at work by eight o'clock.

Locking her car, Esme went through the back door of the funeral parlour and flicked on the lights. She had long got used to being on her own in the building. Her younger sisters, Bella and Isla, found the idea less appealing – 'I don't know how you can sit in there, being the only living, breathing body,' Bella had more than once wondered. Esme was the most pragmatic of the siblings and laughed her sisters' fears away. 'I like the peace and quiet,' was her standard retort. 'After growing up with two noisy younger sisters, it's a nice change.'

Once in the office, Esme switched on the radio and set about making herself a cup of tea before settling in front of the computer to go through emails and check the diary for the day. It was relatively quiet, with just various generations of the Richards family coming in to pay their respects to Albert Richards, their great-grandfather, grandfather, father and brother. He had been born and bred in the village, where he remained all his life, and none of his family lived more than ten miles away. Esme made a note to check the Chapel of Rest was ready for them and that Albert, in his open casket, was looking his best. Being around dead people had long since stopped troubling her. She liked to think of them as sleeping, and often spoke to them as she went about her business.

The clock on the sideboard ticked away the seconds and, after finishing with the emails, Esme moved through to the Chapel of Rest.

'Good morning, Albert. It's only me. Hope you had a peaceful night.' She turned on the lights and adjusted the brightness to a comfortable level before ensuring the chairs were all clean and in order. 'Looks like everything is OK for your visitors. Let's have a look at you. Oh, yes, very nice. I'll be back a bit later to pop some soft music on.'

She closed the door and went back to the office, expecting her father to have arrived by now. The office, however, was empty. This was actually quite strange. Frank Fairfax was never late and Esme was sure that's where she'd inherited her OCD-like tendency for punctuality from. She picked up her mobile and checked for any missed calls or messages, but drew a blank.

Esme called her father's mobile number. After ringing several times, it went to voicemail and she left a message asking him to give her a call.

Rather than dwell on her father's unusual absence, Esme busied herself with checking the funeral arrangements for Albert and ensuring all the necessary jobs were correctly distributed amongst the staff. Fairfax Funeral Parlour had three other employees, who worked part time and between them prepared the bodies, bore the coffins and drove the hearse.

Another half-hour went by and Esme found herself increasingly concerned that she still hadn't heard from her father. She held back from calling her mother – Marion was a worrier by nature and over the years had 'suffered with her nerves', as she put it. Esme didn't want to bother her. She wondered whether her father had perhaps taken the car into the garage for a service but, checking the digital calendar on her desk, could find no mention of it.

Yet another thirty minutes crawled by and Esme had to admit she was now feeling rather anxious about her father's whereabouts. She'd phoned the local garage but was told that Frank had neither booked the car in nor called by with it to report a problem. So when Derek, one of the part-time employees, arrived, Esme told him she was nipping out for fifteen minutes and drove from the village to her parents' home – about two miles outside – to see whether her father had broken down or, God forbid, had an accident and was too injured to raise the alarm. Neither of those scenarios seemed to have played out, for which Esme was grateful; the thought of finding his car in a ditch had been buzzing around in her mind like an angry wasp.

As she drove back into the village, she called Bella on hands-free to check if their dad had stopped by her house.

'No, not seen him at all,' reported Bella. 'Have you tried Isla?' Their younger sister had moved back to the family home last year so she could earn some money to go travelling again, having already spent over twelve months backpacking.

'I'm just going to call her now.' She glanced at the digital clock display on the dashboard. 'She'll be taking her break in five minutes.'

'Keep me in the loop,' said Bella. 'I've got to go, I've got work today.'

'Oh yes, sorry, I forgot – what with all that's going on.'

'No news on what's happened at the school?'

'No, nothing,' said Esme. She pulled into her parking space. 'What a strange start to the week.'

'I'll call round after work,' said Bella. 'I've just got the vicar's house to clean today.'

CHAPTER 2

They said their goodbyes and Esme immediately set about phoning her youngest sister.

'Oh, hi, Isla, just a quickie. I'm trying to locate Dad. You haven't seen or heard from him at all?'

'Dad? No, I haven't,' replied Isla. 'What's up?'

Esme kept it brief but explained the morning's events. 'It's very odd. Dad's not usually so elusive.'

'That is strange. I don't know what to suggest.'

'You didn't see him last night or this morning?'

'Err ... no,' replied Isla, and after a moment's hesitation continued. 'When I got home I assumed everyone was in bed. And I didn't get up until late this morning, so I thought Dad had gone to work. Mum never said anything. Do you think something's happened?'

'I'm sure it's nothing,' said Esme, feeling the need to protect her youngest sister the most. 'It's probably a meeting that he forgot to write in the diary.'

'Yeah. Probably.'

Esme wasn't sure Isla sounded particularly convinced. She was just about to go inside when, to her surprise, Conor's car pulled up.

'Oh, Isla, I'd better go – Conor's here. I'll give you a ring later.'

'OK. I've got to get back to my class now. It's the over-seventies and they like their step-aerobics instructor to be punctual,' said Isla putting on an uppity voice. 'Mustn't keep the matriarchs of Lower Bury waiting.'

Esme slipped her phone into her bag and waited as Conor got out of his car. He gave her something resembling a smile but it was half-hearted and the seriousness in his eyes told a different story.

'What is it?' she said, almost in a whisper. 'What's happened?'

Conor put his hand on her arm. 'Let's go inside.'

Once in the office, he closed the door and looked for a long moment at her. Esme's mind was racing with all the possibilities but she didn't let herself venture down any of them further than the briefest of thoughts. She knew that whatever Conor was about to say, she wasn't going to like.

'Sit down, love,' said Conor, guiding her to the office chair.

'What's happened?' Esme fumbled with the chair before pulling it out and perching on it, her eyes never leaving her husband's.

'Max Bartholomew is dead. He was found in his study.'

'Oh no!' Esme's hand flew to her mouth. 'That's awful.'

'He was hit with a blunt object.'

Esme blinked hard as she took in the information. 'Murdered?'

'I'm afraid so.'

She studied her husband's face. There was something else. 'What aren't you telling me?' she asked slowly.

'Listen very carefully to what I'm about to say,' warned Conor. He walked around the desk and sat on the edge, taking his wife's hand. 'There's evidence to suggest that your father was the last person to see Mr Bartholomew alive.'

'Dad? The last person?' repeated Esme. 'When did Dad see him?'

'Last night. It's on the CCTV – your dad entering the house and then, about ten minutes later, leaving. I've just had a quick look at it over at the schoolhouse. It's definitely your dad. Forensics have given an unofficial time of death that puts him right there at the time.'

CHAPTER 2

'That doesn't mean anything,' blurted out Esme. This was all wrong. How could her father have been there? He would have been at home with her mother. And then, as the awfulness of the situation struck her, she realised Conor was speaking.

'Do you know where your dad is?' he was asking her. 'I can't get hold of him. No one seems to know where he is.'

Chapter 3

BELLA

Prime Suspect

'Esme, calm down a minute!' Bella abandoned the yellow duster on the oak sideboard she'd just been polishing at the reverend's house. 'Say that again, but this time slowly.'

'Max Bartholomew has been murdered. Conor just told me. But that's not the worst of it.'

'What?'

'Just listen, Bella.' Esme paused and Bella could hear her sister trying to control her breathing. For Esme to be so flustered, it must be bad.

'What's worse than that?' Bella asked hesitantly.

'They ... they're saying Dad was there last. That they've checked the CCTV and it shows Dad going in to see Max last night and then leaving.'

'Wait a minute ... that doesn't mean anything,' insisted Bella.

'No, but Dad hasn't been seen since. Mum didn't see him last night – she went to bed early with a headache and when

CHAPTER 3

she woke up this morning, Dad had already left. Or ... he didn't go home last night.'

'Bloody hell.'

'Exactly. Whether Dad went home is neither here nor there. The fact is, he's a person of interest to the police – someone they are keen to eliminate from their enquiries, but that's police talk for suspect.'

'And Conor told you all this?'

'Yes.'

'They're letting him continue with the investigation?' Bella didn't know much about police procedure but she did know from the masses of true-crime documentaries she often curled up with at night that there was a conflict of interest.

'For now, yes,' replied Esme. 'They have someone else overseeing it but they're short on manpower so they need Conor too – but they will, of course, be watching him like a hawk. He's going to have to be extra vigilant.'

'Why on earth would Dad have any reason to ...' Bella gulped. '... to kill Max Bartholomew?'

'That's exactly what I said.'

'What about Isla? Have you told her yet?'

'No. I wanted to speak to you first. How long are you going to be at the vicar's house?'

Bella checked the 1940s clock on the mantelpiece. 'Technically another thirty minutes but I can make it twenty if I get a shifty on. The vicar's over at Upper Bury this morning so he won't know I've nipped off early. I can make it up next time.'

'OK. That would be great. We can go and see Isla together and then we'll have to break the news to Mum. Conor said he'd hold off going to see her until lunchtime.'

Bella finished the call and tucked her phone back into her

pocket. Never had she dusted and polished the sitting room at the vicarage so fast. Holding the spray can in one hand and her duster in the other, she simultaneously sprayed and polished her way around the furniture. Vacuuming at record speed and only clonking the table leg once with the Hoover – fortunately leaving no tell-tale evidence – she had finished the room in five minutes.

The reverend's library received the same high-speed treatment, and less than twenty minutes later Bella was charging out of the door, hopping onto her push-bike and peddling like she was possessed down the gravel drive of the vicarage and out onto Church Lane. She took the short cut over the wooden footbridge that spanned the river and was travelling at such speed that when the path on the other side of the bridge opened out into a parking area, she was very nearly knocked off her bicycle. The green Morris Minor van swerved one way and Bella the other, whereupon the back wheel of her bike skidded out from underneath her. Somehow, she managed to regain control and hop off before she fell off.

'Bloody hell,' she gasped. She looked up and instantly recognised the restored vehicle – it belonged to Ned Shepherd, long-time friend and local gardener.

Ned jumped out of the van and ran over to her. 'Christ Almighty, Bella! Are you trying to get yourself killed?'

'Sorry,' muttered Bella, stepping back over the frame of her bike and settling her foot on the peddle. 'I'm in a rush.'

'You don't say.' Ned shook his head. 'I've no idea what's up with you Fairfaxes. One day it's your dad, the next day it's you – I dread to think which one of you lot I'm going to bump into next.'

'What?' Bella frowned at Ned.

'I'm going to have to look out for you lot,' continued Ned with a laugh.

'No. Stop. What did you say? You bumped into my dad? When was that?'

'Yesterday afternoon.' Ned looked concerned. 'He was coming out of the bank just as I was going in. He marched right out and bundled straight into me. Didn't even say sorry, just stormed off down the street. Not like your dad at all.'

Ned was right – it wasn't like her father to be rude. In fact, he was known for his calm and respectful manner; it kind of went with his job. It would be most unlike him to charge about like that. 'He didn't speak to you?'

'Nope. Don't worry about it, Bells. I'm sure it's nothing.' He gave her a reassuring smile. 'Hey, did you hear what's happened at the school?'

'Yes. Max Bartholomew – I can't believe it. Such a shock.'

'Yeah, I've just been in the shop. Rita told me. Terrible business. She said it's murder.'

The village grapevine was apparently working efficiently. 'That's what Esme told me. Did Rita say anything else?' asked Bella, wondering if her dad's name had been brought into the arena yet. Rita and Henry Samson owned Applewick Village Stores, and if anyone knew anything about anyone, it was Rita.

'No, just that Mrs Bonham hadn't heard from him all morning and when that new schoolteacher – what's his name ...?'

'Dan Starling,' supplied Bella. Mr Starling had come to Applewick Primary School at the beginning of the school year. He was single, in his late twenties, and had proved a hit with pupils and staff alike – not to mention a lot of the mums.

'Yeah, well, apparently Starling volunteered to go around to Mr Bartholomew's house and, through the window, saw him sprawled out on the floor. He broke a pane of glass to get in, thinking he could help him in some way, but it was too late.'

'Poor Dan,' said Bella. 'That must have been a shock for him.'

'I'd say. It was pretty messy, apparently. Lots of blood.'

'I'm glad Mrs Bonham didn't find him. She's a bit too old for frights like that.'

'By all accounts, Starling took control and kept a level head. He phoned the police and wouldn't let anyone go over to the schoolhouse.'

'Good thinking on his part,' replied Bella. 'Look, I'd better get on. I'll catch you later.'

'Yeah, sure. Now, mind how you go. Better late in this world than early in the next,' Ned called after her as she peddled away with one hand in the air, waving.

Bella smiled to herself. Ned was such a dear heart. She'd known him forever, both of them being local and attending the village school, hanging out in the same group of friends. Admittedly, that was a given in a small village like Applewick, where you didn't so much get to choose your friends as have to put up with the other kids – who subsequently became friends through lack of choice. Things had changed recently, though, with the explosion of new housing, and she supposed it was good to get some new blood in the village and breathe life back into a place that had practically been on its knees twenty years ago.

Cycling at a rather less frantic pace, Bella was soon turning into the driveway of the Fairfax Funeral Parlour. She leaned her bike rather haphazardly against the fence at the rear of the premises and rushed in through the door, bringing herself to a halt as she remembered the dignity she should afford the deceased clients and proceeding to walk rather more respectfully into Esme's office.

Her older sister immediately leaped up from her chair and gave her a hug.

'This is so awful,' said Bella, returning the hug. 'I can't believe that Dad's a suspect.'

'I know. I know.' Esme took a deep breath and pulled away from her sister. 'I'm sorry for phoning you like that, but I was in a state of shock. I've given myself a good talking to since then and have come to the conclusion that it really is a misunderstanding. Once they've spoken to Dad and he's explained what he's been doing, I'm sure it will all be sorted and they can get on with looking for the real killer.' She gave a shiver and although she was putting on a brave face, Bella wasn't particularly convinced. It was in Esme's nature to take on the mothering role, to always try to reassure her and Isla that everything was all right, and usually she did a good job of it. Today, however, there was a different feel in the air and it was unsettling, to say the least.

'Have you managed to get hold of Dad yet?' asked Bella, sitting down.

'Nope. Nothing. His phone is going straight to voicemail now. I've given up leaving messages.'

'I just saw Ned. He said he'd seen Dad yesterday afternoon and that he was in an awful mood. Do you know why that would have been?'

'Really?' asked Esme. 'Yesterday afternoon? Dad was here until about five o'clock, when he went home. He seemed OK to me.'

Bella shrugged. It was the least of their worries right now. 'I'm sure it's nothing.' She checked her watch. 'When does

Isla's aerobics class finish?'

'It should be finished already,' replied Esme. 'I did text her to say come straight here once she's done.'

Ten minutes later the three Fairfax sisters were congregated in the office, Esme having broken the news to Isla, who, in typical fashion, was taking everything in her stride.

'Oh, it's really just a silly misunderstanding,' she said, echoing Esme's words from earlier. 'You can't rely on those CCTV cameras, anyway. They're not exactly high definition. It might not even have been Dad. Honestly, I'm sure it will all be sorted by teatime.'

'Conor seemed pretty convinced it was Dad,' said Esme. 'He wouldn't have told me if he wasn't.'

'And with Dad going AWOL, it's not exactly helping his cause,' added Bella. 'Anyway, we need to get to Mum before the police do, and prewarn her.'

Isla let out a sigh. 'I honestly think all this is overdramatic and it's going to worry Mum for no reason.'

'Look,' said Bella, standing up. 'You don't have to come if you don't want to but Mum has a right to know. Sooner or later, it's going to get out that Dad was there.' She looked apologetically at Esme. 'And this isn't directed at Conor, but someone at the station will let slip – and you know what this village is like for gossip. Rita from the shop is already sharing the news. It will spread like wildfire and become so exaggerated that by the time it reaches Mum, Dad will have been depicted as some murdering axeman.'

'I still think it's all being blown out of proportion,' insisted Isla. 'It really must just be some kind of mix-up.'

While Bella felt irritated at her younger sister's lack of concern, she knew her well enough to suspect that under the surface she was paddling like mad, trying to keep a calm exterior. It was a Fairfax trait; they played their cards close to their chests. It was probably what made them very well suited to the funeral trade.

'Just come with us,' said Esme. 'It doesn't matter what we think – we need to be the ones to tell Mum and to be there for her if this isn't sorted out as easily or as quickly as we'd all like it to be.'

Isla relented. 'Sure, especially if it stops Bella ranting at me.'

'I was going to do nothing of the sort,' replied Bella indignantly and not wholly truthfully.

'Of course you weren't.' Isla slipped her arm through Bella's. 'Come on, then.'

Bella watched her mother's complexion go through all the shades of white as she took in what her daughters were telling her, and the implications.

'I don't understand,' she said at last. 'I don't know why your father would go around to Max's house in the dead of night.'

'You don't remember him coming home at all, do you?' probed Bella gently.

'No. I took one of my pills. I haven't been sleeping very well lately and had one of my headaches so I went to bed early and woke up late. When I didn't see your father this morning, I assumed he'd gone to work.'

'Did the bed look like he'd slept in it?' asked Bella, which earned her a glare from Esme. 'It's only what the police will ask.'

'I ... I thought he must have slept in the spare room,' replied Marion.

'I'll take a look,' said Bella. She nipped upstairs and poked her head around the door of the guest room, which used to be her bedroom. It was barely recognisable as her old room now that the walls had been painted in parchment cream – which, to Bella, looked like magnolia. The curtains that hung there now were a caramel colour, aka beige. Her mother had taken the whole neutral-palette theme fully on board. She cast her eye over to the bed, where the duvet cover was perfectly in place, with no sign of a single crease or ruffle. The pillow looked equally pristine, and it was pretty clear to Bella that unless her father had meticulously ironed the bedding when he got up, he hadn't slept in the spare room.

She returned to the others in the living room and gave a shake of her head.

'Oh, God!' cried her mother, putting her hand to her mouth. 'This is so unlike your father. Where's the phone? Let me call him.'

Just at that moment, the sound of the front door closing and footsteps on the wood flooring had Bella and the rest of the Fairfax women turning to look towards the hallway.

'Hello!' It was Frank Fairfax's voice. The living-room door opened and Bella's father filled the doorway. 'Oh, what's this – a meeting of the clan?' He smiled broadly at his family and then, taking in each of their faces, knitted his brows together. 'Everything OK? Esme, why aren't you at the office?'

Everyone began speaking at once as they jumped to their feet in unison and fired a barrage of questions at the new arrival. Frank took a step back and held his hands up in surrender. 'Whoa. Whoa. One at a time, girls, please.'

Esme became the unelected spokesperson of the group. 'We've been worried about you,' she said, and Bella was thankful her sister was taking the lead in this because she didn't imagine her own voice would sound quite so calm. 'You didn't show up at the office. Mum didn't know where you were. We've tried calling your phone, leaving messages.'

'Oh, darlings, I am sorry,' said Frank. 'I've been to see Aunt May.'

'Aunt May?' Bella couldn't help herself. 'Aunt May? At Great Midham?'

'Indeed, unless we have another Aunt May somewhere else,' replied Frank. 'I had a call from a neighbour to say Aunt May was unwell and although she was insisting she was OK, they were concerned.'

'You see, girls, there was a perfectly logical explanation,' said Marion, getting to her feet and going over to her husband. She kissed him on the cheek. 'But you should have told us, Frank. Something awful has happened in the village ...'

Again, it was down to Esme to break the news of the murder.

Frank looked stunned and sat down heavily in the armchair. 'Max is dead?' he said several times, almost to himself, as if trying to understand the words.

'That's not all,' said Bella. She looked to Esme.

Esme perched on the arm of the chair and held her dad's hand. 'Conor said he believes you were the last person to see Max Bartholomew alive and that he would need to interview you. He said you were there last night.'

'What?' Frank looked up at Esme. 'Why did he think that?'

Bella exchanged a look with her older sister and spoke up. 'There's CCTV footage.'

Frank swallowed hard and took a couple of deep breaths. 'I did see Max last night, but he was alive and kicking when I left him.'

Esme squeezed her dad's hand. 'Conor has to question

everyone who knew Max, and you seeing him last night doesn't mean anything,' she said, and although Bella, Isla and Marion echoed Esme's words, Bella was also sure everyone knew it might not be quite as straightforward as that.

The ticking of the clock filled the heavy silence in the room. 'Oh, gosh, is that the time?' said Bella, standing up. She bent down and kissed her mum on the cheek, then did the same to her father. 'School dinners start in ten minutes.'

'Do you need a lift?' asked Frank, and even though his words held his usual thoughtful tone, Bella could tell his mind was elsewhere.

'It's OK, Dad, I've got my bike. See you all later.' Whilst Bella was relieved her father was home, she couldn't shake off the uneasy feeling that all this wasn't simply going to go away.

Pushing her bike into the rack in the school playground, Bella headed over towards the canteen. A separate building from the school itself, the dinner hall was originally intended to be a temporary space but had been there for as long as Bella could remember. She could only imagine how many school dinners had been prepared in those kitchens over the years, and when at one time it looked as though the dinner service might be abolished, the village had got together and bid for the contract to continue to provide hot meals for the children. Bella had been a dinner lady there for the past year, since Jacob had started school.

As she rounded the corner, something made her look to her left towards the edge of the playground, where the commercial-size wheelie bins were kept. To her surprise, Dan Starling was standing there. He saw her a moment later and the guilty look that swamped his face stopped Bella from calling out a hello to him. She thought he was alone, but then Suzanne Edwards stepped out. Suzanne gave Bella a weak smile and, with Dan at her side, walked over towards Bella.

'You OK?' asked Bella.

'Yes. I was just having a moment,' explained Suzanne. 'Dan ... err, Mr Starling, was comforting me. I didn't want the kids to see me upset.'

'Oh, you poor thing,' said Bella, although she wasn't entirely convinced by what her friend was saying. Nevertheless, she offered Suzanne a hug. 'It's dreadful. Are you going to be OK, or do you want to go home?'

'No, I'm fine to do my dinner duty,' said Suzanne.

'Are you sure, Mrs Edwards?' queried Dan. He went to place a hand on Suzanne's arm but withdrew it before making contact.

'Yes, thank you.' With her head bowed, and dabbing at her eyes with a tissue she'd retrieved from her bag, Suzanne hurried into the dinner hall.

'I'm sure she'll be fine,' said Dan. He moved to leave but then hesitated. 'Maybe not say anything about ...' He waved his hand in the general direction of where he and Suzanne had been. 'Don't want to embarrass her or anything.'

'Yeah, sure,' replied Bella. She watched him head back towards the main building and found herself wanting to believe him but, at the same time, not quite able to.

Chapter 4

ISLA

Nothing Adds Up

It wasn't until the following day that the police contacted Frank Fairfax to ask if they could interview him and now Isla was sitting in the living room with her parents waiting for them to arrive when her eldest sister walked in.

'Bella's manning the office,' explained Esme as she planted herself on the sofa beside Isla.

'I bet she's loving that,' said Isla in an attempt to lighten the mood. She received a small smile from her sister as a reward.

'Oh, don't worry, I told Derek to make sure he was there too,' replied Esme. 'He's going to be present when Albert Richards' family come.'

'I thought they came yesterday.'

'Some of them did, but his sister and her family want to come today.'

'Who's that?' asked Frank, his mind clearly elsewhere.

'Just Albert Richards' family,' said Esme. 'Nothing to worry

CHAPTER 4

about.'

Isla had phoned her sister earlier that morning to say that although their dad had been trying to act as though nothing was bothering him, he'd prowled around the house the previous night, unable to settle for more than fifteen minutes at a time, and had even poured himself two fingers of Scotch – something he never did on a weekday. When Isla had got up that morning Frank was already out of bed, and – judging by the empty coffee pods in the bin – his intake of rather more caffeine than usual was notable.

A knock at the door brought a halt to Frank asking anything else about the funeral parlour. Isla jumped up first.

'Oh, Conor,' she said in surprise. 'I didn't expect they'd send you.'

'Hi, Isla,' said Conor, stepping over the threshold. 'For now, I'm being allowed to ride shotgun with my colleagues here. This is DS Lindsey Marsh.'

'Hello,' said the DS. She flashed her badge at Isla and smiled.

'Dad's in the living room,' said Isla, opening the door wide and then following them through. 'Can I get you a tea or coffee?' It seemed weird asking her brother-in-law if he wanted a drink under such formal circumstances. However, both he and the DS declined and Isla sensed this was probably going to be rather more official than she'd imagined.

'Did you want to go somewhere more private?' asked Conor after greeting his in-laws and introducing his colleague.

'Of course he doesn't,' said Esme and then apologised for answering for her father.

'I've got nothing to hide,' said Frank, puffing his chest out and sitting straighter in his chair.

'I'm sure you haven't,' said Conor. 'DS Marsh is going to

lead this. I'm just here to support and observe but I do have to remind everyone, I'm here in my capacity as a police officer.'

Isla resisted the urge to roll her eyes – she felt Conor was taking all this way too seriously. She wished he'd just get on with it, ask her dad the questions and then go. She glanced at Esme, who raised her eyebrows a fraction. It was amazing how one facial expression from her sister could convey so much. Isla took the hint and rearranged the expression on her own face to one that would make her appear more patient.

'So, Mr Fairfax, can you tell us how you know Max Bartholomew, please?' asked the DS as she opened her pocketbook.

'Max and I have known each other for years – since we were kids,' said Frank. 'We both grew up in the village, knocked around together. You don't have much choice in a village the size of Applewick.'

'You were good friends, then?' pressed the DS.

'I guess so. Not so much as we got older. Max went off to university and I went into the family business. He came back to teach at the school and then took on the headship. We see … I mean, saw, each other once a week at the pub.'

'That will be the pub here in the village?' queried the DS.

'Yes. The Horse and Plough.'

'When did you last see Max Bartholomew?'

Isla was aware that everyone in the room was looking intently at her father while they waited for his answer. She was sure they were all holding their breath, as she was. Frank glanced around at his family, swallowed, and if Isla hadn't been familiar with his body language, she wouldn't have noticed the slight tightening of his grip on his knees.

He cleared his throat. 'Last night. About nine o'clock, maybe a bit later. I went to his house.'

'And was that normal?'

'Not really. I needed to check something with him.'

'And that was ...?'

Isla couldn't imagine what her father had needed to check with the head teacher. She'd never known him to go around to the Old School House before, despite the longevity of his friendship with Mr Bartholomew.

'Max was planning a reunion to celebrate one hundred and fifty years of the school and it was going to be his send-off party too. He wanted me to help him compile a list of ex-pupils and staff.'

DS Marsh jotted Frank's explanation down in her notebook. Isla forced her expression to remain neutral as she tried and failed to recall her dad ever having mentioned this anniversary or a leaving party for Mr Bartholomew. She stole a look at her mother but found it impossible to read Marion's poker face.

'How long did you stay with Mr Bartholomew to discuss this?' DS Marsh looked up at Frank.

'I wasn't really paying much attention to the time. I reckon I was only there for about ten or fifteen minutes. Then I had a phone call about my aunt not being well.'

'And where did you go when you left the schoolhouse?'

'Home to tell my wife I was going to see my aunt, but Marion was asleep.'

'And you decided to go anyway, at that time of the night?'

'Yes. I was worried and didn't want to get there too late. The neighbour who phoned sounded very concerned.'

'So, just to confirm, you got a call at about nine fifteen,' said Marsh.

'Yes, about then.'

'And you went home to tell your wife.'

'That's right but, as I just said, she was asleep.'

'Mrs Fairfax, do you remember stirring or hearing your husband at all?' asked Marsh.

Isla felt sorry for her mother; this really wasn't the best thing for her nerves. Marion Fairfax didn't cope very well with stress. Her mental health had taken a battering ten years ago when the family had nearly lost the business and were up to their eyeballs in debt. Isla didn't remember too much about it, but she did have vivid memories of her mother crying a lot and spending whole days in bed. Marion had never really recovered from the stress of those financial difficulties, and the strain of coping now with the news of Max's death and all it entailed was already beginning to show.

'I had gone to bed. I had a headache ... I suffer from migraines,' replied Marion, looking apologetically at the DS. 'I didn't hear Frank come home as I'd taken one of my sleeping pills.'

'Thank you, Mrs Fairfax.' Then Marsh turned to Isla. 'It's Isla, isn't it?'

'Yes, that's right.'

'You live here with your parents?'

Isla nodded. 'Yes.'

'Were you here when your father came home and, if so, what time was it?'

'I was out last night. When I came home, I assumed Mum and Dad were in bed.'

'Did you notice your father's car on the drive?'

'No. He parks it in the garage. I got home and went straight to bed.'

'What time was that?'

CHAPTER 4

Isla hesitated. She really didn't want to say – it would only lead to having to admit where she had spent the night. 'I'm not sure,' she said.

'Roughly,' insisted Marsh.

Isla winced and dropped her gaze, not able to meet her parents' eyes. 'I stayed at a friend's house. I came home about six o'clock this morning.'

'What?' said Marion. 'Where were you?'

'Mum, let DS Marsh ask the questions,' said Esme.

'So, you didn't see either of your parents this morning?' asked Marsh.

'No,' replied Isla, wishing Conor or someone would move the bloody conversation on.

'Where were you this morning, Mr Fairfax?'

'I was still at my aunt's. She lives in Great Midham so I decided to stay the night in case she needed the doctor in the morning.'

'You stayed over without telling your family?'

'I didn't want to wake my wife. Like she said, she wasn't well.'

'And your daughter? I understand you work together.'

'I forgot.' Frank offered an apologetic look in Esme's direction.

'Can your aunt confirm you were with her last night and this morning?'

'Is that necessary?' interjected Conor, who up until that point had remained silent.

'Just covering all bases,' replied Marsh.

Conor hesitated but then gave a small nod. He turned to Frank. 'Any chance someone can corroborate that?'

'I doubt it. You know as well as I do, Aunt May has early

dementia. She probably doesn't even remember I was there.'

'What about the neighbour who called you?' suggested Conor.

'Ah, there's the rub,' said Frank. 'I don't really know who called me. I forgot to ask for their name.'

'They must have had your number, though,' said DS Marsh.

'Probably got it from the emergency contact numbers pinned by my aunt's telephone.'

'Have you got your phone so we can see what number called you? We can work it backwards that way.' It was obvious to Isla that Marsh wasn't going to let it go.

'Well, normally I would be able to look at my call history,' said Frank, 'but, you see, I managed to lose my phone somehow. I've no idea where. I didn't realise until I was about to leave my aunt's. I stopped at the services on the way up there – I could've lost it then.'

A tension-filled silence spread through the room and was finally broken by DS Marsh. 'Hmm. That's inconvenient, but not the end of the world. We can get a copy of your phone records if we need it.'

'Why do you need it?' asked Esme. 'You're making my father sound like he's a prime suspect.' She shrugged off the placating hand Conor placed on her arm. 'Don't. Honestly, I'm sitting here listening to you question my father about his whereabouts, asking him for alibis and phone records. He's done nothing wrong. You should be out there looking for the real person that killed Max Bartholomew.'

'Esme, please,' said Conor. 'We have to do our job.'

'Well, do it properly!' Esme retorted.

Isla was slightly taken aback by her sister's outburst. Esme usually held it together very well. She wasn't flustered by much, so it was a surprise to hear her sounding so frustrated.

'Have you got any more questions?' asked Isla, hoping to defuse the tension and get this all over with as soon as possible.

'As far as you are aware, had Max Bartholomew fallen out with anyone recently?' asked Marsh. 'Mr Fairfax, you were friends with him. Had he confided in you about anything?'

'No. Nothing,' replied Frank. 'He sometimes moaned about work – you know, cutbacks to education, parents or children who had been particularly difficult, but he never named names. There's nothing I can think of at all.'

Isla was relieved when Marsh wrapped up the questioning, thanking them for their co-operation and asking them to let her know if they remembered anything after she'd gone – pretty standard stuff, and hopefully that would be the end of it as far as her father being a suspect was concerned. But as Isla closed the door on them, she knew she'd have her own cross-examination now from her mother. Sure enough, no sooner had she stepped back into the living room than her mother started questioning her.

'Where were you last night? Why didn't you come home? You should have told me. What if I'd woken up and couldn't find you?'

'It's all right, love,' said Frank. 'Don't get yourself upset.'

'Sorry, Mum,' said Isla. 'I didn't realise what the time was. I did text Dad but I guess he'd lost his phone by then.'

'Let's not worry about that now,' said Frank.

'I'll make us all a cup of tea,' Isla suggested, taking the opportunity to escape from her mother. As she waited for the kettle to boil, she was joined in the kitchen by Esme.

'So, where were you last night?' her sister asked, giving Isla a playful nudge with her shoulder. 'Who's the lucky guy?'

'No one important.' Isla tried to contain the grin that was breaking free with little success.

'Oh, I think I know you better than you realise,' said Esme. 'Look at you, you're beaming like the cat that got the cream. Come on, who is he?'

'You mustn't say anything to anyone. Promise?'

'Guide's honour,' said Esme, making the international promise sign with her three fingers.

'It was Dan Starling.'

'Dan Starling!'

'Shh, keep your voice down. Yes, Dan Starling. The teacher.'

'Wow. I wasn't expecting you to say it was him.'

Isla poured the now-boiled water into the teapot her mother always insisted they use. 'Well, there's not exactly a wide choice in the village – and besides, he's really nice.'

'Please tell me it wasn't a one-night stand.'

'Now you're sounding like a mother rather than a sister,' said Isla.

'You've not mentioned him before.'

'No, well, I see him in the pub when I'm working. He comes in a few times over the weekend and usually chats to me at the bar when it's not busy. He asked me if I wanted to go over to Applemere – that's where he lives – and compare pubs.'

'And you did.'

'Yes. I did. Look, Esme, I am a grown woman. I'm twenty-three. I spent three years away at uni and another year travelling around the world. I think I can handle going over to Applemere and staying the night with a man. Anyway, just for the record, nothing happened. He was the perfect gentleman and the only reason I didn't come home was because we'd both had a drink and fell asleep on the sofa.'

Esme eyed her sister. 'Really?'

'Yes. Really. Anyway, don't be worrying.'

'Yeah, sorry, I know. Ignore me.' Esme smiled. 'As long as he's good to you and makes you happy then that's all that matters.'

'I don't want it to be common knowledge, though. I don't even know if anything will happen. Maybe he just didn't fancy me.'

'Oh, stop that. You're gorgeous. How could he not?' Esme gave her sister a hug. 'Right, let's get this tea sorted.'

Isla spent the rest of the day at home with her mother while her father went into work with Esme, adamant that it was business as usual. Isla could tell her mother's anxiety levels were on the rise as Marion spent nearly two hours cleaning the kitchen from top to bottom with copious amounts of diluted bleach. By the time she had finished, the whole house smelt like a swimming pool.

'Why don't you try to have a rest?' suggested Isla. 'We could sit in the garden.'

'Oh, I don't think I could sit still,' replied Marion. 'Not with all this going on. I need to keep busy.'

'Mum, please. There's nothing to worry about. We all know Dad didn't do anything, it's just unfortunate that he was the last person to see Mr Bartholomew alive. They will be asking lots of other people questions too.'

'And going off to see his Aunt May like that.' Marion refolded the tea towels that she'd already folded and placed on the hook moments earlier.

'Come on, Mum,' said Isla, slipping her arm through her mother's and guiding her out towards the living room. 'I know you don't want to, but please just sit and rest for a while. You'll end up giving yourself another headache at this rate.'

Isla put on the radio, tuning it to Radio 4, and helped her mum get comfortable on the sofa, then she sat with her, just holding her hand as they listened to the music. Eventually Marion dozed off and Isla stayed put, not daring to move in case she disturbed her, until it was five thirty and her father arrived home.

'I've brought fish and chips,' said Frank, holding a white carrier bag aloft as the smell of warm salt and vinegar filled the room.

Isla quickly ate hers before having to get ready for her evening shift at the pub, and she left promising her parents she'd be straight home after finishing work.

Tuesday night was Pool League Night for the local pubs and this week the Horse and Plough was playing away to the Ship and Anchor in Applemere, so Isla was a little surprised to see Dan Starling sitting in the corner with a pint when she arrived. He looked over at her, smiled and winked. Isla returned the smile and could feel a small flush of heat rise to her face as she acknowledged the flutter of excitement in her stomach, but was distracted from her thoughts when a customer came to the bar.

'Hello, Henry. What can I get you?' asked Isla. 'The usual?'

'Yes, thanks.' Henry Samson rested his forearms on the bar.

'Been a busy day at the shop?' she asked, making polite conversation.

'It has, actually. Rita went to the wholesalers today so I've been on my own,' replied Henry. 'I hear the police paid your dad a visit.'

Isla stiffened at the comment. 'And I expect they'll be paying

CHAPTER 4

lots of people visits.' She pulled the pump down on the bitter.

'Won't be knocking on my door,' said Henry. He turned and faced the room. 'No smoke without fire, eh?'

Isla looked up at the customers and was thankful that some of them were ignoring Henry; others were paying him attention, though, and nodding their agreement. Isla silently cursed the lot of them, Henry in particular. She'd never liked the man, and he'd been at loggerheads with her dad for years over the ground that ran behind the funeral parlour and the shop, both of them wanting it for extra parking. Henry had tried to buy it but her father had outbid him and bought it himself.

'Take no notice of him,' Mick, the landlord, told her, and then said to Henry, 'We can do without any talk like that.'

Henry shrugged and took a slug of his pint before dropping a ten-pound note onto the bar. 'Free country and all that.'

Mick gently moved Isla out of the way and took the money, ringing it up in the till and handing back the change. 'And it's my pub so I get to make the rules.'

Henry muttered something unintelligible and went back to the table where he and a few other regulars were sitting.

'Thanks,' said Isla. She would have been quite happy to take on Henry herself but appreciated Mick stepping in to support her.

She was more than happy to see Dan approaching now. 'I hope you've not come to give me any grief.'

Dan smiled. 'As if I'd do that.' He placed his glass on the bar. 'Lager shandy, please, and whatever you're having.'

'Thanks. What are you doing here, anyway? Didn't expect to see you tonight – shouldn't you be over at the Ship and Anchor supporting your local team?'

'Now, why would I want to watch a group of blokes playing

pool when I could be here with a much nicer view?'

Isla placed his drink on the bar. 'I'm sure there are other nice views in Applemere.'

'If there are, I haven't seen them yet.' He took a long, slow sip of his drink, his eyes fixed on hers.

'Isla!' It was Mick, breaking into her thoughts. 'I'm not a charity – you do need to charge customers for their drinks.' He nodded at Dan.

'What? Oh, sorry.' Isla tapped in the code for the shandy and a Diet Coke for herself, aware her hands were shaking. How did Dan have that effect on her? Without meeting his eyes again, she took the money from him.

'Put the change in the charity box,' said Dan. 'I'd better not distract you any more. Catch you later.' He glanced over at Mick and, with a brief nod, returned to his table by the window. As he sat down, he looked back at Isla and winked.

'Got yourself an admirer there,' said Mick, coming over to Isla as she emptied the glass wash.

'Just being friendly,' insisted Isla.

'There's friendly and then there's flirting. He was definitely flirting.'

'Don't worry. It's all under control.'

'Hmm. He's got a bit of a reputation, by all accounts,' said Mick in a low voice. 'I'm only saying, keep your wits about you.'

Isla wasn't quite sure how she felt about the warning. 'A reputation?'

Mick shrugged. 'He came in here with Max Bartholomew a few times. I assumed it was a friendly drink after work while he settled in at the school.'

'And wasn't it?' Isla continued to put the glasses away,

CHAPTER 4

making an effort not to look over at Dan as she got the distinct feeling that he was watching her.

'I only overheard snippets, but Max warned him against getting over-friendly with one of the parents. Dan, there, didn't take it too well, from what I could see.'

'Really? Who was the parent?'

'I don't know. As I say, I just overheard a few things. I've seen him in action in here before. Anyway, all I'm saying is forewarned is forearmed.'

'Yeah, thanks, Mick.' Isla sighed. Typical. She'd managed to almost get herself involved with the local Lothario. Maybe last night had been a lucky escape. When Dan left twenty minutes later with promises of being in touch, she couldn't quite summon up the same enthusiasm as earlier. Bugger. Why was she so bloody useless at picking men?

Chapter 5

ESME

An Unknown Visitor

It had been a long week and Esme was glad it was Friday, although she still had to get through the day. It wasn't the first time she had received a body into the funeral parlour of someone she'd known practically all her life, but it was the first time it was a murder victim. As Conor had explained to her, an autopsy was always needed following a suspicious death, even when the cause of death appeared to be obvious – in Max's case, a blow to the head. The wound had been cleaned to a certain extent by the coroner but evidence of the full autopsy – carried out to check for any other possible causes of death or hidden traumas – was clearly visible where poor Max Bartholomew had been stitched back together. It wasn't a pretty sight, and she thanked goodness for Derek's many years of experience in making the deceased look more presentable for loved ones to see. However, in Max Bartholomew's case, the family – a daughter and an ex-wife, who both lived in the nearby town of

CHAPTER 5

Midham – hadn't wanted an open coffin.

Esme watched as Derek and Charlie, another part-timer at the funeral parlour, lifted the body from the trolley and into the coffin that Fiona Bartholomew and her daughter, Tamsin, had picked out the day before.

'Is there anything to go in the coffin?' asked Derek. It wasn't uncommon for family to request certain personal items went alongside their beloved.

'No, nothing,' replied Esme. Mrs Bartholomew didn't want her daughter to put anything in with him. She thought back to earlier in the week when Tamsin had suggested a photograph and Fiona had told her daughter off as if she were a child.

Derek and Charlie fitted the lid and tightened up the screws and bolts. 'Chapel of Rest?' asked Derek.

'Yes please. The ex-wife and daughter are coming over this afternoon.'

Esme went back into the office to see her father and was surprised to find Conor there. She was getting used to the grim look on her husband's face, but today his expression seemed particularly sombre. 'What's happening?' she asked immediately.

'Things have changed – got more serious,' explained Conor.

Frank cleared his throat. 'I've got to go in for a formal interview,' he said, exchanging a look with his son-in-law.

'A formal interview? Are they charging you?' She turned to her husband. 'Does Dad need a solicitor?'

'It wouldn't do any harm to have one with him,' replied Conor.

'When have you got to go?' asked Esme, her mind racing as she tried to decide whether the family solicitor might be able to help or if they had time to find someone more versed in defending a possible murder charge.

'This afternoon.' Her father rose from his seat. 'Conor was kind enough to tell me in person.'

'I don't understand why they're asking for a formal interview. There must be a reason for it, surely.'

Frank blew out a breath. 'I might as well tell you, because if I don't, then sooner or later someone else will.'

'Please,' Esme encouraged.

'When the business was in financial trouble and your mother had her breakdown, I managed to raise enough money to put into the funeral parlour and save it from folding.'

'That's right. A bank loan.'

Frank grimaced. 'It was a loan, but not from the bank.'

Esme was growing alarmed. She didn't like what her father was saying. She wished he'd just spit it out. 'Who from, then?'

'Max. He lent me ten thousand pounds.'

'Max? Max Bartholomew? Oh, Dad.'

'I know, I know. It doesn't look good.'

'Please tell me you paid him back,' said Esme. Her father shook his head. She looked over at Conor. 'And the police know about this, I take it.'

'Yes, we do,' he replied.

'Now, I don't want anyone worrying,' said Frank. 'I'm going to go home and explain all this to your mother. There's no point in trying to hide anything from her – she'll find out soon enough, and this way I can prepare her for what's to come.'

'Oh, Dad,' sighed Esme again, hugging her father. 'This is awful. I can't believe it's happening. It's a nightmare.'

'There, there, love. It will be OK. They can't charge me for something I haven't done – not without evidence, and as there will be no evidence there's nothing to worry about.'

CHAPTER 5

Esme appreciated her father's pragmatic response but suspected he was just trying to reassure her. 'We'll get a top solicitor,' she told him. 'Not being rude, but Mr Conrad might not be the best man for the job – he's more au fait with conveyancing and probate – though I'm sure he can recommend someone.'

'I'll sort it all out,' replied her father. 'I'll get home now and speak to your mother. Conor.' He nodded at the younger man, who returned the gesture.

Esme watched her father from the office window as he got into his car and drove away. Then she turned to Conor, allowing her full fury and desperation free rein. 'How did the police find out about the loan? You told them, didn't you? You told them the business had been in financial difficulties and now they've gone poking around and have managed to drag up something that happened ten years ago.'

'Hey, Esme, it's not like that,' began Conor.

'What is it like, then?'

'I'm a police officer. I can't withhold information.'

'But you've told them something that was private. No one knew about the money problems and they wouldn't have been any the wiser – but you told them, and now look what's happened!'

'That's unfair, love,' said Conor. 'I'm in a difficult position, which is why I've been taken off the case.'

Esme stopped in her tracks. 'You've been taken off the case?'

'Yeah, was told this morning. The new DCI says there's too much conflict of interest, even though we're short on officers and I'm the most experienced one at my level.'

Esme's frustrations drained away. She could see the hurt in her husband's eyes and his dejected body language. He loved his job and took immense pride in what he did. He would see this as a massive blow. She went over to him. 'I'm sorry.' She put her arms around his neck and rose on tiptoes to kiss his cheek and hug him.

'I want your dad's name out of this just as much as you do,' said Conor. 'I'm sorry for you, but I had to do what I had to do. In a way it's a relief, as I was getting into a more and more difficult position.'

'What are you going to do now?'

'Work other cases. The new DCI is a bit of a stickler. He's talking about sending me to another station while the investigation is ongoing.'

'Can he do that?'

'If he feels it's necessary. Look, your dad's right. Without any hard evidence, they can't charge him. It won't stand up with the CPS. In the meantime, we just have to wait patiently while they carry out their investigations to find out who is responsible for Bartholomew's death. There are other leads, but I can't discuss them. Rest assured, this formal interview isn't as bad as it seems.'

'It's just all sounding so much more serious,' said Esme. 'I am sorry for snapping at you like that.'

'Don't worry – I understand how hard it is for you. Look, I need to get back to work.' Conor dropped a kiss on her head. 'See you later.'

Esme forced a smile, still unconvinced despite Conor's reassurances, and once he had gone she found herself wandering into the Chapel of Rest, where the coffin and Max now were. The room, as ever, looked neat and tidy, ready to receive the family members. She wasn't quite sure how much Fiona Bartholomew was being told by the police about the investigation surrounding Max's death as, being his ex-wife, she was no longer his next of kin. Esme supposed that title now fell to Tamsin as his daughter. Esme had never properly met Tamsin, who had been born when Max lived away from the village. By the time he'd moved back to Applewick he was a divorcee and Tamsin was living with her mother. Esme had vague memories of Tamsin coming to stay with her father at weekends, but she'd never mixed with the local children and, looking back, Esme didn't know if that was by design on Max's part or desire on Tamsin's.

Esme debated whether to go home for lunch or, as she often did, pop across the street to the tea rooms run by Kerry Armstrong, a newcomer to the village, who had taken over the café and breathed new life into the business. Esme wasn't sure she was in the mood for pleasantries, but at the same time she didn't want to be seen to be hiding away in case it was misinterpreted as guilt by proxy. Her poor dad. She hated the thought that everyone would be talking about him.

That last thought settled it. She stood up and grabbed her handbag before calling out to Derek that she was off out for lunch, then headed across the road.

The bell above the café door tinkled as she walked in and, whether it was her imagination or paranoia, Esme felt as if all the customers turned their heads to stare at her. She smiled at a couple of the regulars and took the free table by the window.

'I won't be a minute,' Kerry called over, and as if this was a signal to the customers, they all resumed their conversations. 'Hello, Esme. How are you?' Kerry arrived at the table a few moments later with her order pad and pencil in hand.

'Not too bad, thanks.' Esme was relieved that, at least outwardly, everything seemed to be as normal with Kerry. She ordered a sandwich and a pot of tea and took out her reading book. She liked to give herself some down time during the day to escape into a fictional world because as much as she enjoyed working for the family business, it wasn't exactly a place for uplifting chit-chat with your customers and colleagues.

Ten minutes and one chapter later, Kerry appeared with her order. 'There you go. Sorry about the wait – I'm on my own today,' she explained.

'Oh, what's happened to Pippa?' asked Esme.

'She's off sick,' replied Kerry and then, taking the seat opposite Esme, she leaned forward and spoke in such a low voice that Esme had to lean in herself to hear what was being said. 'I had to send her home yesterday. I found her in the back, crying. She's not been herself all week.'

'Is she OK?' Esme frowned at the news. She liked Pippa Bonham, who was the daughter of the school secretary and an old school friend of Isla's. They'd been an unlikely duo, as Pippa was a quieter character than Isla, and although the two girls had remained friends over the years, Pippa had never shared Isla's sense of adventure and had always stayed close to home, content to work part time in the café and at the village nursery attached to the school.

'I'm going to call her later and check,' said Kerry. 'It's probably boyfriend trouble – you know what it's like when you're young.'

'I'll mention it to Isla. Maybe she can give her a call.'

'Great minds think alike; I was going to suggest that myself.'

Forty minutes later, having enjoyed her lunch and the escapism her book offered, Esme was back at the funeral parlour greeting Max's ex-wife and daughter and showing them into the Chapel of Rest.

CHAPTER 5

'If you need anything, please just ring the bell here,' said Esme, indicating a discreet doorbell on the side of the wall. 'It rings through to the office so I can pop in when you need me.'

'Thank you,' said Fiona Bartholomew. 'Has anyone else been to visit Max?'

'Err, no,' replied Esme. 'No one else has contacted us. Were you expecting anyone in particular?'

'No. I just wondered.' Fiona took a seat at the front of the chapel, placing her hands in her lap. Her daughter followed suit and Esme took this as her cue to leave, exiting the room without a sound. The carpeted floor of both the Chapel of Rest and the corridor to the office soaked up any noise footsteps might make so that all mourners could hear was the gentle sound of music playing in the background as it filtered into the chapel and throughout the public areas. This also acted as an indicator to staff that family and friends of the deceased were paying their respects and so prevented anyone intruding on such a private time.

Esme planned on taking the opportunity to check through the invoicing and was just about to open the appropriate file on the computer when she stopped, the words of Conor rattling around in her head. Their father had injected ten thousand pounds into the business two years ago and what she now found disturbing was that he had never mentioned the true source of the funds. Admittedly, she hadn't been so involved in the accounting then and her father still liked to keep on top of that side of the business, but it bothered her that although he'd never said outright that it was a bank loan, he'd always given that impression. She knew he had wanted to do everything possible to avoid a repetition of the financial problems they had before. In hindsight, she should have been more aware of what was going on with the finances.

Esme clicked on the online-banking icon and then went over to her father's desk and rummaged around in the drawer until she found the book where she knew he wrote down important numbers and passwords. She'd always warned him about the dangers of this but, for once, she thanked him for his simplistic security measures.

It only took her five minutes to find and open the bank statements from two years ago and, with the help of the search tool, she keyed in £10,000. Seconds later, three results showed up. Two were easily identifiable from the clients' invoice numbers but it was the third that made Esme's heart lurch. Her father had referenced the ten-thousand-pound bank transfer as *Bartholomew Funeral Plan*, which, to anyone looking at the books, would appear to be a straightforward and honest transaction. But given what Esme knew now, it was more ominous than that.

As she sat back in her chair playing out various scenarios of how her dad's formal interview might go later, she became aware of the silence. Derek had gone home so it was just her and Max's family present, but that wasn't what interrupted her thoughts; the music had stopped. Damn, the machine must be playing up.

The music system was located in a small cupboard just outside the Chapel of Rest, allowing Esme to access it without disturbing Fiona and Tamsin. As she approached the door of the chapel, she became aware of loud voices coming from inside – which was surprising, as usually visitors treated the Chapel of Rest with a reverence such as that expected in a church or a library and conversations were carried out in hushed tones. These voices didn't sound hushed at all, or

CHAPTER 5

genial. In fact, this sounded more like a disagreement, verging on an argument:

'I know he's your father and you want to think the best of him, but I can't sit here and pretend he was anything other than a cheat.'

'No one is asking you to,' replied Tamsin. 'But what happened between you and Dad happened a long time ago. The man you remember isn't the one I knew. He was honest. Kind. Loving. He always wanted what was best. So, yes, I am going to stand up in front of everyone at the service and say all that.'

'You say what you like. We both know the truth. You hadn't even spoken to him for weeks because of what he was going to do. Good job the police don't know.'

'I don't want to talk about this anymore,' said Tamsin.

'You know, I'm not surprised he came to a sticky end. Not that I would wish it on him, but he could be very dogmatic about things and was always upsetting people.'

'Oh, Mum, stop it. You're just making yourself sound bitter.'

There was silence for a moment and Esme debated whether to switch the music on and risk warning Fiona and Tamsin that she'd heard them or just to creep back to her office.

'I'm going now.' It was Fiona. 'I'll wait in the car.'

Esme spun on her heel and nipped back down the corridor, thankful for the carpet to dull her footsteps. She slipped in behind her desk and caught her breath while she tried to concentrate on the computer screen in front of her. She heard the door to the Chapel of Rest open and then close, suggesting Fiona was leaving, and then she heard the iron catch on the nineteenth-century entrance door lift and the distinctive groaning sound, like a disgruntled old gentleman being disturbed from his forty winks, as the door opened and then closed with a heavy thud.

Esme put the overheard conversation out of her mind while she used her mobile phone to take a photo of the ten-thousand-pound transaction showing on her computer screen. She wasn't entirely sure why but had in her mind that she would probably show it to Bella and possibly also Isla at some point. Clicking out of the banking system, she let out a small breath. It didn't sit comfortably with her to be snooping around the business bank account – she felt as if she was going behind her father's back – but she had needed to see the transaction for herself.

The bell linked to the chapel gave a discreet buzz and Esme went through to see Tamsin.

'We're leaving now,' said Tamsin. 'Mum's waiting outside for me. Thank you for helping us arrange everything.'

Esme accompanied Tamsin down the hallway to the main entrance. 'You know you can come in anytime between now and the funeral if you want to sit in the Chapel of Rest with your father again.'

Tamsin nodded. 'I appreciate that.' She went to go but paused. 'Was my dad liked by the people in the village – you know, the parents and staff?'

Esme was taken aback by the question. She quickly gathered her thoughts. 'He was very well respected.'

'That's not the same as being liked, though, is it?' replied Tamsin with a sad smile before turning and walking across the street to where her mother was waiting in the car.

Esme let out a sigh and went back to the office, annoyed that she hadn't given a better answer. If she was honest, she didn't know how much Max was liked or disliked as a person. She was perfectly satisfied with how he ran the school as a head

CHAPTER 5

teacher, but – as would be the case anywhere – she knew there were some who didn't share that sentiment. She was aware that Bella's friend Suzanne had been complaining about his handling of a situation between her son and another boy in his class. Esme didn't always have time to stand and chat in the playground so she wasn't quite up to speed with it all, but last week Suzanne had been particularly cross and had been talking about taking her complaint to the local education authority. Whatever Max had done or hadn't done, Suzanne was less than impressed.

The telephone in the office rang and Esme answered it. 'Good afternoon, Fairfax Funeral Parlour. How can I help you?' It was someone from Applemere requesting their services. As Esme dealt with the caller, she heard the main door open and then shortly after that the door to the Chapel of Rest. She cursed herself for not locking the door but assumed it was probably Tamsin going back into the chapel – maybe she'd forgotten something. Esme couldn't make the telephone cord stretch far enough to see down the hallway. She'd been meaning to get a new office telephone, a wireless one, but her dad had claimed a sentimental attachment to the retro 1970s model.

As the phone call with the new customer ended, Esme heard the click of the chapel door closing. 'Hello!' she called, scooting out from behind her desk. 'Hello! Can I help you?' She stepped out into the hallway and just caught a glimpse of a black coat as someone shot through reception and out the main door too fast for her to see who it was. The heavy oak door slammed shut.

Esme ran down the hallway and heaved open the door, stepping out onto the pavement and looking up and down the road. The street was empty. Where on earth had the person gone? Whoever it was must have sprinted down the road. Esme went back inside, locking the door behind her. For the first time since she'd worked at the funeral parlour, she wasn't keen on being there on her own. She gave an involuntary shiver and retraced her steps back down the hallway, stopping outside the chapel. Out of habit, she poked her head round the door just to make sure everything was OK and was startled by what she saw on top of the coffin. A single white rose.

Esme went over to the coffin and picked up the rose, examining it as if it would yield some answers. She was sure it hadn't been there when she came in to see Tamsin. She would have noticed it, surely. That could only mean one thing – the person who had been in such a hurry to leave without being identified must have left it. Who on earth could that be, and why did they do it? She didn't like this one bit and, taking the rose with her, hurried out of the chapel. All she wanted to do now was get home as quickly as possible and away from the funeral parlour. Since Bella always picked Amelia and Dylan up from school when she collected Jacob, taking them all back to her house, Esme would get the chance to speak to Bella when she went over to retrieve the twins. She was very keen to know what her sister would make of the whole thing.

Chapter 6

BELLA

One For All and All for One

'So, have you finished your homework now?' Bella asked Amelia and Dylan.

'Yep. All done,' replied Amelia, smiling proudly as she turned her book around to show her aunt. 'We have to design a poster for our Greek topic.'

'Excellent. It looks really good. Well done.' She turned to Dylan, who sheepishly opened his book. Ah, bless him. Dylan wasn't a natural artist and clearly wasn't engaging with the topic, his drawing being rather more basic than his twin sister's to say the least. Bella went for the positive spin. 'And you've finished too. Good work. I like the drawing there of the Parthenon.'

'It's just a temple.' Dylan closed his book and shoved it into his bag. 'Can I play in the garden now?'

'Of course you can,' said Bella. 'Once you've helped with the dishes.' She grinned as her nephew pulled a face of displeasure but nevertheless scuffed his way over to the sink and picked up a tea towel. Amelia joined him and as Dylan dried the dishes, she put them away, telling Bella all about the swimming party she'd been to at the weekend.

Bella enjoyed looking after Esme's children and they were really patient with Jacob, who loved his cousins being there. For those few hours after school, her little cottage was filled with chatter and laughter – along with the occasional dispute, usually between the siblings, but she didn't mind that; it was just nice to have a full house and it fed into her romantic notion of one day having the conventional family life she'd always imagined for herself. It was just a shame her ex-partner, Gavin, hadn't shared that aspiration. Married life had never been on the cards as far as he was concerned, and although the arrival of Jacob had led to them living together, that had proved to be temporary – by the time Jacob was two years old Gavin had moved out.

Bella tided up the rest of the kitchen and once the kids had finished the dishes, they piled out into the garden. It wasn't anywhere near the size they were used to at home but that didn't seem to bother them and Dylan was soon kicking a football about with Jacob, Amelia hot on his heels.

The doorbell buzzed and, glancing up at the clock, Bella was surprised it was already after five thirty. She opened the door to her sister. 'Hiya. Come on in. The kids are in the back garden.' They went through the lounge and into the kitchen diner at the back of the house. 'Ooh, a rose. Is that for me, or from a secret admirer?' Bella nodded at the bloom in her sister's hand as she filled the kettle. 'Cup of coffee?' She paused. 'Is everything all right? You look very tired.'

Esme pulled out the wooden kitchen chair and sat down,

dropping the rose onto the table. 'I'm OK. Just worried about Dad.'

Bella listened as Esme brought her up to date with the developments of the day, telling her about Fiona and Tamsin's heated discussion, the bank statements, and finally about the rose. Bella put two cups of tea on the table and took the chair opposite. 'Wow. That's one hell of a day. And what does Conor say about the interview?'

'Not to worry and that it's just a formality.'

'I had no idea about the money,' confessed Bella.

'Neither did I. Dad usually tells me everything – at least, I thought he did. Now I'm wondering if there's anything else I should know. I could do without any more surprises.' Esme rubbed her closed eyelids with her finger and thumb.

Before Bella could say anything else, the doorbell sounded again. She was pleased by the unexpected appearance of Isla on the doorstep. 'Come on in. Esme's here.' But then she noticed her sister's drawn expression. God, not another one having a bad day. 'You look as though you need a cup of tea too.' Bella ushered her younger sister into the kitchen and made her a drink. 'What's up?'

Isla leaned her head back and looked up to the ceiling. 'I've been such an idiot,' she said, before flopping her head down on her folded arms. 'Such an idiot.'

'Spill,' ordered Bella.

Isla sat up. 'I've been going around all week like some stupid schoolgirl waiting for her latest crush to call her – and then finding out the exclusive attention she thought she was getting wasn't exclusive after all.'

'Oh dear,' said Esme. 'Is this Dan we're talking about?'

'Dan?' interjected Bella. 'Dan who?'

'Dan Starling,' Esme informed her in a tone that matched the eye-roll.

'Him! When did all this happen? What have I missed? How come you know and I don't?' Bella tapped the pine tabletop.

'Oh, don't,' said Isla. 'I've been so naive. He's been coming in the pub, all chatty, and I thought he liked me. He asked me over to Applemere the night …'

'The night Max was killed?' asked Bella.

'Yes, that night.' Isla held up her hand. 'Nothing happened. We got drunk and fell asleep.'

'Classy,' said Bella.

'Anyway, he came in the pub yesterday and was all flirty again so I assumed that he genuinely liked me.'

'As you would,' said Esme, offering support in the indirect way Bella knew she often did.

'Mick told me Dan was a serial flirt and had been in with other women. Apparently Max had even warned Dan about not getting involved with one of the parents.'

'Really?' Bella looked at her older sister. 'You don't look very surprised by any of this.'

'Isla mentioned it to me the other day after Conor and that DS had been,' explained Esme.

'I just thought it was all a bit of gossip,' said Isla. 'I didn't really want to believe what Mick was saying, but Dan has my number and hasn't once rung me. I thought he might come over to the pub tonight, and I did something really stupid.'

'Please don't tell me you rang him?' groaned Bella.

'Worse.'

'What?' Even Esme sounded surprised now.

'I hung around for him after school.'

'Oh, God. What happened?' Bella gave her sister's arm a

squeeze.

'I was waiting on the bench in front of the hedge when I heard him coming out. He was talking to a woman. I don't know who it was but they were laughing – make that *giggling* – together in that way people do when they obviously fancy each other.' Isla let out a long sigh. 'Dan said something about seeing her tonight and then made a joke about getting home to change the bed sheets for her.'

'Ouch,' said Esme.

'Bastard!' said Bella. 'Did you see who was with him?'

'Not really. I couldn't see over the hedge properly. I just saw the black baseball cap she was wearing – it had the Apple Runners logo on it.'

'So, someone from one of the Apples,' said Esme, using the colloquial shorthand for the local villages of Applewick, Appledown, Appleside and Applemere. 'Did he see you?'

'Yes. He looked a bit flustered for a split second but very quickly composed himself and then came around and hustled me in the direction of the car park, away from whoever it was he'd been talking to. He said he would love to see me tonight but he had a heap of marking to do.'

'Bastard twice over,' said Bella, feeling sorry for her sister, and then, trying to find a positive, added, 'At least nothing happened when you stayed the other night.' She got up and put her arm around Isla's shoulder. 'Better to find out now than later.'

Isla leaned her head against Bella's. 'I know, but I really liked him. *Really* liked him. I'm so rubbish when it comes to men. I think I'm going to give up and go and live in a monastery.'

'Convent,' corrected Esme. 'Monks live in monasteries. Nuns live in convents.'

Bella shook her head. Esme could be so precise, even though she never intended to come across that way. She gave Isla another hug. 'Ignore the Madam Pedantic over there.' Her younger sister gave a small laugh while her older sister did her best to look offended and poked her tongue out at them.

'I'm so gullible at times,' said Isla.

'The thing is,' said Bella, 'Dan Starling is the sort of man who comes across as very charming, very likeable, and he talks to people in a way that makes them feel special. He has this effect on so many women. You should've seen him with Suzanne Edwards the other day.'

'What do you mean?' asked Isla.

'She was upset about what had happened to Max. Dan Starling was being very consoling.'

'Another piece of evidence to add to his Prince Charming status,' muttered Isla.

'Sorry, sweetie, I don't mean to make you feel worse. I'm just trying to show you that it's easy to fall for his charms,' said Bella. 'I know the dinner staff were all mooning over him when he first came. They call him Applewick's Dish of the Day.'

'Does that include you?' asked Isla.

There was no malice or accusation in her sister's voice so Bella chose to answer honestly. 'I'm not going to lie, when he first arrived I was very much taken with him – as were most of the women in the village – but he's not really my type. And, remember, I've not exactly got a good track record with picking the right man. Esme's the success story there.'

'Esme has always been the success story,' said Isla, not unkindly. 'Anyway, I don't know why I'm wallowing in self-pity. There are much more important things to think about – like Dad.'

CHAPTER 6

'And Mum,' added Esme.

'She's not good, is she?' said Bella. 'I called in this morning to sit with her for a bit but she was on edge the whole time. It's really got to her, all this Max Bartholomew business.'

'It's very difficult at home,' sighed Isla. 'I just wish there was something we could do.'

'There is something we could do,' said Esme, with such authority that both Bella and Isla sat to attention.

'And that is?' prompted Bella.

'We can find out who killed Max ourselves.' Esme spoke in such a way that it was more like an announcement of some foregone conclusion than a whimsical suggestion.

Bella let out laugh. 'Oh, you are funny, Esme. There's me all this time thinking you were the sensible, level-headed one and now you've come out with an idea like that.' She stopped laughing as Esme fixed her with an unflinching stare. 'Oh, God, you're bloody serious, aren't you?'

'Deadly,' said Esme. 'No pun intended.'

'How on earth are we supposed to do that?' Isla sounded as incredulous as Bella felt, which was reassuring.

'Come on, Esme, you're not really serious, are you?' Bella tried again.

'I am, and there's absolutely no reason why we can't at least try to work on some different leads or suggest other suspects to the police.'

'You really think the police are going to listen to any of us?' Bella sat back in her seat and folded her arms. 'Of course we're going to come up with every possible alternative to Dad by virtue of the fact we're his daughters. They won't take us seriously.'

'Aha! I've already thought of that,' replied Esme with an

air of triumph. 'No, you're right, they probably won't take us seriously, but you're forgetting I have a husband in CID. Now, him they would take seriously.'

'But you said earlier he'd been taken off the case.' Bella wasn't at all convinced.

'And he has, but he's still at work, he's still a serving police officer – a detective – and he can still make suggestions to the team,' responded Esme. 'All we have to do is come up with some other suspects, preferably with a motive and opportunity, and then I'll get Conor to tell the team working the case.'

Bella exchanged a sceptical look with Isla before replying to her older sister. 'I don't think it's as simple as that.'

'Look, I know it won't be plain sailing,' admitted Esme, 'but I've got to do something to try to help Dad. And Mum. It's awful seeing how it's affected Mum already, and I know Dad is putting on a brave face.'

'I can't argue with that,' said Isla, flicking her hair over her shoulder. 'But how can we find anything out?'

'We just need to keep talking to people about Max,' said Esme. 'We need to work out a strategy, work out who might've had a motive, then try to put them at the scene. That's the difficult bit, I know, but we have to at least try.'

'And, between us, we know enough people to ask around without causing too much fuss or attracting too much attention,' added Isla, who was clearly warming to the idea.

'Exactly!' declared Esme. 'We can get together like this most days and exchange information and get to the bottom of it all.' She turned to Bella. 'You're not saying very much.'

Bella wanted to be as enthusiastic as her sisters, and she couldn't deny that she wanted to help her parents just as much as they both did, but it all seemed so fanciful and, quite honestly, futile. 'I think we should leave it to the experts,' she said at last.

'The experts who seem intent on proving Dad is guilty,' objected Esme.

'If Bella doesn't want to help, we can still do it on our own,' said Isla.

'Yes, we could,' agreed Esme.

'Hey! That's not fair. You know we always do things together,' Bella complained, knowing by the time she finished the sentence that she was going to cave in. There was only her pride left to defend now.

'So, you're in?' asked Isla.

'Under duress. And, for the record, let it be known that I don't think this is a good idea.'

'But you're in,' pressed Isla.

'Yes, I'm in.' Bella huffed as she watched her two sisters high-five each other for their efforts.

'Excellent,' said Esme, pulling a notebook out of her bag. 'Now, before I go, let's just quickly go over what we know.'

Bella looked out of the kitchen window at the children. Amelia was pushing Jacob around in his go-cart. There wasn't much room in her back garden but the kids still managed to have fun out there. She turned back to her sisters. 'I don't think we know very much.'

'I'm not just saying this because I'm fed up with Dan,' said Isla, 'but Mick also told me that Dan and Max had words one night in the pub; that Max warned Dan about being over-friendly with the parents. Like I said before, he's got a reputation as a serial flirt.'

'You also said Dan was comforting Suzanne Edwards,' said Esme. 'Do you think there's anything in that?'

'Oh, I doubt it,' said Bella. 'Suzanne's married.'

Esme shrugged. 'So?'

Bella returned the shrug. 'I don't think it was anything like that.'

'I'm still going to make a note of it.' Esme scribbled in her book and then looked up. 'Suzanne runs, doesn't she? Is Suzanne an Apple Runner?'

'I'm not sure, actually. She did mention recently about joining the club but I don't know if she did.'

'First job goes to you, my lovely Bella,' said Esme, who was clearly getting into the role of lead detective. 'Find out if she did join, and also if there's anything going on with Dan.'

'Oh, of course, she'll be more than happy to tell me she's having an affair,' replied Bella, not bothering to tame the tut that followed.

'We need to find out if Max was in any kind of relationship,' said Esme, tapping the pen on the table.

'Find out who left the rose on the coffin,' said Isla. 'The likelihood is that it was a woman, and it might be a married woman. Maybe a jealous husband decided to teach Max a lesson.'

'Good point.' Esme pursed her lips.

'Oh, heck!' declared Isla, jumping to her feet. 'I've got to be at the pub in five minutes. I need to go.'

'Let's get together again to work out what we know, what we want to know, and how we're going to find it out,' said Esme. 'We can go through everything then and devise a plan of action. What about Monday afternoon?'

'Sounds good to me,' said Isla, knocking on the window and waving goodbye to her nephews and niece. 'Where shall we meet?'

CHAPTER 6

'What about at the funeral parlour?' It was Esme. 'Dad's been going home at lunchtimes to be with Mum, so there won't be anyone there. Shall we say meet at one thirty?' Esme looked at her sisters, who agreed in unison.

Isla was heading down the hallway now. 'Must dash!'

'Oh, Isla, before you go,' called Esme as her sister reached the front door, 'I was in the café today and Kerry was saying Pippa Bonham was a bit down in the dumps. She thinks it's man trouble. You couldn't have a chat to her and make sure she's OK, could you?'

'Ah, poor Pippa,' replied Isla. 'Not sure I'm the best person to talk to about relationships but I'll give her a call tomorrow.' She blew kisses back into the house before she hurried off to the Horse and Plough.

'I'd better grab the kids and go too,' said Esme, popping her notebook back into her bag. 'Conor will be home before us at this rate.'

'Don't take this the wrong way,' said Bella, resting her hand on her sister's arm, 'but we should be concentrating on getting Dad an alibi before we get carried away with playing amateur detectives.'

'Yeah, I know, but if we can't prove it wasn't Dad then we need to prove it was someone else.' She gave Bella a kiss on the cheek before calling Amelia and Dylan in from the garden. 'Don't worry, I have a plan.'

After her sisters had gone and she'd got Jacob in the bath, Bella idly scrolled through Facebook on her phone. A post on the village group page brought her to a halt. It was announcing that entries were still open for The Apples 10K race the following month. Several people had commented and it was the second reply showing that caught Bella's attention.

Suzanne Edwards
Just registered! Yikes! @AppleRunners

Bella clicked on @AppleRunners and was taken to their Facebook page. She scrolled through the pictures, coming to stop at a group photo of several runners standing in a line, arms linked. Bella scanned the faces and there was Suzanne Edwards, second from right, wearing a black baseball cap with the Apple Runners logo on it: a green apple with a pair of running shoes underneath.

Chapter 7

ISLA

The Flight of the Starling

Isla's shift at the pub the previous night had been run-of-the-mill and although she had told herself to forget about Dan Starling, every time the door to the pub opened, she'd found herself looking up in hope that it might be him. Every time it wasn't, she'd scolded herself for being so weak. She really shouldn't be wasting time on him at all.

Now, Saturday morning, it was disappointing to realise she hadn't changed her mind about how she felt about him and was actually checking her phone every ten minutes in case he'd texted her. She really needed to get a grip of herself. Bella would no doubt tell her off if she knew she was mooching around like this.

'You don't seem yourself today. What's up?' asked her dad as she slouched on the sofa nibbling at a slice of toast. 'You're not even dressed yet.'

'It's not that late. It's only ...' She checked her watch and was surprised to see it was gone ten already.

'Mid-morning,' supplied her father.

'I'm just a bit tired,' said Isla, hoping to fend off any further questions. It was then she remembered what Esme had said about Pippa Bonham. 'Actually, I'm going out in about half an hour.' She hopped up from the sofa. 'I'd better get ready. How's Mum?'

'She's resting this morning,' replied her father. 'Got a headache.' He tagged on a smile, which Isla could see was an effort for him.

'Any luck finding your phone?' she asked.

'No. I rang the garage where I stopped the other night but they haven't seen it,' replied Frank. 'Will probably have to get a new one. It was only a cheap thing, anyway. Not like the fancy ones you and your sisters have.' He let out a sigh as he got to his feet and looked out of the living-room window. 'I suppose I should wash the car.'

Isla felt a wave of sympathy for her dad. He really was having to shoulder so much. The formal interview yesterday afternoon had gone well, according to him, but Isla wasn't convinced he was totally levelling with the family. Apparently the police now needed to trace the neighbour who'd rung him, as this would help prop up his timeline and version of events. She gave her dad a hug. 'Why don't you rest too? You've got to remember to look after yourself. Shall I make you a cup of tea? Have you had breakfast?'

'Oh, I'm fine, love.' Frank patted his daughter's hand. 'I'm better off busy, anyway. Don't be worrying about me now.'

Isla sighed, knowing it was no use trying to talk her dad around. She could see he was set on doing things his way. As she got ready to go out, she made a note on her phone to speak

CHAPTER 7

to Esme about Aunt May's mysterious neighbour. They really needed to find out who'd made the call as a priority.

Isla walked into the village. It was a sunny day and the good weather had been a universal signal for the residents of Applewick to undertake gardening duties. She knew a lot of them to say hello to – it came with growing up in a small rural village – and as she passed Rose Cottage, where Miss Needham, who must be as old as God's dog, was weeding her flowerbed, Isla wondered whether she was looking at her future self: a lifelong resident of Applewick, born and bred in the family house – subsequently inherited – who was destined to be left on the spinster shelf and outlive everyone else of the same generation.

Not wanting to become stuck in a rut, Isla was hoping to take another year out to do some more travelling as soon as she'd saved enough money. The travel bug had certainly taken hold of her – but so had the desire to find a special someone to spend the rest of her life with. She let out a small huff and shook her head.

Pushing open the door to Applewick Teapot Café, Isla was pleased to see Pippa behind the counter. 'Hi, how are you?' she asked. 'I haven't seen you for ages.'

'Hi. I'm OK, thanks. Didn't expect to see you in here.' Pippa offered a tepid smile.

'Oh, hello, Isla,' said Kerry, coming into the café area from the kitchen beyond. 'Nice to see you.' Isla couldn't help thinking Kerry wouldn't win any Oscars for attempting to act surprised to see her. 'I tell you what,' said Kerry, turning to her employee. 'Why don't you take a break and have a chat with Isla here? You can have a proper catch-up. It's not as if we're rushed off our feet with customers.'

Pippa's eyebrows nearly disappeared into her hairline. 'A break? But I only just got here.'

Kerry smiled broadly. 'It's OK. I'm feeling generous.'

Isla withheld the wince she was on the verge of giving at Kerry's total lack of subtlety, and shrugged when Pippa threw her a questioning look. 'Be nice to catch up.'

'Come on, you can take an iced bun each and sit outside. Lovely and warm today.' Kerry was slipping Pippa's apron from over her head and simultaneously taking two buns from the counter display.

'Don't know what's got into Kerry,' said Pippa as they settled themselves down at a picnic bench in the garden.

'I'll have to come in here more often,' said Isla. She took a bite of her bun, mentally calculating how many sit-ups she'd have to do to compensate for the sugary treat.

'I haven't seen you for ages – must be about four weeks or so.'

'Yeah, sorry about that. I don't even know what I've been doing that's kept me so occupied. Working the pub in the evenings, taking a few exercise classes during the day.' It was a lame excuse, which sounded even lamer now Isla was saying it out loud. She had to admit, she'd been a rubbish friend.

'I'm surprised you're still about,' said Pippa. 'I didn't expect you to hang around so long after your backpacking adventure.'

Isla licked her thumb. 'I'm saving up. I'd like to go to Australia next but I don't think that will happen for at least a year or two.'

'You're not looking for a career, then?'

Isla shook her head. 'Not yet. Maybe when I've seen a bit more of the world.'

'Don't you think it's a waste of a university education?' Pippa ran her finger back and forth along the edge of her plate.

'You don't know what you're missing,' declared Isla, avoiding the question. Everyone was always reminding her of her degree in sports science and how she wasn't doing anything with it. She hated having to constantly justify herself. She'd get a career job when she was ready to pursue a career. At twenty-three, she wasn't at that stage yet. She eyed Pippa's untouched iced bun. 'Aren't you hungry?'

'Not really.' Pippa pushed the plate towards Isla. 'You can have it if you want.'

'I'd better not,' replied Isla, recalculating the sit-up to calorie ratio. 'What have you been up to, anyway?'

'Not much.'

Bloody hell. It was hard work trying to talk to Pippa. Isla decided to go straight for the jugular. 'Is everything all right, Pippa, only you seem a bit down?'

Pippa stared at her hands in her lap. 'I'm OK.'

'You don't sound OK.'

Pippa lifted her head and looked away for a moment before speaking. 'I ... I've ... I'm upset about what happened to Mr Bartholomew.' She pressed her lips together and swallowed. 'I can't believe someone has killed him. It's awful to think there's a murderer in the village.'

'I know, it's terrible what happened, but I'm sure the police will make an arrest soon. Try not to let it worry you.' She studied her friend's face and, leaning in, spoke more softly. 'Is that really what's upsetting you?'

Pippa nodded, dislodging the tears that had gathered in her eyes. She wiped her face with a napkin from the plate. 'I'm just a bit emotional, that's all.'

'Is it boyfriend trouble?' ventured Isla.

A small silence followed as Pippa picked at the wooden table edge. 'I don't want to bore you.'

'You won't be boring me at all. If it makes you feel any better, I'm in the same boat – finished with before it even got started.'

Pippa sniffed and wiped her nose with the napkin. 'Mine had started. And it was serious.'

'Oh, I'm sorry,' said Isla. 'I had no idea.'

'I didn't tell you. I didn't tell anyone,' admitted Pippa. 'We liked keeping it to ourselves. It made it feel special, like it was just the two of us in the world. No one to pass judgement. No one to have their say. No one to spoil it. I wanted it to stay as perfect as possible. But it doesn't matter now. It's all over and there's no one to have to face or show my pain to. And you mustn't say anything, either.'

'I won't. I promise.' Isla didn't think she'd ever seen her friend looking so sad. It hurt her to witness it. Pippa must have been madly in love. She was just about to ask if she knew the man when Pippa spoke again.

'Was it like that for you? Were you imagining a future only to have it kicked out from under you?'

Isla might not have been so dramatic about it, but she felt that showing solidarity and empathy was more important than technicalities right now. 'I made a complete fool of myself over Dan Starling,' she confessed.

It seemed to get Pippa's attention. 'Him? Not you as well.'

'Hmm. If you mean am I another female who has fallen under his spell, then, yes, it seems I am,' confessed Isla. 'I thought he liked me but I'm finding out he's like that with everyone.'

'I can't stand him.' The was a certain amount of force accompanying the statement. 'I hate him,' finished Pippa, leaving no room for misunderstanding.

'Really? You must be the only female in the village who hasn't been flattered by his charms.'

'He's not as nice as he makes out. Believe me,' said Pippa, sitting up in her seat and frowning. 'You know, he was facing a disciplinary.'

'What for?'

'Being over-friendly with the parents. One parent in particular.'

'I've heard that, but surely it can't be grounds enough for a disciplinary. He must've done something else.'

'He's weird,' said Pippa. 'In a kinky way.'

It was Isla's turn to look surprised. 'How exactly? Or don't I want to know?'

'Into odd stuff.'

'Like bondage?' Isla was trying to think whether she'd had any inclination of this the other night when she'd been with Dan.

'And more.' Pippa fixed her eyes on Isla. 'Like I said, kinky. He's goes over to the More Than Vanilla club in Great Midham.'

The private members' club in the nearby town was well known for its alternative nightlife and had been closed down twice in as many years but each time had reopened a few months later under new ownership. It was definitely a venue for the broader-minded members of society. 'How do you know all this?'

'My dad's on the board of governors,' replied Pippa. 'Mr Bartholomew had spoken to him off the record, wanting his advice. Apparently Dan left his laptop open in the staffroom and Mr Bartholomew saw it. Said it wasn't any way for a primary-school teacher to carry on, and that he certainly shouldn't be having that sort of thing open while he was on school premises.'

'Wow. I didn't expect that of him. Had the complaint been lodged, do you know?' Isla hoped her attempt at sounding casual had worked. She was dying to know if anything official had happened – all this was information about someone who could hold a potential grudge against the head teacher.

'I think Mr Bartholomew was going to do it this week.'

'But he never got the chance,' said Isla, almost to herself.

'You all right, girls?' It was Kerry, calling from the doorway. 'We're getting a bit busy now – I could do with some help.'

'No problem. Just coming.' Pippa rose from the picnic bench. 'Thanks for the chat. I'll catch you later.'

As she left the café through the garden to avoid Kerry cross-examining her, Isla thought about the other thing Pippa had told her about – Dan Starling and his kinky fetish, whatever that was. She checked her phone and wasn't surprised to see she'd not had any messages or missed calls from him. He had definitely given her the elbow. But she couldn't help wondering if the disagreement between Dan and the head teacher might have been enough to bring about Max's murder. It seemed ludicrous to think Dan could be a murderer. When she was with him the other night, he'd never once given her cause to doubt she was safe. Murder aside, she hadn't even had any idea that he might be into something a bit different. There was, of course, no law against it, but if he was looking at stuff on his computer at work then she could see Max's problem with him. But it all seemed a bit too far-fetched to end in murder.

Heading back home, she was so lost in thought that she crossed the road without even looking. The sound of a car horn and screech of tyres had her leaping back onto the path. Isla couldn't believe it when Dan Starling popped his head out of the car window.

'Isla! You nearly got yourself run over!'

'Sorry. I was miles away,' confessed Isla, and despite what Pippa had just told her about him, her stomach gave a little flutter at the sight of his hypnotic blue eyes and she just couldn't ignore the feeling of being drawn to him. At the same time, the thought of her dad being questioned by the police jostled for attention. She walked around to the driver's side. 'How are you? It's awful about Max Bartholomew.'

'I'm shocked, to be honest,' said Dan. 'I can't quite believe what's happened but I'm bearing up. Someone's got to keep the school going.'

'I'm sure everyone appreciates what a difficult position you're in.'

'Look, I'm sorry I haven't been in touch but, what with everything, I don't know if I'm coming or going.'

'It's OK. You don't have to explain. So, erm, what are you doing tonight?' Isla wanted the ground to swallow her up. She sounded desperate even to her own ears.

'Ah, I'm really sorry but I've got something on tonight.' Dan pulled an apologetic face. 'I'm meeting up with some mates in Great Midham.'

'Cool, no problem, I'm actually going out as well – I just wondered if you needed to go for a drink to get away from it all,' replied Isla hurriedly. 'Another night, maybe.'

'Yeah, sure. I'd like that.' He reached out and covered her hand with his. 'Right, I'd better shoot off. And you, young lady, had better pay closer attention when crossing the road.' He winked and put the car into gear, before pulling away.

Isla watched as he drove off, not really sure how he could have such an effect on her given all she knew about him – but she couldn't ignore how attracted to Dan Starling she was. She felt so conflicted and knew she should be running a mile from him but she really didn't want to believe what Pippa had said. She dwelled on the thought, however, that if there was actually any truth in Pippa's revelation, it could give Dan a possible motive to kill Max, which would only help her father's case and give the police another lead to look into. As she continued walking home a small idea began to take form in her mind, mutating into something rather more tangible. It was a plan – a risky one, but it would tell her what Dan was really like and it might even help her find out who the Apple Runner woman was. Isla didn't know whether to believe Dan about going out with his mates tonight – he could be going out with that woman, for all she knew. She really didn't feel she could trust him. Well, she had at least three reasons there to go ahead with her plan. Yes, it was high-risk, but she was willing to take the chance.

Chapter 8

ISLA

An Eye-Opening Evening

'Oh, thank you, Sam! I owe you,' said Isla. 'I'll ring Mick now and let him know you're covering my shift.'

'No problem. I wasn't doing anything else tonight and the extra money is always handy,' replied Sam. 'Plus, now I don't have to do tomorrow lunchtime.'

Isla finished her call with Sam Boddington, who lived over at Appledown, grateful he'd been more than happy to swap shifts. She wasn't exactly looking forward to doing the Sunday lunch shift the next day, but at least now she was free tonight. It had been a while since she'd got dressed up for a night out and, looking at herself in the mirror, was only sorry it wasn't for an actual date rather than a stalking mission. She pulled at the hem of her dress – it was a bit on the short side but would have to do.

Her phone bleeped a text-message alert to tell her the taxi was outside and, as she left, she popped her head around the living-room door. 'See you later,' she said to her parents. 'I'll be back tonight but not until late. Just heading over to Midham to meet some friends.'

'OK, love, mind how you go,' said her dad. 'Ring me on the house phone if you can't get a taxi back.'

Isla always appreciated her dad's offer of a lift – it was reassuring, and although she knew he wouldn't mind coming to get her in the slightest, she'd never needed to call him so far.

Twenty minutes later, the taxi pulled up in Great Midham town centre and Isla headed for West Street, where the More Than Vanilla club was located. She'd looked it up online earlier and, since she wasn't a member, had booked a guest ticket for the night. It had been pricey but, she hoped, worth it. She knew she was taking a gamble in expecting Dan would be there tonight, but she'd decided to give it a shot.

The More Than Vanilla club was housed in a Georgian-style double-fronted building and was one of several early-nineteenth-century properties on the road to have been converted into commercial premises. The others ranged from fashion boutiques to private dentists and, at the end of the street, the local Conservative club.

Isla approached the entrance, where a doorman was standing at the foot of the steps leading up to a black-gloss door. She showed the digital ticket on her phone, which the doorman scanned before letting her in. As she stepped into the reception area, she was greeted by a dull thud of music coming from the other side of an interior door covered with black silk and cushioned-button fixings.

'Do you have a mask with you?' asked a woman as she took Isla's coat.

CHAPTER 8

'A mask?' Isla was rather taken aback by the question.

'Yes, Saturday night is Masked Ball Night,' explained the woman. She brought up a box from behind the counter and took out several black eye masks, spreading them across the shiny surface. 'Take your pick. These are on the house.'

Isla chose one that flicked up at the sides and was decorated with a few sparkly sequins across the top. Stretching the elastic around her head, she slipped it on. She was then allowed through the interior door to where the music boomed loudly, flashing disco lights momentarily blinded her and the heat from the vast number of people in the room was stifling. The room was filled with clubbers, all wearing their masks – some rather more elaborate than others. She felt self-conscious in her rather conservative little black dress as she took in the flamboyant clothing and – it would be fair to say – costumes that some were wearing; others were wearing rather less, which involved a lot of black plastic.

Isla spotted the bar on the other side of the dance floor filled with gyrating bodies moving in time to the music. She threaded and shuffled her way through people and tables towards the bar, declining several men's offers for her to join them on the floor.

This was completely different from anything she'd experienced before. Having spent over a year travelling the world, she wasn't exactly oblivious to the diversity of life; however, witnessing such a scene in Great Midham was something else. Finally, she reached the bar and after waiting a few minutes and shouting her order across to a barman who could easily have been at a Mardi Gras festival, with her vodka cocktail in hand she decided to explore the other rooms in the club. Despite feeling very much out of her comfort zone, Isla made an effort to appear relaxed and unfazed by her surroundings as she made her way through to the next room, gently swaying and bobbing her shoulders to the music.

This room was darker, having less lighting, and didn't feel as full. People stood around and were able to speak to each other more easily without the music being so intrusive. There were several snugs around the edge of the room and although it was hard to see clearly, as Isla glanced at the one nearest to her she could make out two people in the middle booth enjoying a rather amorous snog.

'Hey, you look lost, honey,' came a voice in her ear. Isla spun around and it was only the deepness of the voice that indicated it was a man. 'You new here?'

'Err ... yes. Someone mentioned the club to me. Thought I'd check it out,' replied Isla, trying to sound more confident than she felt.

He looked her up and down, lifting his mask for a moment to get a better look. 'You sure you got the right address? This don't seem like your sort of place.'

Isla gave a nervous laugh. 'Possibly!'

'My name's Floss.'

Isla shook his extended hand. 'Pleased to meet you.' As Floss held on to her hand and gave her a questioning look, she gathered herself. 'Oh, sorry, Isla.'

'Nice name. Well, Isla, you enjoy yourself, and if you need anything, make sure you ask for me. Everyone knows me.'

'Actually, Floss, can I ask you something now?' She was going to seize the opportunity while she could.

Floss nodded and smiled. 'Ask away.'

'I thought a friend of mine might be here. You wouldn't happen to know if someone called Dan Starling –' She stopped mid-sentence as Floss held up a hand.

'I can't say. We don't all use our real names here, honey.' Floss studied Isla. 'You're not here checking up on your boyfriend, are you?'

'Oh, no! Not at all!' Isla cursed herself. She'd been sussed out within just a few minutes. 'I just wondered. I should call him, anyway.'

'Yeah. You call him, Isla. Mind how you go now and, word of advice, don't go asking for people – no one likes it. They want to feel safe here. Know what I mean?'

'Yes, of course.' She moved away before Floss could say anything else.

Isla spent the next half-hour moving from room to room as she explored the first floor, where it appeared to be calmer with people talking and relaxing on sofas that were dotted around the place. All the doors of the upstairs rooms had been taken off to give an open feel, yet the space was still cosy. She refused several offers to join various groups chilling out together and made her way back downstairs, finally accepting that with everyone wearing masks, it would be impossible to spot Dan amongst the clubbers. As she leaned back against a wall, a screech of laughter to her left caught her attention and a woman dressed in a full black-PVC suit with a dog lead clipped to her neck choker ascended from another set of stairs and trotted across the room behind the man who was leading her. Isla could tell the man wasn't Dan just by his build, but the steps down to the basement intrigued her. She hadn't noticed them before and, after taking a final swig of her drink, she left her glass on a table and headed over.

The staircase was illuminated by some ultraviolet strip lighting and Isla hesitantly made her way down, peering around the corner when she reached the bottom. She was faced with the start of a long corridor lined with people, mostly couples but occasionally a threesome, all pawing and kissing each other. She was just about to turn and beat a hasty retreat when the man nearest to her caught her hand and pulled her towards him and another man.

'Ooh, fresh meat,' he said with a chuckle. 'Hello, darling.'

Isla gave a polite laugh. 'Sorry. I didn't mean to come down here.'

'Oh, don't apologise, we can make you feel welcome.' The man nuzzled against her neck and she felt the hand of the other man wind itself around her waist.

'No. Honestly. No.' Isla wriggled away.

'Oh, that's not very nice when we're only trying to look after you,' said the first man again.

'She doesn't need looking after,' came a new voice from behind Isla. She felt herself being pulled away from the duo and jostled around behind her rescuer. 'She's with me.'

'No worries. She's all yours.'

The man who'd come to her rescue was wearing a white short-sleeved T-shirt and black jeans, which was something of a comfort to Isla after all the strange outfits that so many were wearing. He turned and ushered her up to the ground floor.

'Thank you,' said Isla and then gasped as the man lifted his mask. 'Dan!'

'What on earth are you doing here?' he asked. 'I saw you and was just coming over but you disappeared down there.' He nodded towards the staircase.

'I didn't know. I was just curious.'

'Yeah, well, you know what curiosity did to the cat.'

'I should probably leave,' said Isla. 'I made a mistake.'

'Hmm, you probably did.' Dan accompanied her out to the reception area. 'What were you doing here?' he asked as he helped her on with her coat.

'I don't know,' replied Isla with a sigh. 'Being stupid.'

'Looking for me?'

She shrugged. 'Maybe.'

Dan dropped a kiss on her head. 'Whatever you think it is, it's not.'

'I don't know what I think,' admitted Isla.

'And whatever is happening here isn't illegal,' he added. 'Do you want me to call you a cab?'

'No, it's OK. I can sort it out.' She paused at the door. 'Did you come here with your mates?'

Dan didn't answer immediately but studied her, hands on his hips and mask now pushed into his back pocket. 'What do you think?'

'That's not an answer.'

'I didn't come here with another woman, if that's what you want to know.'

Isla nodded. 'Goodnight, Dan.'

She stepped out onto the path feeling like a complete idiot – something she seemed to make herself into on a regular basis where Dan Starling was concerned. She delved into her bag to look for her phone so she could get a taxi and it was then that she realised her purse wasn't in there. Bugger. She must have dropped it when she was at the bar. She looked at the building and didn't want to go back in at all. It was only her small zip-up purse that she took on nights out; her main purse with her bank cards was safe at home. Fat lot of use that was.

Isla sighed at her own stupidity. She'd have to ring Esme

and see if she wouldn't mind picking her up. She didn't want to ring her dad as that would mean he'd have to leave her mum or bring her with him – neither of which sat comfortably with Isla.

Esme answered on the fourth ring. 'Hi, Isla. All OK?'

'Not really. I need to ask a favour.'

'What's up?'

'I'm in Great Midham. I've lost my purse. I hate asking, but you couldn't come and pick me up, could you, please?'

'What are you doing in Great Midham? Shouldn't you be at work?'

'I'll explain later.'

'OK. Whereabouts are you?' asked Esme.

'Err, outside the More Than Vanilla club.' Isla flinched as she waited for the predicted response from her sister.

'What? That place? Don't tell me you've been in there!'

'OK, I won't.'

'Oh, for goodness' sake, Isla. Wait there, I'll be over straight away.'

'Thanks.'

'Don't go anywhere.'

Some thirty minutes later, it wasn't Esme who turned up to collect her but Conor. Esme had sent a text pre-warning Isla that Conor had overheard their phone conversation and insisted he go to collect her. His BMW pulled up alongside her and she climbed in.

'More Than Vanilla – honestly, Isla, what were you thinking?' asked Conor, turning the car around. As they drove away from the club, Isla saw Dan Starling standing on the pavement watching them. He didn't go unnoticed by Conor, either. 'What the hell is he doing there? You weren't with him, were you?'

'I bumped into him. Actually, he got me out of a tricky situation when someone thought I was up for a threesome.'

'For Christ's sake,' scolded Conor. 'Stay away from that place.'

'I am a grown woman,' protested Isla.

'Yeah – a grown woman who needs her brother-in-law to come and bail her out.'

'I lost my purse, otherwise I would've got a taxi. I can look after myself.'

'Yup, I know – you've been around the world travelling and come back in one piece.' He gave her a sideways look and smiled. 'I'm just pulling your leg. What sort of brother-in-law would I be if I didn't worry about my wife's little sister?'

'I know. And I am grateful,' said Isla, following up with an apologetic smile.

'All the same, stay away from that place – and from Dan Starling.'

Isla shifted in her seat to look at her brother-in-law. 'Why?'

'It doesn't matter. I just don't like the man, that's all.'

'I think a lot of men in the village feel the same way.'

Conor made a huffing noise. 'I'm saying it from a professional point of view. I don't like him. I don't trust him.'

'Ooh, copper's instinct,' teased Isla, trying to lighten the mood. She didn't like to think Conor was cross with her. 'Or is it insider information?'

'Something like that,' muttered Conor in a way that told Isla it would be pointless trying to get anything else out of him, so she sat back in her seat for the rest of the journey home.

Chapter 9

EMSE

Esme Investigates

'I'll be all right on my own,' said Esme when Conor, for the umpteenth time, expressed his disapproval of her plan to visit Aunt May. 'But you could come with me if you're that worried.' She looked through her bag to check she had everything she needed – purse, phone, keys, notebook.

'You know I can't,' replied Conor. 'Much as I would like to keep an eye on you, if my bosses find out I'm there while you're cross-examining potential witnesses then I'll be on gardening leave before you know it.'

'I'm simply going to chat to the neighbours so I can thank whoever it was that phoned Dad,' said Esme. They both knew full well that wasn't the entire truth but Esme had decided that as long as she didn't specifically tell Conor what she was going there for then he couldn't get into trouble. She acknowledged with an exaggerated raise of her eyebrows that he knew exactly what she was doing.

CHAPTER 9

Conor rested against the kitchen island watching her zip up her bag. 'Just be careful. I don't want you being charged with obstructing a police investigation or perverting the course of justice.'

Esme leaned over and kissed her husband. 'I'm doing nothing of the sort. Honestly, don't worry.' She looped the strap of her bag over her shoulder and picked up her car keys. 'Oh, by the way, you don't happen to know if there are any ANPR cameras between here and Great Midham, do you?'

'Not off the top of my head but I can't imagine there'll be any on the back road. Obviously there are cameras in Great Midham town centre, but if you're thinking in terms of tracking your Dad's car then I don't think he would have passed any.'

'Drat.'

'And they won't be able to track him via his mobile if he lost it, like he said.'

'He did lose it,' insisted Esme. 'Dad wouldn't lie about that.'

'Sorry, I didn't mean to imply … it was just force of habit, police talk, that's all.'

'Do you know if the police have found anything on the school CCTV other than Dad going and leaving?'

'Oh, come on, love, you know I can't divulge anything.'

'For God's sake, Conor, this is Dad we're talking about.'

'Put it this way, I don't know any more than you do on that score.' He pushed himself up from the island and went over to Esme, wrapping his arms around her. 'No one's telling me anything at the station. I feel like a leper. All the team are giving me a wide berth because they're frightened I'm going to ask them about the case. As soon as I walk into the room, a deathly silence falls over everyone.'

Esme rested her head on his shoulder. 'I'm sorry. I didn't

even think about how it must be for you.'

Conor shrugged. 'I can't blame them. It's as awkward for them as it is for me.'

Esme returned his hug, feeling sorry for her husband. It would be tearing him up not to be involved – he loved his job, and was good at it; being excluded from a murder case right on his doorstep must feel like torture for him.

Amelia came skipping into the kitchen. 'I've got cheerleading practice!'

Esme pulled away from Conor. 'That's right. Dad's going to take you today. I'm going to visit Aunt May this morning.'

'I don't have to go with you, do I?' Dylan gave Esme a pleading look as he followed his sister into the room, sliding his feet along the tiled floor.

'No, you can stay with your dad and take Amelia to her practice.'

She turned to Conor. 'I'll be back by lunchtime.' Then, calling goodbye to the children, she hurried out to the car before her husband could protest any more.

Esme hadn't mentioned to her sisters that she was going over to Great Midham as although the idea had been percolating in the back of her mind, it wasn't until this morning that she'd had the sudden and overwhelming urge to do something proactive and had decided that the trip just couldn't wait. She'd not been sleeping well since her dad's more formal interview and despite him not actually being charged with anything, Esme had the distinct feeling that if the police persisted in not looking at any other possible suspects, it would only be a matter of time before they managed to collate more evidence against him. Conor had assured her this wasn't the case, but a sense of anxiety that she was not at all used to had been pitching up in her stomach and Esme now felt that the only way to combat it was to actually go out and do something.

Thirty minutes later she was turning into Orchard Avenue, an Edwardian street lined with terraced houses that had small front gardens and no off-road parking. Finding somewhere near Aunt May's house to leave the car was a rarity – especially on a Sunday morning, when most of the residents of the street were home – but she managed to park about five doors down and, opening the black wrought-iron gate to her aunt's house, proceeded up the terracotta-tiled path to the open porch. Inside was a key safe, which she hoped still had the same number. It was handy for the carers who came in every morning to make sure Aunt May was up, washed and dressed. Her aunt was in her nineties and showing signs of dementia but still seemed to be coping well living independently. The situation was under constant review, though, and the meals-on-wheels team were in every lunchtime and then the carers again at teatime. Aunt May had never married and so all responsibility for her well-being fell to Frank and the Fairfax family.

The safe number not having changed, Esme let herself into the house and called out to her aunt. She had phoned and spoken to her that morning to say she was coming but Esme wasn't convinced May would remember. 'Hello ... Aunt May ... It's me, Esme.' She went into the living room and found May sitting in her chair by the window.

'Oh, hello, dear. Have you come to bring me my lunch?'

'No, Aunt May, it's me, Esme. Frank's daughter. I spoke to you this morning and said I was popping in to see you.' Esme gave her aunt a kiss on the cheek.

'Oh yes, of course, Esme. That's right. My great niece.'

Comforted that Aunt May remembered who she was, Esme went to make a pot of tea and brought it back into the living room. She poured a cup for each of them and, not wanting to dive straight in with the questions, took her time to chat to May and ask her how she was getting on. Esme shared news about the children and took out a couple of photographs from her bag to show May. 'That's Amelia and Dylan. They'll be going off to secondary school in September.' She was just wondering how she was going to steer the conversation around to her dad when Aunt May saved her the trouble.

"How is Frank these days?"

'Oh, my dad, erm, yes, he's fine,' replied Esme. 'Didn't he come to see you last week?'

'Did he?' Aunt May's brow furrowed and she put her finger to her lip in thought. 'Last week. I'm not sure. He might have done. Did he cut my grass? No, wait, that wasn't him, that was the nice young man from number nineteen.'

'Dad came over last Monday night,' said Esme. 'He came quite late because he was worried about you. He stayed the night and then went home in the morning.'

'Stayed the night? Let me think. Frank, you say?' Aunt May shook her head. 'I don't know. He might have done. I'm sorry, I can't always remember everything. He did come and see me, but I can't remember when that was.'

'Do you remember him staying the night?' Esme felt a sense of hopelessness wash over her as her dad's one and only alibi crumbled.

'Well, I know he has stayed before. I suppose he did.' She smiled at Esme. 'Yes. It's probably just me.'

Esme was sure Aunt May was just pacifying her now and that she really had no recollection of Frank visiting at all. They

CHAPTER 9

continued to chat about the garden and what the children were up to for another hour until Esme left with the promise of coming to see her again soon.

Before walking back to her car, Esme knocked at the house next door. A young woman around her mid-twenties answered.

'Sorry to bother you,' said Esme. 'I'm the niece of May Fairfax, next door to you. I don't suppose it was you or someone in your house who rang my dad, Frank Fairfax, last week because they were concerned about May, was it?'

The young woman shook her head. 'I can ask my mum. Wait there.' She returned almost immediately with a woman about Esme's age.

'Hi, I'm Sarah. Sorry, it wasn't me that rang. Is everything all right?'

'Oh, yes, it's fine, thank you. I just wanted to thank whoever it was.'

'You could try number twenty-five – that's Jenny. She sometimes pops in to see May. It might have been her. Or else the lady up the road – not sure of her name ... lives at number sixteen, or eighteen maybe – it's the house with the blue door and matching gate. She brings May some shopping now and again.'

Esme thanked Sarah and went around to number twenty-five first. She knew Jenny to say hello to and was given a warm welcome. 'No, I didn't ring your dad,' she said after Esme quizzed her. 'I do have his number, but I've never had cause to ring.'

'Could it have been the lady up the road, do you think? Number sixteen or eighteen. Your other neighbour thought it might be her.'

'Well, that'll be Doreen, but she's away on a cruise with her husband. They went a week yesterday, so it couldn't have been her.'

'I know it's a long shot, but do you remember seeing my dad at all, or his car parked in the road?' She could tell from Jenny's reaction that she thought it an odd question, but Esme didn't see she had any choice but to ask.

'I don't remember seeing your dad, sorry. I do know the front-room light was on. I put the bins out at about ten o'clock and I remember thinking May was having a late night, but that in itself isn't unusual. Doesn't May remember?'

Esme shook her head. 'Not really. She can't quite distinguish one visit from another.'

'Yeah, she does get a little confused, but she's very independent for her age and seems to manage OK.'

'The carers and the meals on wheels are a godsend,' replied Esme. 'Anyway, don't let me take up any more of your time. I need to be getting home.'

'All right. Nice to see you, and if I speak to any of the other neighbours, I'll ask them, although I don't really know who it could be.'

Esme felt even more deflated as she drove back to Applewick. She'd been so sure she'd be able to find out who'd phoned her dad. It must've been one of the other neighbours – it just had to be. The alternative didn't bear thinking about.

Chapter 10

BELLA

An Inside Job

Bella was particularly pleased with herself on Monday morning. She'd managed to get Jacob to school before Mrs Bonham had come out ringing the bell to signal the start of the day.

'Early bird,' commented Suzanne when Bella joined the small cluster of mums who were chatting while keeping one eye on their respective children as they raced around the playground. 'How's things?' The pointed way in which she said it told Bella that Suzanne was referring to her father. It certainly didn't appear to be a secret that he had been a person of interest to the police.

'All fine,' replied Bella. She wasn't going to get into a conversation about it in front of everyone. 'You off to yoga?' She eyed the rolled-up mat under her friend's arm.

'Yes, for my sins,' laughed Suzanne.

'I keep thinking I should do something active,' continued Bella. 'Maybe yoga, or even running.'

'Oh, you should come along to Apple Runners. In actual fact, I think there's a beginners' group starting up soon,' Suzanne enthused. 'One of our more experienced runners takes all the newbies through their paces for the first twelve weeks so you get to build up your stamina and distance. You could sign up for The Apples 10K.'

'Whoa! Steady on. I only said I was thinking about it. I'm not sure I'm ready for ten kilometres any time soon.' Bella caught sight of Jacob chasing after one of the other children and returned her attention to Suzanne. 'So, do you have many runners at the club? Anyone I'd know?' But the sound of the bell ringing out brought a halt to the topic. 'Oh, Mr Starling's ringing the bell today,' remarked Bella.

'He can ring my bell any time,' laughed one of the other mums and nudged Bella with her elbow. Bella glanced at Suzanne to gauge any reaction but she was already rounding up her son to go into class.

Bella herded Jacob over to his class line and kissed him goodbye. 'Have a great day. Love you.'

'Oh, Mrs Bryers,' said Dan coming over to Bella.

It's Miss Fairfax,' corrected Bella as she grinned and waved at Jacob marching into his classroom. She blew him a kiss and then turned to Dan Starling. 'I was never married to Jacob's father.'

'Oh, yes, sorry.' He pulled an eek sort of face by way of apology.

'Not a problem,' replied Bella, swishing her hand as if wafting away a fly. 'Things have a way of working out for the best.' She wasn't quite sure why she said that; she wasn't in the habit of referring to her private life so freely.

'Don't they just?' Dan gave a conspiratorial grin before

CHAPTER 10

continuing. 'Anyway, Mrs Bonham wondered if she could have a word. Don't worry, it's nothing serious ... nothing to do with Jacob. She just wants to speak to you about some cleaning she needs doing. A one-off, but I'll let Mrs Bonham explain.'

'I'll go and see her now,' said Bella. She walked across the playground and into the school with Dan. 'How are the children coping with what's happened?' she asked.

'Most of them seem OK. The younger ones don't really understand the severity of it but a few of the older ones have been unsettled. We're working with the parents and school counselling services.' Dan held the door open for Bella and they proceeded up the corridor together. 'The service is available to staff and parents as well. I mean, if you need anyone to talk to, that is.'

'Thank you. That's good to know.' Bella paused at the door to Dan's classroom. 'And you? How are you doing?'

Dan ran a hand through his hair. 'I can't pretend it's not an utter shock. Very disturbing indeed. Max – Mr Bartholomew – was such a respected man. He was an inspiration to me and really mentored me. I still can't quite believe what's happened.'

'Yes, I think everyone is in shock. And you're having to step up to take on head-teacher duties?'

'Yes. Yes, I am. To be honest, it's rather bittersweet. I mean, it was the intention for me to take over from Max one day; I just didn't expect to have to do it in such circumstances.' The frown lifted. 'But I'm rising to the challenge and really hope it becomes a permanent arrangement.'

'Won't you have to go through an interview process, though?'

'Yes, there is that, and with the board of governors' support and backing, I hope I'll be seen as fit to take over.'

'Oh, Bella, just the person,' came a voice as Mrs Bonham appeared in the narrow passageway. 'I see Mr Starling managed to nab you.'

'I'd better let you go and teach,' said Bella to Dan. She could see how the mums found him so charming and easy to speak to – he confided in a person as if they were his best friend and he was telling them something secret. She followed Mrs Bonham down the corridor to the reception area. 'How can I help?'

'I know you do cleaning for the vicar and at the doctor's surgery; I wondered if you'd consider cleaning the Old School House. Not the whole house, just ... just Mr Bartholomew's study.'

'The study. Isn't that where he ... he was found?' It wasn't the most appealing job she'd been offered.

'Yes, I'm afraid so. I've rolled up the rug, but where the police have been in and carried out a search, well, both Fiona Bartholomew and I thought it might be best to clean up.'

'Is it bad?' Bella didn't know why she found the thought so distasteful – it wasn't as if she hadn't seen a dead body before at the funeral parlour, and she wasn't averse to rolling up her sleeves and getting stuck into some serious cleaning, but the thought that it was where someone had been murdered was what unsettled her. Still, the money was always handy – and then it dawned on her that it would give her the perfect excuse to have a little poke around. She might find out something that would help prove her father was innocent. 'Shall I take a look?' she suggested, infusing her words with enthusiasm.

There was no direct access from the school to the Old School House so Bella followed Mrs Bonham out of the main gates and around to the path that led up to the front door. It was there

CHAPTER 10

they came face to face with Suzanne Edwards.

'Mrs Bonham, I was just coming to see you,' said Suzanne without a smile.

'I'm busy at the moment, but if you wait in reception I'll be with you as soon as I can.'

Bella could detect a hostility between the two women and watched on in fascination at the passive-aggressive exchange.

'How long will you be? Only I have a yoga class to get to.'

Mrs Bonham squared her shoulders and pinched out a reply. 'I wouldn't like to put a time limit on it. As you can see, I'm in the middle of something with Miss Fairfax but I'll be with you shortly.'

'Oh, I haven't got time to wait.' Suzanne fished an envelope from her bag and thrust it towards the secretary. 'It's self-explanatory.' With that, she marched away from them without another word.

'What a madam she is,' muttered Mrs Bonham.

'Suzanne?' Bella wasn't sure if she'd understood; it wasn't like Mrs Bonham to speak that way about a parent.

'Awful woman. She should be ashamed of herself.' Mrs Bonham walked up the path to the schoolhouse. 'She's been causing so much trouble for Mr Bartholomew.'

Bella hurried after her, eager to coax out some more information. 'Really? That's awful. What has she been doing?'

'I shouldn't really say.' Mrs Bonham opened the front door but paused on the step. 'She believes her son can do no wrong and thinks he's being bullied by other children when it's actually her own child that's the nasty one.'

'Oh dear. The trouble is no one likes to admit their child isn't very nice,' replied Bella, feeling the revelation was an anti-climax.

'Yes, I know, but she can't leave it there. Has to go writing to the board of governors and the LEA.' Mrs Bonham shook her head. 'And then she ...' Mrs Bonham stopped mid-sentence as if suddenly remembering her professional position.

'What else?' asked Bella gently, while screaming inside her head because she sensed that Mrs Bonham had just stopped herself from revealing something far more important than playground squabbles.

'Let's go inside and see the study,' said Mrs Bonham, her matter-of-fact approach signalling the end of that particular conversation.

Stepping over the threshold of the Old School House, Bella shivered. It wasn't literally cold inside but the projected knowledge that some awful crime had taken place here left the house feeling chilly and unwelcoming. An intense silence coated the walls and clung to the furniture but it was the smell that was the most foreboding thing, and it intensified as they went into the study. It was the smell of blood and death. Bella had never quite been able to describe this smell but she was very much aware of it whenever she was at the funeral parlour.

Bella looked around the room. The rug Mrs Bonham had mentioned was rolled up and fastened with duct tape – Bella guessed this was where the smell of dried blood was coming from. The carpet itself was faded around the edges, revealing the original deeper blue colour that had been protected by the rug. There was a distinct brown patch where the blood must have soaked through the rug.

'I've got some industrial carpet cleaner that should get that stain out,' said Bella. She took in the rest of the room – the traditional desk in front of the window, the bookcases lining both sides of the chimney breast. On the opposite wall hung several photographs of Max throughout his teacher career and on the desk stood a framed photograph of a young woman about twenty years old, whom Bella vaguely recognised as his daughter. Cupboards lined the lower half of the wall; the doors had been left open and several sheets of paper scattered the floor. The desk drawers hadn't all been closed properly either, and there was a pile of papers and files stacked on one end of the desk. 'Did the police leave it like this or was it Max's way of working?'

'Oh, good Lord, it wasn't Max. He'd have a fit if he could see it. No, it was the police. I told them to leave it in the end. They did try to tidy up but I just wanted them out. I know they've got a job to do, but it was all too much – it seemed so disrespectful.'

Bella quoted Mrs Bonham a price for cleaning and said she could come back later that day. 'Do you need to check with Mrs Bartholomew about the price?'

'Technically I should, but I'm not going to. She'll only try to haggle with you. If I tell her I've agreed it, there's nothing she can do about it.'

'I don't want to cause any problems,' said Bella. She also didn't want to carry out the cleaning if Fiona Bartholomew wasn't going to pay up.

'Don't worry. I'll make sure you're paid straight away and if not, I'll pay you myself. I'm quite happy to take on the likes of Fiona Bartholomew – another woman who liked to make Max's life as difficult as possible. She was always hassling him for money even though they were divorced. I expect she's already calculated how much the daughter will inherit and how she can get her hands on it.'

'I didn't realise,' said Bella. 'They've been divorced a long time and she's arranging the funeral; I just assumed it was all amicable between them.'

'That one can hold a grudge, I don't mind telling you,' replied Mrs Bonham. 'She may like to come across as the grieving widow, but she's not. She's already tried coming in here to have a look around at what she can grab.'

'I had no idea. What about the daughter?' Bella was going to make the most of this while Mrs Bonham was in the mood for talking. The woman had been the school secretary for as long as Bella could remember and had certainly had a good working relationship with the head teacher, so could prove to be a useful source of information.

'Put it this way, the apple didn't fall very far from the tree where mother and daughter are concerned.'

'It's a shame Mr Bartholomew never married again,' ventured Bella, using Max's formal title to please Mrs Bonham and to try to encourage the older woman to divulge more information. She could see Mrs Bonham prickle at the suggestion and wondered whether she'd had some feelings for the head teacher herself.

'He was dedicated to the school and the children,' she replied, going over to the bureau and picking up a photograph of Max standing outside the school gates, which Bella judged to have been taken about thirty years ago when he first came to the school. 'Applewick Primary School was his true love.' Mrs Bonham gazed at the photograph, lost in her own thoughts for several seconds, with an expression somewhere between admiration and sadness. Bella gave a small cough, which brought Mrs Bonham out of her reverie. 'Right, well, I must get on. You'll come back when?'

Bella checked her watch. 'After lunch, if that's OK.'

'Perfect.' Mrs Bonham looked at the clock on the mantelpiece. 'Oh, goodness, I've got to dash. The vicar's due at the school any minute to talk to the children and try to reassure them. I really must go.' She pressed the door keys into Bella's hand. 'Lock up and drop them back to me once you've done the cleaning.'

Mrs Bonham rushed out of the house, leaving Bella alone in Max's study. That oppressive feeling of death weighed down on her again and she wished she hadn't agreed to the cleaning job, but she couldn't get out of it now.

Chapter 11

ESME

The Plot Thickens

Esme had to practically order her father home at lunchtime. They'd got the funeral of Albert Richards taking place the following day and Frank had been going over and over all the arrangements, making sure the hearse was clean and filled up with petrol, and generally fussing where there was no need.

'I have it all under control,' said Esme. 'You don't need to worry about anything. Please, just get off home now – Mum will be wondering where you are.'

'Yes, of course. Sorry.'

'And don't apologise, Dad. There's no need.' Esme gave her father a reassuring smile.

'I know, I shouldn't. You're perfectly capable of running this place and you don't need me at all,' said Frank. 'I just like to keep busy.'

'Go and be busy at home,' said Esme, helping her father on with his jacket. She was certain he was only flapping because

CHAPTER 11

he wanted to take his mind off the murder, and she imagined being at home with their mother – whose anxiety levels were rocketing at the moment – was quite draining at times. Her poor dad really was shouldering a lot of emotional weight. 'Later in the week, once we've had the Richards' funeral and then Max Bartholomew's on Wednesday, I'll do you a swap. I'll go and spend the afternoon with Mum and you can stay here at work. How does that sound?'

Frank straightened his jacket and fastened the button. 'You're a good girl. Don't know what I'd do without you.'

Esme sagged down in her chair once her father had left. The strain all this was putting him under was clear and she wondered how much more he'd be able to cope with. What if the police didn't find the real killer – what then? She felt sick at just the thought and resolved there and then to do everything she could to stop her father being charged with Max's murder.

Her mobile rang on her desk and she saw it was Conor, which instantly had her scrambling to answer it as her mind rushed forwards, willing him to tell her the case against her dad had been dropped.

'Hi, love,' said Conor and Esme knew from his serious tone that this wasn't going to be an uplifting conversation after all.

'What's up?' she asked, not feeling any need for social niceties.

'I've just been talking to one of the DCs from the station. He's working the Bartholomew case,' explained Conor. 'He's a good lad and he let me know a couple of things on the quiet.'

'Which are?' Esme didn't care how Conor had come by the information.

'They've had a look at your dad's phone records and have got the number he was called from – but it was a pay phone in

Applemere, not a private number in Great Midham.'

'That can't be right,' protested Esme. 'There must be a mistake.'

'I'm sorry, but there's not been a mistake. Look, I've got to go. Just thought I'd give you the heads-up as they're probably going to be talking to your dad again.'

'But it proves he got a phone call.'

'Yes, but who from we don't know. There's always the possibility that he could've made the call himself.'

'Why would he do that?' Conor didn't answer and the reason slowly dawned on Esme. 'To give himself an alibi.' The words were a whisper.

'The call was logged at nine thirty-three. Doesn't quite match up with the times your dad gave of getting the call at nine fifteen.'

'He was a bit vague about the times – maybe he just got it wrong,' suggested Esme.

'If it was just five minutes, you could give him the benefit of the doubt, but we're talking fifteen minutes,' said Conor. 'The CCTV shows him leaving Max's house at nine seventeen. That gives him enough time to drive to Applemere and use the pay phone to make a call to his mobile.'

'Dad wouldn't do that. And besides, he'd know the timings wouldn't match the CCTV footage.'

'If he was aware of the cameras, that is.'

'No, sorry, Conor, I refuse to believe it.'

'I'm just telling you how it looks to the police,' said her husband. 'Look, I've got to go. Speak to you later.'

When she got off the phone, Esme slumped in her seat. Things were going from bad to worse.

CHAPTER 11

Bella and Isla were sitting in the office with their sister for the lunchtime update meeting they'd arranged.

'So, how are we going to tackle things?' asked Isla.

Esme picked up her notebook from the desk. 'I've been writing a few thoughts down about what we know so far and what we need to know. Of course, there will be a lot of stuff that we don't yet know we need to know.'

'It's like a bloody riddle,' said Bella.

Esme gave her a reproachful look. 'If you can think of a better way to go about it then please do share.' She was aware of the spike in her voice but she wasn't in any mood to justify herself to her sister. Not today.

'Touchy,' commented Bella.

'Let's not get into an argument before we've even started,' said Isla. 'Let's just get on with it.'

'Hear, hear,' said Esme, earning herself an eye-roll from Bella that she ignored as she prepared to get the planning under way. She didn't want to tell her sisters about her phone call with Conor just yet – she wanted them to be thinking clearly without getting distracted by how damning that information could be. 'OK, I thought we could write down the names of anyone who has a possible motive, what that motive is, and what opportunity they had to carry out the murder. After that, we can work out how we will investigate them.'

'Sounds good. So, our first suspect ...' began Isla.

'Wait a minute,' interrupted Bella. 'I think the most important thing is to prove Dad didn't do it. I know finding another suspect would help but, ultimately, we want to show that it couldn't have been Dad because he was at Aunt May's. Everything after that is secondary.'

'Good point,' said Isla, who Esme felt was trying her hardest to act as peacemaker between her and Bella.

'Yes, we must do that too,' said Esme. 'In fact, this morning I went to see Aunt May. I was hoping she'd be able to give Dad an alibi but she's quite confused about dates. She can't really remember when he was last there, so her word wouldn't stand up in court if it came to that. I also asked the neighbours if they'd rung Dad but none of them did.'

'Won't the phone records prove who it was, though?' asked Bella.

'I was coming to that. I suppose I might as well tell you now,' said Esme, deciding she had no other option, and she went on to explain what Conor had said.

'Oh, God,' said Bella. 'That's not what we needed to hear.'

'There's no way Dad did what they're suggesting,' said Isla in alarm. 'He just wouldn't. He's just got the timings wrong, that's all.'

'We all know Dad is not a murderer,' said Esme. 'That's why we need to concentrate on proving someone else did it alongside proving he didn't. I know from what Conor's said in the past about cases that there's always pressure from above to solve the crime and make an arrest – especially so with a murder, like this one. The local press will keep on pestering the police for regular updates and the superintendent for the area won't want something like this dragging on. It's too high-profile and too serious to be forgotten about.'

'OK. Let's not waste any more time,' said Bella, and Esme was relieved she now seemed to have both sisters fully on board.

'Right then, we need to find out who the caller was. Someone from Applemere seems logical and, therefore, not a neighbour. Who other than a neighbour would phone Dad to tell him that Aunt May was unwell? That's question one.' Esme wrote it in

CHAPTER 11

her notebook.

'We'd still need to prove Dad did go over to Aunt May's, though,' said Bella. 'I don't know how we'll do that but we need to be thinking about it.'

Esme wrote another note to that effect and highlighted it in yellow. 'Other suspects? Now, there's Fiona Bartholomew – Max's ex-wife – but, so far, we haven't got a motive or opportunity.'

'She was always tapping Max up for money,' said Bella. 'That's what Mrs Bonham told me. Does she stand to inherit from his death?'

Esme wrote the question down. 'We should also consider his daughter, Tamsin, because if Fiona doesn't inherit then I presume she does.'

'Dan Starling,' said Isla in a small voice.

'Ah, yes. Now, tell Bella what you found out and what happened last night.'

Isla relayed the events to her sister.

'Oh, Isla, you are an idiot,' said Bella, not unkindly. 'Fancy going over to that place. Couldn't you have just watched to see if Dan went in?'

Isla looked down at her hands. 'I could have, but I wanted to see if he was with anyone. Just to … oh, I don't know … to convince myself he wasn't worth even thinking about.'

'You deserve far better than him,' said Bella, squeezing her younger sister's hand.

Isla gave a weak smile. 'I know. It's like a form of emotional self-harm.'

'No wonder you look so tired today,' said Bella.

'I wasn't drunk and I didn't have a late night. Conor came and got me around ten o'clock but Dad's car alarm went off in the night and then I couldn't get back to sleep after that. My mind was buzzing, thinking about how stupid I'd been.'

'Well, no more punishing yourself. And that's an order. From both of us,' replied Bella.

'So, we have to add him to the list since he had a motive,' said Isla in a more matter-of-fact tone, which Esme felt she'd put on as much for her own benefit as for theirs. 'He was in danger of being reported by Max for improper conduct with a parent. He also wanted the headship.'

'Do we know who the parent in question is?' asked Bella.

'I should imagine it's whoever the Apple Runner is that Isla heard with him,' said Esme. 'If we find out who she is, we might be able to apply pressure on her to confess – which would add weight to Dan's motive.' She wrote in her notebook: *Who is the Apple Runner?* 'We also need to find out who left the rose. If it wasn't Tamsin popping back in, then who was it? A secret lover of Max's?'

'I could ask Pippa Bonham,' said Isla. 'She was quite keen to talk about Max and, what with her dad being on the board of governors, she might know something about it.'

'Good idea,' said Esme. 'Anything else?' She looked at both of her sisters.

'I was asked by Mrs Bonham if I could clean Max's study,' Bella said. 'When we went around to the house, Suzanne Edwards gave Mrs Bonham a letter.' Bella went on to recount the frosty exchange that took place between the two women and Mrs Bonham's later comments. 'She really can't stand Suzanne. You should've heard her. Anyway, she had to shoot off to an assembly and left me with the keys to go back there later. The room needs a tidy-up after the police rummaged through everything looking for clues.'

'Wonder what the letter was about,' mused Isla.

'I'll make a note of it,' said Esme. 'But I'm not entirely convinced Suzanne and Mrs Bonham not liking each other is very relevant. I feel we're missing something.'

'She's an Apple Runner, you know,' said Bella. 'I checked the website the other day, and Facebook. Do you want to know who else are Apple Runners?'

'Well, duh!' Isla pulled a face at her sister.

'Tamsin Bartholomew. Fiona Bartholomew. Jessica Samson. Pippa Bonham. Any one of them could've been having an affair with Dan Starling that upset Max, with the exception of Pippa, seeing as she's single, but including Suzanne. How about we turn the tables and ask: what if Max was threatening to expose them if they didn't stop the affair? Then, they would have a motive to kill him.'

After jotting down the names in her book, Esme rattled her pen on the leather centre pad of the desk. 'OK, this is what we have so far.' She turned the notebook around for her sisters to see.

Who phoned Dad from Applemere?

Who was the Apple Runner with Dan Starling?
Suzanne Edwards
Fiona Bartholomew
Tamsin Bartholomew
Jessica Samson

<u>Suspects</u> <u>Motive</u>
Fiona Bartholomew Money.
Tamsin Bartholomew Money.
Dan Starling Job and/or affair

Suzanne Edwards Bullying issue re her son. Very close to Dan – affair?

Jessica Samson Possible affair with Dan

'And I suppose any one of those women could potentially have had an affair with Dan that Max might have been blackmailing them over,' concluded Esme.

'Or, look at it another way,' said Isla. 'Could one of them been having an affair with Max and it was Dan doing the blackmailing?'

Bella let out a sigh and shook her head. 'It's all just speculation, though. We need facts.' She got to her feet. 'I must get off to clean that study. I'll try to speak to Suzanne and see if I can get any info out of her.'

'And I'll speak to Pippa again,' volunteered Isla. 'She might know a bit more about what was going on behind the scenes at the school than she's letting on – seems her dad has been happy to share insider info, what with being on the board of governors.'

'We've got Max's funeral on Wednesday,' said Esme. 'I'll see who attends and maybe discreetly chat to some of them. If the killer is there, they may let something slip or appear nervous. Oh, I don't know. To be honest, I feel like I'm grasping at straws. I'll have to be very careful, but I'll try to talk to Fiona Bartholomew – she didn't have a good word to say about Max to her daughter. She might feel able to speak more freely after a few sherries at the wake.'

Chapter 12

BELLA

All That Glitters is not Gold

As soon as the meeting with her sisters was done, Bella made a hasty exit and headed back to the Old School House to get the cleaning over with. She wasn't relishing the thought of going into the place on her own, but the money would be handy.

As she cycled down the High Street towards the school she saw Ned's Morris Minor van parked outside the shop and Ned coming out through the door.

He saw her and waved. 'Hi, Bella!'

She slowed to a stop and greeted him as he came over. 'Hiya.'

'Glad to see you're cycling more carefully today.'

'Ha. Very funny.' Bella liked Ned. He was so easy-going and had this way of making life pressure-free. 'What are you up to? On your lunch break?'

'Yeah. I've just been doing the garden at the vicarage. I'm off to Applemere now to look at a new job for a nurse – she wants a pond and some landscaping doing. Could be a good earner. You don't fancy a ride out, do you? We could grab a drink at the Ship and Anchor or have a stroll along the harbour. I'll get you back in time for school pick-up.'

'Oh, Ned, that's a lovely idea and any other day I'd jump at the chance,' replied Bella. It wasn't unusual for her to take a ride out with Ned if she had the time; she enjoyed his company and the break in routine. They would often stop at a pub somewhere for a drink, although Ned never drank alcohol if he was driving. They found they could just enjoy each other's company, sometimes without the need even to talk, which was a relaxing feeling born out of years of familiarity. 'I'm just on my way to a cleaning job.' She could see the disappointment on his face even though he was clearly trying to hide it. 'Are you going to the funeral on Wednesday?'

'Is that going to be our social?' quipped Ned. 'Pretty sad if we have to use a wake to meet up.' He grinned at her.

'That's what our lives have come to after all this time in the village,' Bella laughed. 'Actually, I've got a favour to ask.'

'When haven't you?' said Ned, and Bella knew he was referring to the many occasions when he had helped her out with some DIY project or other.

'I need to take a rug to the dump sometime this week. It's too big and too dirty to go in my car.'

'Sure, no problem. I can sling it on the trailer. Is it from your place?'

'No. It's from Max's study. The one where, you know, he died.'

Ned pulled a face. 'Ah, that's what you meant by dirty.'

'Sorry. Is that OK?'

'Yeah, sure. No worries. Just let me know when you want it moved.'

'Thanks, Ned. I owe you.' She hopped back onto her bike. 'See you later.'

The thought of sitting with a cold drink outside the pub at Applemere watching the boats bob around in the harbour taunted her as she cycled up the High Street. It had been ages since she and Ned had spent any time together. They both seemed to be so busy at the moment and she knew things would only get busier for him now that summer was just around the corner. She'd turned him down the last time he'd asked her, too – also for a genuine reason, but it didn't make her feel any less guilty. She would ring Ned later and fix up a date to see him; he was a good friend and she appreciated his uncomplicated company.

Bella let herself into the Old School House armed with her bag of cleaning equipment and the industrial carpet sanitiser she'd picked up from the funeral parlour – it was sometimes needed after they'd brought in recently deceased clients. She shuddered and pushed the thought away; she really didn't need to add her own uneasy feelings to the spooky atmosphere that already occupied the house.

To break the silence while she worked, Bella switched on the old Bush radio that was sitting on the bureau. Chatter from the local radio DJ filled the room and was much better company than the lurking presence of not just death but murder, and Bella worked quickly.

First, she scuttled around collecting up the papers that had been abandoned on the floor and made a neat pile of them on the desk; she had a quick flick through but found nothing of note, most of them relating to education in some way or another. Next, she went over the surfaces with her duster and polish, buffing the oak bureau, bookcases, desk and chair, none of which appeared to have been attended to in quite a while. Max must not have had a housekeeper or Mrs Bonham would surely have asked them to carry out the cleaning. Bella finished off by scrubbing the carpet and managed to remove the faint stain of Max's blood. She sloshed out the water into the kitchen sink and went back into the study to vacuum the rest of the carpet. She would come back for the rug when Ned could take it in his trailer.

Job now done, all that was left before she could head off was to empty the wastepaper bin. She remembered spotting the wheelie bins lined up at the back gate from the study window and so carried Max's bin out through the back door and down the garden path. She could hear the children running around in the playground on the other side of the fence, shouting and squealing with laughter. It was a joyous sound that gave Bella some much-needed relief after the exhausting ninety minutes she'd just spent in the study. She thought of Jacob – no doubt one of those happy, carefree voices – and smiled as she remembered being one of the school's children many years ago enjoying the fifteen minutes of freedom that afternoon playtime offered.

As she lifted the lid of the wastepaper bin to empty out its contents, something shiny on the path reflected the May sunshine and caught her attention. She bent down and picked up a silver Paper Mate ballpoint pen. Wondering if it had been meant to be discarded as rubbish, she took an envelope from the wastepaper bin and tested out the pen on the back of it. Blue ink swirled in flawless patterns. Someone must have dropped it, she decided – probably Max.

Back in the study, Bella was about to place the pen on the desk when she noticed some wording engraved on the barrel: "25 years of dedicated service". Max had presumably received it as a gift a few years ago when he'd reached that milestone anniversary at the helm of the school. It was a poignant reminder of how much the school community was going to miss his leadership and how deeply he'd loved his job. Everyone knew he was dedicated to that school and its pupils. He'd always had the children at the forefront of his mind and had even managed to stave off closure some years ago when pupil numbers had dwindled; his enthusiasm and sheer determination had convinced the LEA to offer a reprieve, and ever since the expansion of the village in recent years, with new housing built on the north side of the river, pupil numbers had been thriving. Max had also been instrumental in setting up the village nursery school, which inevitably became a feeder setting for Applewick Primary School. What a shame he wouldn't be here to see his golden anniversary.

Bella replaced the pen and, after locking up the Old School House, made her way over to the main school site in search of Mrs Bonham. She pressed the buzzer at the glass-fronted reception area and to her surprise it wasn't Mrs Bonham who appeared but her husband, Keith, popping his head up from under the desk.

He slid open the glass door. 'Hello, there.'

'Oh, hello, Keith,' said Bella. 'Have you got a new job?'

Keith got up from his knees and stretched out his back. 'No, I'm just fixing the computer system. It overheated because the fan's not working. An easy fix.'

'But still beyond me,' said Mrs Bonham, entering the reception room. She turned to Bella. 'How did you get on?'

'All done,' said Bella, passing over the keys. 'And here's an invoice for the cleaning to give to Fiona Bartholomew. I'll come back later in the week for the rug – Ned Shepherd's going to take it to the tip in his trailer.'

'Righto, just call in and I can give you the keys. Now, let me settle that invoice with you,' said Mrs Bonham, taking her purse from her bag. 'I'll get the money from Fiona when I see her next.'

Despite Bella's protests that she didn't mind waiting, Mrs Bonham insisted on paying her in full. 'There you go. Now, will I see you at the funeral on Wednesday? Keith and I are going, of course. As is Pippa.'

'Yes, I'll be there. What's happening about the teachers – are they able to go?'

'They are. We have some supply teachers coming in to cover for the day. We did think about closing the school but, then, what would the parents do with the children if they're attending the funeral?'

'I wouldn't want to take Jacob,' said Bella. 'I expect it will be well attended, though.'

'Yes, I'm sure it will. I've said it before and I'll always say it, Mr Bartholomew was a well-respected and much-loved teacher and member of the community. I can't imagine anyone from the village would've wanted to harm him. Well, apart from the odd one.'

'Maureen,' warned Keith, stopping his wife from saying too much.

Mrs Bonham gave Bella a knowing but sympathetic smile. 'I'm sure they'll find out who did it soon enough. Don't be worrying about your dad. We all know what an upstanding member of the community he is. It will all be fine.'

Bella swallowed the lump in her throat and became aware of tears building in her eyes. She blinked hard and managed to say a muffled thank you before fleeing from the building. She had ten minutes before Jacob was due out of school but she could see parents already beginning to queue at the gate, waiting to collect their children. Wiping the tears that had escaped from her eyes, she sat down on the bench by the hedge and delved into her bag for a tissue.

One was thrust under her nose from in front of her. 'Here, you look like you need this.'

Bella looked up and, accepting the tissue, saw that it was Suzanne Edwards. 'Thanks.' She dabbed her face before blowing her nose.

Suzanne sat down next to her. 'Need a shoulder to cry on?'

'I'm all right. Just, Mrs Bonham said something and it had this unexpected effect on me.'

'Something not very nice, I take it,' replied Suzanne.

'Actually, she said something kind about my dad. You've probably heard he's been questioned about Max's murder. She told me not to worry and it set me off.'

Suzanne raised her eyebrows. 'That's one for the books. Me and her don't get on, as you probably guessed earlier.'

It was as if someone had handed Bella the golden ticket. She wasn't going to waste the opportunity. 'I did notice, actually. What was all that about?'

Suzanne gave a big sigh. 'Archie's been having trouble at school with a couple of the other boys. It's got progressively worse and I'd been to see Max several times but he just wasn't taking it seriously. To cut a long story short, I complained to the LEA about the way he handled it. Mrs Bonham took exception to that and stopped me in the street one day to tell me so. Naturally, I told her to mind her own business or else I'd be complaining about her next.'

'Oh, I didn't realise all that was going on.'

'I hadn't said anything as I was hoping the school would deal with it. I didn't want to fall out with the other mums about it, but I've had the school on speed dial for the past few months. I've dreaded having to pick Archie up and find out what's happened that day.'

'How's Archie's teacher been? He has Mr Starling, doesn't he?'

'Yes, and Dan's been wonderful – very supportive. I can't praise him enough,' gushed Suzanne, her eyes lighting up as she spoke. 'I made that clear when I sent off my letter of complaint.'

'It may be handled differently now that Mr Starling is Acting Head.'

'I hope so. I've actually withdrawn my complaint now.'

'Oh, is that what the letter you gave to Mrs Bonham was about?' asked Bella, making sure her tone sounded even. She really wanted to prise some information out of Suzanne.

'Yes.' Suzanne didn't meet her eye but instead looked away towards the entrance, further down the path. 'The gates are open, we'd better go. You OK now?'

Bella got up, racking her brains for a way to pursue the conversation. 'Are you going to the funeral tomorrow?' she asked as she walked alongside Suzanne.

'I don't know. I'd feel a bit of a hypocrite if I went.'

'You really feel that strongly about it that you won't go to his funeral?'

Suzanne spun around to look at her. 'It's up to me. I don't need anyone's permission not to attend, you know.'

'Sorry, I was just surprised, I suppose.'

Suzanne let out a deep sigh. 'No, it's me who should

CHAPTER 12

apologise. I'm sorry for snapping, it's just I've had the police over to see me today – asking all sorts of questions. I feel frazzled.'

'The police?' Much as Bella was sorry for the distress this would have caused Suzanne, it offered her some hope that the police were actually looking at other potential suspects. Or were they just trying to round up witnesses to strengthen their suspicions surrounding her father? 'Why were they asking you questions?'

'I don't really want to talk about it,' replied Suzanne. 'It's personal.'

'But to do with Max?'

Suzanne stopped walking and looked down at her feet. 'I complained to the board of governors about something he did, but I didn't really want to; I felt under pressure to, that's all.'

'Under pressure? From Jason?' asked Bella, wondering if it was Suzanne's husband who'd been behind it.

Suzanne hesitated, seeming about to deny it but then mumbling that, yes, it had been Jason. 'Of course, that's given the old witch in there another reason to hate me. You mustn't say anything, though. I just want it all to go away.' She began walking again.

Bella fell into step with her. 'I'll keep it to myself.' She didn't count telling her sisters, seeing as they knew already. 'Although, I'd never have thought Max would do anything … inappropriate. Are you OK?'

'I'm fine. Sometimes it's the people you least expect it from that are the ones to take advantage of their position.' The words came out in a rush on one breath before she strode off across the playground to collect her son, leaving Bella to sort through their conversation in her head. Although she knew what Suzanne's complaint was, something about her friend's explanation didn't feel right – but Bella couldn't quite put her finger on what.

Chapter 13

ESME

An Ungracious Exit

From her seat next to her sisters at the rear of the church Esme watched as their dad, with Derek, Sam and Charlie, shouldered the coffin up the aisle towards the wooden doors at the front. Fiona and her daughter Tamsin followed, their gazes fixed straight ahead, and behind them trailed Max's brother and his wife, who had driven down from Yorkshire, and a cousin from London with her family. Max appeared to have no other relatives than these, and Esme was glad so many of the villagers had turned up to give the head teacher a decent send off.

The coffin was carried out to the churchyard, where the grave had been dug in readiness – as a lifelong resident of Applewick, Max was entitled to burial at the local church. Overlooking the river to its front and enclosed by woodland behind, this was one of the prettier churchyards of the Apples and Esme always found in it a sense of calm and tranquillity despite the loss it represented to local families. She took a moment to look at the handful of wreaths and bouquets placed by the graveside. Fiona Bartholomew had asked that any financial donations be made to the school fund for a sensory garden that Max had been hoping to raise enough money to get done during the summer holidays – Ned Shepherd had said he'd do it at cost price and had been excited about working on a project for the village school.

Distracted by her thoughts of the sensory garden, Esme almost didn't register the bouquet of white roses nestled amongst the other flowers. She crouched down to look at the name tag.

To a dear friend, colleague, mentor and wonderful teacher,
   You will be very sorely missed.
   RIP
   Maureen, Keith and Pippa Bonham

The roses in the bouquet were the same variety as the one left on Max's coffin at the funeral parlour. It was then that Esme noticed a single white rose lying on the grass next to the grave. At first she assumed it had fallen out of the bouquet, but the white ribbon tied around its stem told otherwise. There was no name card attached.

'Come on, Esme. Everyone's going to the village hall now.' Conor put a hand under her elbow to help her up. 'Beautiful flowers, aren't they?'

'Yes, they are.' Esme looked around at the mourners, wondering who might have been the giver of the single rose. No one appeared to have the slightest interest in what she was doing; no one was watching to see if they'd been rumbled. As she walked with Conor out of the graveyard and over the bridge to where the car was parked, she pulled her pocket diary from her bag and slowed her pace down as she scribbled a note.

'What are you doing?' asked Conor as they got into the car. He peered over to see what she'd written. 'Who sent single rose?' he read out.

'It's rude to read over someone's shoulder,' said Esme, shoving her diary back into her bag.

Conor studied her face for a moment before starting the engine. 'You're not doing anything crazy like playing some sort of Miss Marple, are you?'

'Don't be silly.'

'Because if you are, you need to stop.'

Esme fastened her seat belt without looking at her husband. 'All ready. Let's go.' She continued to stare straight ahead, knowing his gaze was resting on her, before Conor grunted and then started the engine.

The wake was held in the village hall opposite the school, which Esme felt was fitting for the head teacher, and as she watched the mourners fill the large room she felt sure Max would have been touched to see so many faces from throughout his life.

In her capacity as one of those mourners, Esme mingled and was able to share anecdotes about the deceased without being intrusive. Although her primary concern was to show respect for Max, Esme was also gradually working the room trying to glean any bits of information that could help prove her father innocent, and it was Fiona Bartholomew who turned out to be a source of interest.

'I didn't realise Max was so well liked,' Fiona commented to Esme as she sat on a chair holding a glass of sherry in each hand. She drained one of them and placed it on a table that was within reach. 'Could do with bigger glasses.'

'It's a great turnout for him, that's for sure.' Esme sat down beside her.

'To be honest, though, how many of these people can truly say they were friends of Max?' carried on Fiona. 'Most of them are colleagues or villagers. And it's not nice to think that one of them is probably responsible for his death.'

'No, it's not a pleasant thought at all. But do you really think it was someone he knew? Who would hold that much of a grudge against him?' Esme hoped that by playing the innocent she could coax something useful from Fiona.

'You'd be surprised. Who's to say Max wasn't being difficult? I should know – I was married to him. There was many a time I'd have willingly strangled him with my bare hands.'

'We could all say the same about our spouses,' said Esme, tagging on a laugh.

'The difference is, most people wouldn't mean it,' replied Fiona. 'I'm sure there are one or two in this room who would've been glad to do it. Strangle Max, that is. Although it seems a cricket bat was their preferred method.'

Esme raised her eyebrows. 'Cricket bat?'

'It's missing from his study and, without getting into the gruesome detail, his injuries are consistent with blunt-force trauma – as they like to say on all those forensics shows.' Fiona took a gulp of her drink. 'Rather brutal, don't you think? I mean, to hit someone so hard around the head that it kills them there's got to be a significant amount of force, so either someone very strong or …' She paused for what Esme assumed was dramatic effect.

'Or …?' she prompted.

CHAPTER 13

Fiona slugged the remainder of her sherry down and leaned in close to Esme. 'Or they were driven by something much more powerful.' She moved even closer. 'Love.'

'Love? But who?' Esme raced through the possibilities, tilting her head slightly away from Fiona to avoid the sherry fumes. She suspected the woman had drunk far more than the two sherries.

'I've no idea, but Max knew lots of things about lots of people. He always did. Kept it all in his little black book, as they say. He made it his business and he wasn't averse to using that to his advantage.' Fiona stood up and staggered on her feet.

'You mean he was blackmailing someone?' Esme jumped up and caught Fiona's arm to stop her from stumbling over.

'I don't know. I'm just saying what he was like.'

'Have you told the police?'

'Of course, but I don't think they're interested. They think I'm a vindictive ex-wife.' Fiona gave what could only be described as an evil laugh. 'And they'd be right!'

'Mum! Oh, God, look at the state of you.' Tamsin took her mother by the arm and gave Esme a weak smile. 'I'm so sorry. I think it's all been a bit too much for her.'

Esme told her not to worry and Tamsin explained, 'We booked into River House Airbnb for tonight. I didn't think either of us would fancy driving back to Mum's. I'll take her back now.'

'Here, let me help you,' said Esme. 'We parked our car outside so I can drive you.'

They slid Fiona into the back of Conor's car and in just a few minutes were heaving her out again and guiding her inside the Airbnb. They plonked her rather unceremoniously on the bed, where she promptly fell asleep.

123

'Thanks ever so much,' said Tamsin as she followed Esme back out to the car. 'Look, I don't know what Mum was saying to you but she talks a lot of rubbish at times, especially where my dad is concerned, and especially when she's had a drink – combine the two and she tends to get carried away with her storytelling.'

'Don't worry, she wasn't really saying anything much,' replied Esme, feeling a wave of sympathy for Tamsin. 'How are you coping? Do you need help with anything?'

'That's kind of you. I'm OK. I hadn't spoken to my dad for a while.' She wrapped her cardigan around her body and looked out across the river in front of them. 'We had a disagreement about something and never got the chance to resolve it.'

'That must be tough,' said Esme, resting a hand on Tamsin's shoulder. 'Try not to torture yourself with that. Families fall out but underneath it all we still care about each other.'

'I said some horrible things, though.' She used the cuff of her sleeve to wipe her face.

'Take it from someone who's a parent, when our children say horrible things, yes, it's a bit of a blow, but we know they don't really mean what they've said – it's just an outlet for frustration.'

'I know, but I'm in my mid-thirties not a petulant teenager.'

'It probably feels worse today. In time you might be able to put it behind you and focus on the good memories you have of your dad.'

'I don't know if I'll ever be able to do that. It was a bad argument. I didn't agree with something he wanted to do. I should have left it; I didn't one hundred per cent know he was going to do it.'

Esme was desperate to know what this thing was but just

couldn't bring herself to ask outright. 'Maybe you can console yourself with the idea that he might not have done whatever it was he said he was going to do.'

Tamsin looked lost in thought now as she gazed across the riverbank towards Applewick Church. 'You're close to your dad, aren't you?' she asked, turning to look at Esme.

'Yes, I am.' Esme wasn't sure where this was going and was aware that to any onlookers in the know about the local murder case, the two of them were probably an odd sight – the daughter of the victim talking to the daughter of the prime suspect.

'Would you stand by your dad, whatever he did?'

Esme didn't know how to answer. What sort of a question even was that, given the circumstances? She thought hard about how to construct her response. 'I think ... I would always love my dad for being my dad but I may not always love his every action. Again, a bit like when your kids are naughty. Yes, I think that's how I'd see it. Does that help at all?'

Tamsin returned her focus to the church. 'I guess I'll never be able to put that theory to the test.' She closed her eyes briefly, sniffed, and wiped her cheeks with her cuff again before facing Esme. 'Thanks for your help. You're very kind. I think I would have liked you as a friend when I used to come and visit Dad as a kid.'

'I think I would have too.' Esme's heart went out to the other woman.

'Thank you for making today run smoothly. Mum will be in touch to settle the account.' She turned away and walked slowly up the path with her arms folded across her body and her head down.

Esme got back in her car to return to the wake as she'd

arranged to take her parents home afterwards. She'd been surprised when her mum had said she wanted to attend the funeral and hadn't been convinced it was a good idea given the state of Marion's nerves of late – but she'd appeared to be coping well enough with the occasion earlier. Before leaving with Tamsin and Fiona, Esme had spotted her mum sitting with Bella and Ned, the latter ever happy to chat all things garden with her.

Esme drove back to the village hall and stopped to give way to another car that was turning into the car park. It was a black Audi and Esme gave a start as she clocked that the passenger was DS Marsh. She knew the woman had only been doing her job, but Esme had taken a dislike to her when she'd been at the house interviewing her dad.

'What on earth are they doing here?' Esme muttered to herself as Marsh and another officer got out of the car and made their way into the hall. Esme parked her car and hurried in after them. What she witnessed next made her stomach lurch with fear and her heart race as panic set in. She could hardly believe what was happening.

Marsh walked over to Frank, who was sitting with Bella, Ned and her mother. She said something to him and then, with an outstretched arm, indicated for Frank to follow her out of the hall. Esme knew the police didn't haul people out of occasions such as funerals for no reason.

Conor was talking to the other officer and Esme could see the concern on her husband's face. He turned to Marsh and they exchanged some words. By now, Marsh was guiding Frank across the hall; they were right in front of her.

'What's going on?' asked Esme, making to grab her dad's arm.

CHAPTER 13

'Mind out of our way, please, Mrs Fairfax-Murphy,' said Marsh. She put an arm between Esme and her father.

'Dad! What's happening?'

'Don't worry, love. It's all just a misunderstanding,' said Frank but there was a tremor in his voice that Esme had never heard before.

Before she could say anything else the trio were out of the door. She looked back at her mother, who was crying. Bella was comforting her and Isla was dashing across the hall towards them. Conor, on the phone, was striding towards Esme. He put an arm around her and pulled her towards him, all the while continuing to talk on his mobile. He guided her out of the hall and then, unlooping his arm, ran over to the unmarked police car, where Marsh was now handcuffing Frank.

Esme ran over to the car too.

'Anything you say may be used in evidence against you ...' Marsh was rattling off the arrest speech.

'Stop! You can't arrest him. He hasn't done anything!' Esme could hear herself shouting at Marsh, who was completely ignoring her.

Conor paused his phone conversation and caught the door when Marsh went to close it. He glared at the DS and then bent down to look into the car. 'Don't worry, Frank. We've got a solicitor on the way. Don't say anything until you've spoken to him.' He stopped Marsh from shutting the door once again, staring straight at her, seeming to be defying her to challenge him. 'I'm still your superior,' he growled. Marsh hesitated before letting go of the door and taking a step back, whereupon Conor closed it himself.

DS Marsh got into the front of the car and Esme thought her knees were going to buckle as her father was whisked away in front of her eyes.

Chapter 14

ISLA

A Starling Confession

'Everyone just calm down a minute, please,' said Conor, raising his voice to be heard over the noise in Bella's living room where they had all congregated while the police carried out a search back at the family home. Isla couldn't help feeling sorry for him; it was a tough gig to control the females of the family – that's what her dad always said, anyway. 'Ladies, PLEASE!' It had the desired effect. Conor blew out a breath. 'If you all just sit down and listen, I can tell you what I know.'

'Yes, listen to Conor,' said Isla, backing him up.

'Thank you, Isla.'

'I can't believe they arrested him like that at the wake,' continued Marion. 'And then to search our house. Can they do that, Conor? Why couldn't they wait until he was home, or give us some sort of warning? This is awful.'

'I'm sorry, Marion, but it's a common tactic to arrest someone when they least expect it and then to immediately carry out a search of the home. It's not very effective policing to let the criminals know you're coming.'

'Conor!' reprimanded Esme as Marion gasped.

'Sorry, I'm not saying Frank's a criminal.'

'Let Conor tell us what he knows,' said Isla, sympathising with her brother-in-law's struggle.

'Yes, let's all be quiet a minute,' agreed Bella.

'Right.' Conor cleared his throat. 'I've been on the phone to my mate, who's actually at the house now, and I'm afraid it's not good news.'

'I don't think we needed your mate to tell us that,' muttered Bella and then, after a glare from Esme, she followed up with a quick 'Sorry.'

Conor rubbed his forehead in what was clearly exasperation. 'So, there's some new evidence against Frank,' he began. 'They were looking at the CCTV in Applemere to try to see who made the call but that phone box isn't covered by any cameras. So, they looked at the nearest camera, which is at the petrol station, and unfortunately, instead of seeing anyone who might've been going to the phone box, they saw Frank stopping at the station to fill up his car. That was just a few minutes before the call was made.'

'They think Dad phoned from the call box to make it look like someone else had,' said Esme, her heart sinking further than she would ever have imagined it could.

'Yep. There's more, before you all start shouting again,' warned Conor. 'There's a witness who saw him, or at least someone who they thought was your dad, walking out of the lane that runs behind the Old School House somewhere between ten and ten thirty that night. It puts him there, which is consistent with him being inside the house at the time of death.'

A fragile wail cut through the room as Marion clutched Esme's arm. 'That can't be right.'

'I'm sorry, Marion,' said Conor.

'But the CCTV shows him leaving at nine fifteen or something like that,' said Isla.

'He could have gone over to Applemere to make the phone call and then returned to Max's, gaining entry at the back where there is no CCTV footage,' said Conor.

'Who's the witness?' asked Isla.

'I don't know, and there's no way I'll be told that. My mate has to be careful – he's not supposed to be telling me anything.'

'It must be someone from the village if they saw Dad and were able to recognise him,' observed Isla. She hated the idea that this person who was instrumental in her dad's arrest was someone they probably all knew, someone they had probably spoken to this very afternoon at the wake.

'Is that it?' Bella asked Conor. 'As if that isn't enough. Did your mate not say anything else?'

'Your dad was also seen earlier in the week having what looked like a heated exchange with Max outside the funeral parlour.' He looked at Esme. 'Last Thursday, apparently, around five o'clock.'

'I left early that day,' said Esme. 'I had the dentist. Dad never mentioned it, though. What were they arguing about?'

'I don't know. The witness didn't hear them but was driving past and noticed they both looked agitated.'

'I'm sure there's a logical explanation for that,' Bella said.

'I'm sure there is, but it's only Dad's word,' said Isla. 'They can't exactly ask Max to corroborate any explanation Dad might give.'

'There's something else,' said Conor. Isla wouldn't have thought anyone could look graver than Conor was already looking but now he took his expression to a whole new level.

'What?' she asked, her voice faint, knowing this was going to be the body blow of evidence against her dad.

'The search they're carrying out this afternoon ...'

'Bastards, doing that while we're not there,' said Isla.

'Isla!' reprimanded Esme.

'It's true.'

'Never mind that, what the bloody hell have they found?' butted in Bella.

'In the garage rafters, right at the back, they found a cricket bat. Max's cricket bat. In other words, the murder weapon.'

Another wail emanated from Marion as Isla and her sister gasped in disbelief. 'No. That's not true. It can't be!' Isla jumped to her feet. They've got that wrong. Surely there's been some mistake. She looked at Conor but his face was one of deep sorrow.

'I'm sorry. I can't believe it myself but that's what they've found. They're going to be running it by forensics but they're pretty certain it's the murder weapon.'

'It can't be,' said Esme, echoing her sister's words. Marion was weeping now, with Esme and Bella comforting her from either side while looking stunned themselves.

'Oh, God, this is just too awful,' Isla gasped. She felt breathless. Her chest tightened and her windpipe felt constricted. She needed fresh air – this room was suffocating, crushing her, compressing the air from her lungs. As she rushed out of the door, across the hallway and out through the front door she heard Conor calling her but he didn't follow.

Isla stumbled down the path and onto the pavement. Her

CHAPTER 14

dad had been arrested. He was probably being charged with murder right now. They'd found the murder weapon in his garage. This was an absolute nightmare.

She didn't know where she was going, she had no destination in mind, but ten minutes later she was crossing the wooden bridge and marching along the river path. The sight of the church ahead stopped her. She'd never been particularly religious but she felt a sudden and overwhelming desire to seek help from some higher place, and how much higher could you get than God?

It turned out not even God was on her side. When she lifted the iron latch and then tried to turn the handle she was met with resistance. It was locked. Isla sat down on the wooden bench in the porch holding her head in her hands. She felt too numb and too shocked to cry. She just couldn't countenance her dad being a murderer, and yet – even with no other qualification than having watched all the CSI police shows – she knew that the evidence against him must be more than a coincidence. Motive. Opportunity. Evidence. All three boxes ticked.

As Isla sat there contemplating the awful situation her father was in, she became aware of voices approaching. She really didn't want anyone to see her, especially if she looked as dragged down as she felt, and she wasn't at all in the mood for talking. She pushed herself back into the corner of the porch so that, through the leaded side window, she could catch a glimpse across the stone wall of whoever was approaching while remaining unseen.

It was Pippa Bonham and her parents. She figured they must be on their way home from the wake to number 1 Orchard Cottages, which was reached by the river footpath or via the road to Appleside if you were going by car. She could see that Pippa had her head bent down as she walked alongside her father, with her mother slightly ahead of them. Keith's face held a frown and his voice carried across the otherwise silent graveyard.

'You've got to pull yourself together, Pippa. All this moping around – it's not good for you.'

'Your father's right,' said Mrs Bonham over her shoulder. 'Drawing attention to yourself like that back in the hall!'

Pippa stopped walking and glared at her mother. 'Oh, we can't have that, can we? Don't want anyone asking questions, now.'

'Stop that,' hissed Mrs Bonham, spinning around on her heel to face her daughter.

'Stop what? Telling the truth?' Pippa gave a derisory laugh. 'Everyone's going to find out sooner or later.' She barged past her mother and marched off down the path, leaving her parents gaping at each other before hurrying after her.

Isla remained in the porch for some time, not really sure what she'd just witnessed or what the Bonhams were talking about. Could it be Pippa was pregnant? That would explain how emotional she was these days. Isla really couldn't think what else it could be.

Sighing to herself, she thought she should make her way back to Bella's but decided she'd take the long way there. She sent Esme a text just in case they'd all started getting frantic about where she was.

Sorry, just needed some fresh air. Going for a walk. Won't be long. X

CHAPTER 14

She had a text message back almost immediately.

OK. Mum's going to stay at Bella's for a couple of hours. Conor and I are going to the house to make sure it's all tidy after the police search. Will ring you later. X

Isla felt both relieved and guilty. She was glad her mum was with Bella – she'd enjoy seeing the children when Bella picked them up from school, and they'd be a good distraction for her. On the other hand, Isla did feel bad she wasn't going to the house to help Esme, but she just didn't want to go home yet. It would mean seeing the garage and knowing the murder weapon had been there all that time and then facing up to the fact that her dad was in police custody. She tapped out another message to Esme.

How long does Conor think Dad will be held? X

Instead of retracing her steps over the footbridge, Isla continued down Church Lane, passing the vicarage with its gardens that stretched a good hundred metres along the lane to the main road. Two swans glided along the river and she was reminded of paddling here as a teenager during one particularly hot summer's afternoon. When she'd told her dad about it he'd been furious, saying how dangerous it was with the underwater weeds and with currents that could swipe a person down to Applemere and out to sea in a matter of minutes. Looking back, she could only blame the foolhardiness of youth; she'd thought she was invincible.

Her mobile pinging out a message alert broke her thoughts.

Technically he's being detained and interviewed under caution. Because it's murder, they can detain him for up to 96 hours before they have to charge him. X

Isla put her phone in her pocket, the message doing nothing to lift her mood or suggest her dad would be released anytime soon. She knew enough to understand that they wouldn't have taken him into custody if they weren't confident of their evidence, and finding the cricket bat would only serve to strengthen their case against him.

She was on the new bridge now – although, at ten years old, it wasn't exactly new. A bit like the "new" estate where Esme lived, on the other side of the road, which was about the same age, it was still seen as new when compared with the original houses in the village.

As she leaned over the white railings and looked down at the river again, watching the two swans disappear under the footbridge by the church, she heard a car cross the new bridge and then slow to a halt before reversing back to where she was standing. She turned around and was surprised to see Dan Starling in the driver's seat.

He lowered the window and leaned across the passenger's side. 'I thought that was you. Not planning on going for a swim, are you?'

'Not today.' She'd seen Dan at the church service and then later at the wake, but she had made a conscious effort to avoid talking to him. 'I'm just on my way home.'

'The long way around?'

'Wanted a walk, that's all.'

'I can't tempt you with a lift?' He sounded hopeful.

'You're going in the opposite direction,' remarked Isla.

CHAPTER 14

'Ah, yes, so I am. Wait one moment.'

Isla watched as he put the car into gear, drove forwards, swung around at the entrance to Church Lane and then drove back to her, albeit now parked on the wrong side of the road. 'How's that? Better?'

Isla couldn't help laughing. 'You're now facing oncoming traffic,' she said, trying to look reproachful.

Dan let out an exaggerated sigh. 'Damn. You'd better get in so I can rectify that.' He raised his eyebrows and gave her such a cheeky smile that Isla knew she was going to accept.

'Only to my house, though.'

'Nice to see you smiling,' said Dan as he pulled away from the bridge. 'I was hoping to get a chance to speak to you today but you were glued to one sister or the other all afternoon.'

'Tactical manoeuvre,' confessed Isla.

'About the other night at More Than Vanilla,' he began, his voice not unkind.

'Oh, please, don't,' said Isla, putting her hand over her face. 'I'm really sorry about that. And I'm so embarrassed, too.'

'You don't have to apologise.' He reached out and moved her hand away. 'It was quite sweet, really.'

'Now, I know that's not true,' said Isla, gazing out of the window, not able to look him in the face.

'It is! Cross my heart.'

She made herself look at him. 'Can we just forget about it?'

'Sure, but only when I've told you what I was doing there.'

'Do I want to know?'

'You might be surprised.' He turned the car onto the High Street. 'You mustn't laugh, now.'

'OK. I can't think why that place would make me laugh, but I promise.' She was intrigued.

'It was for research,' he replied.

'Research. For what?'

'I'm writing a book. A police procedural, and one of my characters goes to a club not unlike More Than Vanilla,' he explained. 'I've got a few contacts there I talk to for research. I don't go there for pleasure, so to speak.'

Isla felt the relief wash over her in tidal proportions. 'You're a writer?'

'Aspiring,' he confessed. 'I haven't got an agent. I'm not published or anything like that – this is my first serious stab at writing a book.'

By now they were pulling up outside her family house and Isla was grateful Dan had chosen to park where they were shielded from any onlookers by the hedging that surrounded the property. 'I feel even more of a fool now,' she said. 'Is that really the truth?'

'Of course. Again, cross my heart.' He drew his finger across his chest one way and then the other. Then he undid his seat belt and turned to face her. 'I really like you, Isla. I know it probably seems as though I've been avoiding you, but it's been a crazy week or so and – now, this may sound strange but hear me out – I like you enough to not want to hurt you.'

Isla's tidal wave of relief diminished to a faint ripple. 'That's the corniest way of telling someone you're not interested.'

'It's not meant to be. It is actually the truth. You're young, you're beautiful; you should be with someone your own age – someone who's going to treat you the way you deserve.' He trailed a finger through her hair, sending a shiver to her core.

'Ten out of ten for honesty, then,' said Isla. 'At least you're admitting to being a bastard.'

'I wasn't going to say bastard, exactly,' said Dan. 'I'm just

CHAPTER 14

not into commitment or anything long-term. I've recently come out of a divorce and I need time to chill.'

It took the sting out of the rejection a little and Isla couldn't help feeling sorry for him. She got out of the car and went around to the driver's side, leaning in at the window. 'Do you always manage to charm your way into making people feel sorry for you?'

'Mostly,' he said with a grin. 'I only say no to the girls who are worth it. You remember that, Isla Fairfax.' He gave a mock salute before turning the car around in the road and tooting the horn as he accelerated away.

Isla didn't know whether to laugh or cry. That was the most backhanded compliment she'd ever received.

Chapter 15

BELLA

Ned Makes a Discovery

In the end Marion had stayed with Bella because she hadn't wanted to go back to the house the previous evening and Bella had been happy to have her stay over. She sensed that Isla was having a hard time coping with it all and that she perhaps needed a bit of respite from being under the same roof as their mum.

'Why don't you stay again tonight?' Bella suggested as Marion nibbled her toast.

'I don't want to put you out,' said Marion. 'You can't be comfortable on the sofa.'

It was true, it wasn't an ideal sleeping place, but having only two bedrooms in her cottage didn't give Bella a lot of choice. 'Oh, I was fine. It was actually very cosy.' It was stretching the truth but Bella could cope with another night. 'Jacob likes you being here,' she added, which sealed the deal.

'Just tonight and then I really must go home,' said Marion.

CHAPTER 15

'Hopefully they'll let your father out today.'

Bella placed a hand on her mum's shoulder. 'Don't get your hopes up, Mum, just in case.'

'I'm trying to stay positive.'

'I know, and you're doing a great job. Now, I've got to get Jacob ready for school and then I've got some work to do this morning. Heather said she'd be over just after nine.'

Heather Tindle was an old friend of Marion's who lived over at Appledown and had offered to keep Marion company. It was a relief to Bella as she didn't like the idea of leaving her mother alone but, equally, didn't want to have to ask Isla to come over as that would defeat the whole object of giving her sister some breathing space.

Going into the playground, Bella was aware her father's arrest was the talking point of the community. She wasn't sure whether it was just because of her hypersensitivity to the fact that everyone would be gossiping about it, but as she went through the school gates she felt as though every adult in the playground stopped talking to look around at her. This included the usual huddle of her mum friends from Jacob's class, amongst which was Suzanne Edwards.

She felt someone slip an arm through hers. 'Chin up, Bells. Literally, chin up. We've nothing to be ashamed of.' It was Esme. Bella had never been so pleased to see her sister. They walked through the playground towards the group. 'Morning, ladies,' said Esme in her usual upbeat manner. There were some awkward hellos and much avoiding of eye contact.

Bella took inspiration from her sister's stoicism. 'Is there an assembly today?' She looked around at the faces of her so-called friends, finally settling on Suzanne's.

'Erm, yes. It's two fifteen this afternoon,' replied Suzanne.

'It's a whole-school assembly.'

'Not sure if I can make it,' said Esme. 'What about you, Bella?'

'Yes, I'll be there. Jacob would be upset if I wasn't.' She injected a defiance into her voice, challenging anyone to say anything about their father being arrested. The bell rang out for the start of the school day and the group seemed relieved to disperse.

'If anyone thinks I'm going to skulk around the playground like I'm guilty by proxy, they have another think coming,' said Esme. 'Mum OK?'

Bella loved her sister for her pragmatic approach and ability to thumb her nose at the rest of the villagers. 'Mum's fine. Heather Tindle's popping over to keep her company. Ned's helping me get rid of the rug from Max Bartholomew's today.'

'Excellent. Conor's going to try to find out what's going on with Dad and ask the solicitor to give us an update.' Esme put her arm around Bella's shoulders and gave her a squeeze. 'It will be OK. We need another meeting – maybe tomorrow. I'll speak to Isla. Got to dash. See you later, Bells.'

Bella collected the keys for the Old School House from Mrs Bonham and walked around to the back of the property, where Ned was meeting her with his trailer. So, this was where someone had allegedly seen her father leaving on the night of the murder. She'd love to know who that was. She wondered how they could've been so certain it was her dad since there wasn't any street lighting at the beginning of the track that accessed the back of the school and provided the residents of Lantern Road rear access to their properties. The nearest streetlamp was at the start of the terrace.

Ned arrived a few minutes later and together they went

CHAPTER 15

through the gate and into the back garden. 'Nice space,' commented Ned. 'You could do loads with this.'

'Yes, it's a good size, isn't it?' Running through the middle of the lawn was a stone path, on one side of which was a hedge, an apple tree and well-stocked flower borders, and on the other was a wooden fence separating the garden from the school playground.

'That's odd,' said Ned, coming to a halt. He nodded at the fence. 'That bird house on the grass there is leaning against the fence – hardly likely to encourage birds to nest in it.' He crossed the lawn and inspected the wooden hut. 'Oh, that explains it.' He lifted the roof up and took out a small camera. 'It's one of those cameras used for watching wildlife; goes off when it senses movement.' He looked around and pointed to an area near the rear gate where there was a gap in the fence and a metal dish on the ground. 'He was probably watching hedgehogs. Looks like he was leaving food out for them.'

'I didn't have Max down as a hedgehog fan,' said Bella with a passing interest. 'Put it back. Come on, let's get that rug and go. I don't like it here – gives me the creeps.'

'I've always wondered what it was like in here,' said Ned, replacing the camera and following her up the path. 'As a kid, I imagined it to be full of books and the whole place really dark and dingy.'

'You won't be disappointed, then,' said Bella. She laughed at the look of apprehension on his face. 'It's not that bad – just obvious that a man has lived here on his own for many years.'

'Yeah, he never married again, did he? Didn't even have a girlfriend or anything.'

'No – never heard of one or saw him out with anyone female.' She turned the key and opened the back door.

'Strange that.'

'Perhaps he just liked his own company.' They were in the kitchen now and Bella closed a drawer that was half open as they walked through.

'Maybe he had a secret life,' said Ned in a conspiratorial tone. 'Maybe he was a spy really and this was just his cover job.'

Bella laughed at her friend. She was used to his sense of humour, which never failed to bring a smile to her face. She'd always been grateful for his upbeat take on life, especially during some of her darkest days when her relationship with Jacob's dad didn't so much hit the rocks as nosedive straight off a cliff face into a raging storm.

'The rug's in the study, just through here.'

'Now, this is a dark and dingy room full of books,' marvelled Ned, completing a full 360-degree turn. 'My nan had a bureau just like this one.' He went over to it and looked at the photographs. 'Is that Bartholomew? He looks so young. In my mind he's always been about sixty. Oh, look, that must be Tamsin he's with there – she must be about five in this picture.'

'Even then he looked old,' said Bella, coming over to stand beside Ned.

'I saw her last night,' said Ned.

'Tamsin?' Bella picked up a piece of paper from the floor wondering how she'd missed it the other day and decided a draught from the window must have blown it off the desk. 'Yeah, Esme said she was staying at River House.' Ned lived a few doors down from River House in what used to be a tied cottage that his father had inhabited when working for the Needhams, who farmed several outlying fields to the west of the village.

CHAPTER 15

'She was coming down the path with Keith Bonham and Pippa,' continued Ned. 'Pippa looked very upset. You'd think she was the one whose dad had died, not the other way around.'

'I think Pippa's going through a tough time at the moment,' said Bella. 'Strange that she was at River House. I didn't realise she knew Tamsin that well – it's not as though Tamsin ever mixed with anyone in the village, and she must be a good ten years older than Pippa.'

'Keith would have known Max from way back. They both grew up in the village. I assumed it was to do with that,' said Ned, standing up and looking at some of the books on the bureau shelf. 'You know – offering condolences and asking if they can help in any way, that sort of thing. I was putting the milk bottles out when I saw them.'

'Mm ...' responded Bella, no longer concentrating on what Ned was saying. She was looking at the desk. 'That's odd. I could've sworn I put the pen on the desk there.'

'What's that?' said Ned.

'I found a pen out in the garden the other day when I was cleaning. I left it on the desk and it's not there now.'

Ned shrugged. 'Perhaps someone's used it.'

'But who, and why?'

'I don't know. People need pens all the time; it could've been Max's ex-wife, his daughter, or even Mrs Bonham. It might not even have been Max's pen.'

'I just assumed it was. It had something like "twenty-five years of dedicated service" engraved on it.'

'Still doesn't mean it was his.'

'I suppose not,' said Bella. Ned was now peering at the bureau and tapping his knuckles on the underside of the piece of furniture. 'What are you doing? Ned! You can't touch anything.'

'Just checking something,' he said, pulling open the door and kneeling down. He reached underneath, fumbling around for something. 'If it's anything like my nan's, there should be a little catch under here. Ah, there we go.' Ned got to his feet. '*Et voilà*! A secret drawer.' He pointed to the now-protruding plinth that separated the top half of the bureau from the drawers on the lower half. He pulled the plinth, opening the drawer. 'Bloody hell, Bells!'

Bella followed his gaze. 'Bloody hell, all right!' One half of the drawer was filled with bundles of ten-pound and twenty-pound notes, each wad wrapped in an elastic band. 'There must be hundreds of pounds here.'

'All neatly stashed away. I guess old Bartholomew didn't believe in a savings account.'

Bella stared at the money for a moment before speaking. 'We'll have to tell the police. I'm assuming they never found this drawer. You'd have to know it was there – you wouldn't just come across it.'

'What else is in there?'

'Don't touch anything!' Bella pulled Ned back. 'Fingerprints. It might be some sort of evidence and you go putting your hands all over it.' She took out a pair of plastic gloves from her bag. 'I use them for cleaning,' she explained when Ned raised his eyebrows. There was an envelope and Bella carefully removed it from the drawer and slipped the letter out from inside.

'Should you be doing that? asked Ned.

'Not at all,' replied Bella. 'You can wait outside if you don't want to be an accessory. Not that I'm planning on getting caught.'

'No, you're all right. I want to see what's in the letter. I'm guessing it's important – otherwise it wouldn't be in here with all that cash.'

The letter was printed and had a handwritten Post-it note stuck on top.

Don't think I won't hesitate to send this to the governors and share it on social media. I'm sure The Apples News **will be most interested. Pay up or else!**

Bella then read out the letter, which was not signed or dated.

Dear Board of Governors,

It is with deep regret that I have to contact you but I was subject to an incident recently involving Mr Max Bartholomew, Head Teacher of Applewick Primary School.

While I was in his office discussing a matter concerning my son, Mr Bartholomew made an inappropriate comment and sexual advance to me. I was totally shocked but managed to tell Mr Bartholomew in no uncertain terms that his behaviour was unacceptable and tantamount to sexual harassment. I am deeply upset by the incident and as I would not wish any other female to be put in a similar position, I feel I have no alternative but to make an official complaint.

I am considering taking this matter to the police too but am interested to hear from you beforehand.

'Wow!' Ned shook his head. 'Sexual harassment! Who'd have

thought? Hard to believe, though.'

'Doesn't mean we shouldn't,' said Bella. She placed the letter on the desk and took her phone from her bag, then proceeded to take a photograph. 'And before you say anything, no I shouldn't be doing this either but it might help to clear my dad. This could prove that Max had someone else out to get him. Pity we don't know who it's from.'

She replaced the letter in the bureau and then made a call to Conor to tell him about their discovery. Her mind was whirling with all the information she and her sisters had gathered so far – there was so much to sift through it was hard to make sense of any of it. She had to admit, she had a newfound admiration for the police and the work they did in solving crimes.

Chapter 16

ESME

Runners and Riders

'Is Mum OK?' asked Esme as Isla sat down beside Bella in the office of the funeral parlour. It was Friday afternoon and their mother had gone back to her own house that morning, saying she felt terrible kicking Bella out of her own bed and, anyway, she would prefer to be in hers.

'Yes, she's having a nap,' replied Isla. 'She knew I was popping out, but I don't want to be long.'

'Let's get straight down to business,' said Esme. She already had her notebook open in front of her. 'Time is against us – the police have until Monday teatime to charge Dad or release him. If they release him, he could still be rearrested if they get any more evidence.'

'They obviously haven't got enough to charge him at the moment,' said Bella. 'I've heard nothing about the money and letter Ned and I found. Basically, the police arrived, thanked us and dismissed us, saying they'd be in touch for a statement.

Has Conor said anything?'

'Only that he hadn't heard anything about the money or note. They currently have opportunity and the murder weapon, with a loose motive. They're asking for more forensic tests on the cricket bat, which Conor says could take a while. It doesn't all happen overnight like on the TV.'

'Hopefully the cricket bat will prove Dad isn't linked to it,' said Isla. 'You know, I've been thinking about that bat. Someone obviously planted it in the garage to set Dad up. I think whoever it was must've put it in there that night I went over to the More Than Vanilla club. I remember I was really tired the next day because the car alarm had gone off in the early hours.'

'That makes sense,' said Bella. 'They probably knocked the car and set the alarm off.'

'The police might get some forensic evidence from the bat that they can link to someone else,' said Isla.

'It might, of course, just prove they have no forensic evidence at all,' said Esme. Conor had warned her not to rely too heavily on this aspect. 'So, we need to get our act together.' She was trying to focus all her efforts and concentration on finding new evidence that would support their dad's innocence. She couldn't let herself dwell on the possibility of him being charged – she knew she'd fall apart if she did, and that was the last thing anyone needed right now. She cleared her throat. 'After Bella phoned me last night and told me about the money and the letter in Max's study, I put together a new list of things we need to find out.'

'Just out of interest, how much money do you think was there?' asked Isla, looking at Bella.

'There was six thousand pounds exactly,' replied Bella. She

took out her phone, tapped at the screen and showed it to her sisters.

'You took a photo?' Isla's eyes widened.

'And counted it.' Bella closed her phone.

Isla frowned. 'Is that legal?'

Bella gave a shrug. 'It's academic. The police don't know. And don't worry, I wore gloves. Anyway, it's not the ten thousand Dad owed Max, although that doesn't mean it's not some of it'.

'It could be something entirely unrelated,' said Esme as she turned the notebook around so her sisters could read what she'd written. 'These are our next questions.'

1. Who phoned Dad from Applemere?
2. Did Dad take a loan from the bank to repay Max? If so, why would he then kill him?
3. Was Max about to pay blackmail money, and who to?
4. Who was the Apple Runner with Dan? Can she tell us more about Dan and his disputes with Max?

Bella tapped the page with her finger. 'You should also add: "What is the connection between Tamsin Bartholomew, Pippa Bonham and Keith Bonham?" Ned happened to mention he saw Pippa and her dad talking with Tamsin, and Pippa had seemed very upset. I don't know if it's significant at all,' said Bella.

'Oh, and I saw Pippa with her parents,' added Isla. 'They were walking back along the river path to their house, I assumed. I was sitting in the church doorway.'

'The church doorway?' Esme gave Isla a quizzical look.

'Don't ask. I was just having time-out,' said Isla. 'Anyway, they were in the middle of some sort of argument. I didn't hear much, just Pippa basically saying something like, everyone was going to find out sooner or later.'

'Wonder what she meant,' mused Bella.

'No idea,' replied Isla. 'I wondered if she might be pregnant or something. For goodness sake, don't quote me on that, though.'

'Of course not,' said Esme.

'It might not be anything to do with Max's death,' said Bella.

'I'll make a note of it all the same,' said Esme, jotting a few words down on the paper. She tapped the pen absently on the desk once she'd finished, before looking up at her sisters. 'Back to Ned seeing Pippa and Keith talking to Tamsin, that might be more easily explained. Mrs Bonham was the school secretary; she had a good working relationship with Max. It's reasonable to assume Max was on friendly terms with Keith and Pippa, especially as Keith was also on the board of governors. I'll add that as well, but I think we need to concentrate on whether Max was being blackmailed.'

'I've been thinking about that,' said Bella. 'I wondered if it was something to do with Suzanne. When I spoke to her, she just said her complaint about Max was to do with her son's bullying – but there was also something else she didn't want to talk about. She said it was pointless now. What if she sent the blackmail letter that we found in the drawer?'

'Would she do that?' asked Isla.

'Possibly,' replied Bella. 'She didn't mind sending the bullying complaint. I'll try to talk to her again. I might just ask her outright.'

CHAPTER 16

'We need to find the Apple Runner,' said Esme. 'Which, of course, could be Suzanne.'

'Agreed. I'll do my best when I talk to her,' replied Bella.

'We must also consider other possibilities,' said Esme. 'It could be someone else.'

'I know you both think Dan might've done it,' said Isla, a defensive tone creeping into her voice, 'but I'm sure you're wrong. OK, I admit, he might be a bit of a ladies' man – and, yeah, more fool me for getting involved with him in the first place – but I saw him the other day and he explained that the reason he was at the More Than Vanilla club was for research. He's writing a book. He said that Max had seen some of the research photos on his laptop and got the wrong end of the stick.'

Esme sighed and gave her sister a smile. 'I know you want to believe the best of him,' she said, 'but all that sounds very convenient. I'm not so sure about him. And if Max had found out about the More Than Vanilla club and seen the stuff on his laptop, maybe he was threatening to sack him. Maybe Dan didn't take that well. Maybe they got into a fight in Max's study. And it got out of hand. And Max died as a result.'

'There's no evidence to suggest that, though,' retorted Isla. 'Much as I want to find someone else to blame, I don't think it's Dan. OK, so you've given him a motive, but that's all.'

'We need to see if we can place him at the scene somehow,' said Esme. She hated seeing her sister so hurt but she wasn't as easily convinced of Dan's innocence. 'And finding who the Apple Runner is might lead us to finding out more about Dan – how he really felt about Max and where he was on the night of …' She stopped mid-sentence.

'Yes,' said Isla defiantly. 'He was with me. At his place.'

There was an uneasy silence in the room as the sisters contemplated the alibi. It was Bella who spoke first. 'You were at his place, but you fell asleep because you'd drunk too much. What time was that?'

Isla looked embarrassed. 'I'm not sure. We went to his about nine o'clock.'

'And you fell asleep when?' asked Esme.

'I can't really remember but it was quite soon after we got there.' She frowned. 'I can recall looking at the clock and I think it was something like half past nine. I don't remember anything else until the next morning.'

'I know this is going to sound a bit out there, but you don't think he could've spiked your drink, do you?' asked Bella. 'That's pretty quick to be out like a light until the following morning. If he did, he still would've had time to drive back to Applewick and kill Max, then drive back to his place again where you were still sleeping. When you awoke in the morning – there he was, with you none the wiser.'

'Oh, please don't say that,' cried Isla, covering her face with her hands for a moment. 'I don't think he'd do that – I mean, where would he get the stuff from to spike my drink?'

'If he goes to More Than Vanilla, I'm pretty sure he'd have plenty of opportunity to buy the stuff there,' said Esme. She felt so sorry for Isla. This whole business with Dan wasn't getting any better. 'If we can find out who the parent was that Dan might have been having an affair with, which is likely to be the Apple Runner, which might be Suzanne, then we might be able to push for some answers.'

Isla let out a long sigh. 'That's a lot of mights.'

'Have you got a better idea?' asked Bella. 'Sorry, didn't mean to snap. I just feel so desperate and helpless.'

CHAPTER 16

'We all do,' added Esme, trying to ease the strain between her sisters. 'We just have to keep digging. Sooner or later, we're going to make a breakthrough.'

'I admire your confidence,' said Bella.

'PMA. Positive mental attitude,' responded Esme, hoping to instil some level of confidence in her sisters, too. She continued briskly. 'I'll go to the bank and see if Dad borrowed any money via the business account. I'll also get Dad's solicitor to ask him about the phone call – was the caller male or female, young or old? What exactly did they say? It might help. I'm not sure how, but it's worth a try.'

'When I speak to Suzanne,' said Bella, 'I think I'm just going to be direct and ask her if she's having an affair with Dan. I know that she and Jason haven't been getting on well for a long time. He's a bit controlling, from what she's said. Perhaps she was looking for comfort from elsewhere.'

'Good thinking,' said Esme. She turned to Isla. 'Do you think you could speak to Pippa Bonham? See what her connection with Tamsin is; find out if Tamsin confided in her about anything.' Esme stopped and held her pen in mid-air.

'Hello, she's thinking,' said Bella, giving Isla a wink.

'I've just remembered about the rose on the coffin,' said Esme. 'There was a bouquet of roses from the Bonhams at the funeral with the same type of rose as the one left on the coffin. Also, there was a single rose at the graveside – again, exactly the same.'

'Max's secret admirer,' said Bella.

'My thoughts exactly,' confirmed Esme. 'I'm going to ring around the florists. There's The Flower House near here, and another shop over in Appleside. I'll claim the name tag went missing and we're just making a list of floral donations for the family. It's not unusual for us to do that, so it won't seem like an odd question. If we can find out who left the rose, it might give us another lead.'

'All done?' asked Isla. 'I want to nip back and check on Mum before I go to see Pippa.'

'All done,' replied Esme.

'I hereby declare the meeting of the Applewick Village Mystery Club closed.' Bella rapped her knuckles on the desk in a gavel-like fashion before she and Isla got ready to make a move.

Once her sisters had left, Esme got to work on the investigation, deciding to call in at The Flower House in person. The bow window with the Georgian window panes was painted a glorious bottle green, with plants and flowers filling the space. Little terracotta pots, each labelling a different herb, hung by garden string from the top of the window and a wooden step ladder was standing at one side with pots of rosemary and lavender filling the steps. An old-fashioned butcher's bike in a green that matched the window frame was propped up outside, with "The Flower House" painted on its crossbar panel and a wicker basket attached to its front that was full to the brim with an assortment of artificial flowers. Jackie, the owner, was putting together a table decoration and Esme explained the reason for her visit.

'White roses ...' said Jackie, leaving the table decoration and picking up her order book. She began to flick through the pages.

'Yes, there was a bunch from the Bonhams and then one rose all on its own,' explained Esme. 'I didn't know if it had come out of the bouquet or if someone had sent it – the card seems to have got lost.'

'Here we go. Yes, the Bonhams ordered a bouquet of ten

white roses for Max Bartholomew.' She ran her finger down the order book. 'Sorry, I can't see an order for just one.'

'And you don't remember anyone coming in and asking for one white rose?'

'No. Sorry.' Jackie closed the book. 'I don't keep them in. I had to order the roses for Mrs Bonham, so I would have had to do the same for a single rose and there's definitely no order.'

'Not to worry. I'll try the florist in Appleside on the off chance.'

Esme left the shop and went back to the funeral parlour. Once at her desk, she looked up the number for Appleside Florists and went through the same scenario with them over the phone. No one had been in to order a single white rose and it wasn't something they kept in stock. Esme flopped back in her chair and muttered a curse under her breath.

It was then the thought struck her. Deciding to close up early, she hurried up the High Street towards the churchyard. As she crossed the footbridge she saw the vicar coming up the river path. Blast! She didn't really want to get into a conversation with him and have to explain what she was doing here but it was too late now to avoid him.

'Ah, hello, Esme,' he called, waving in her direction.

'Hello, Vicar,' she called back and then, in a flash of inspiration, took her phone from her bag and made out she was taking a call. She mouthed an apology to him. The ruse worked and the vicar smiled, swishing her apology away as they passed each other. Esme carried on walking past the gate to the churchyard and further along the river path until she was certain that by now the vicar would be well and truly ensconced in his house. She backtracked, still holding the phone to her ear in case she bumped into him but making it into the churchyard undetected.

Esme wove her way around the gravestones until she came to Max Bartholomew's grave, situated in the second part of the graveyard beyond a stone wall. The flowers from the funeral were still laid out neatly on the grave but they were past their best now, their petals curling and their leaves drying out from the heat of the sun. Esme knelt down and counted the roses in the bouquet. The she re-counted, just to be certain. Eight. The rose on its own made nine. What of the tenth rose? Was that the one left on the coffin? If it was, how had the mourner got hold of it before Wednesday?

Esme walked back to the funeral parlour to pick up her car, not feeling she'd achieved anything. It seemed logical that if Jackie had ordered ten roses, they must be the eight in the bouquet, the one on its own by the graveside and the one left on the coffin, but why and how they were separated she couldn't fathom. Would it have been Pippa or Mrs Bonham that left the two single roses? Somehow, she couldn't imagine either of them doing that.

Her next stop was the bank across the road. As an official partner in the business, Esme had access to all the banking records but she'd never really got that involved with the accounts. It was something her father liked to do and she'd been happy to let him. She wished now she'd been more astute where finances were concerned.

Having a bank in Applewick was a rarity for a small, rural community these days, even if it was only open two mornings and one afternoon each week. Every year there were rumours that it would be closing completely and future banking would have to be carried out in Great Midham but, so far, the village had been lucky. The sub-office was manned by two members of staff – Arnold, the sub-office manager who had been with the bank for years, and the clerk, Caroline. Both were nearing retirement age and Esme predicted it would be at that point the village bank closed its doors for good.

'Hello, Mrs Fairfax-Murphy,' greeted Arnold, who, although friendly, liked to keep up certain traditional values in using full and correct titles.

Esme returned the greeting and exchanged pleasantries with both members of staff before getting on to the purpose of her visit. 'Sorry to bother you,' she began, offering what she hoped was a charming smile. 'I'm just sorting out some paperwork for the accountant on behalf of my father and he's asked me to check something. Of course, as you probably know, I can't actually ask Mr Fairfax at the moment.' She paused and the two bank officials shared sympathetic looks with her.

'Yes, terrible business. We are very sorry to hear what's happening to your father,' said Arnold. 'How can we help?'

'When Mr Fairfax called in last week, can I just double-check what it was about? Only, the accountant seems to think it was to do with a loan or an overdraft and I know my father mentioned it but I can't find any correspondence confirming this.' She smiled and looked straight at Arnold as if this was the most natural thing in the world to ask for and there was no question of breaking client confidentiality.

For the briefest of seconds Arnold looked uncertain. 'I'd have to check if it was a company or a personal matter.'

'Of course, either way, the accountant needs to know. I mean, he could ask the manager at Great Midham but I said I'd come in and speak to you – after all, you know everything about the bank. I said to the accountant: Arnold is practically the bank himself and, based on his many years of service and experience, I would trust his judgement anytime over that of these young, fresh-faced managers who, in the good old days, would still be in junior positions.' Esme hoped she hadn't over-egged it, but she knew from conversations with her dad that Arnold didn't like having to answer to the youngsters, who were indeed young enough to be his grandchildren.

Arnold stood a little straighter and flattened his tie against his chest. 'That's very kind of you to say, Mrs Fairfax-Murphy.' He looked proud of himself. 'Your father did indeed call in last week to meet with one of the youngsters. Unfortunately, these lending advisors don't have the ability, authority or experience to make personal decisions – they simply input the data and wait for the computer to say whether any lending can be agreed.'

'And what was the outcome?' probed Esme, conscious she'd been away from the office for nearly an hour.

'As I say, it's all done by computer. If it had been down to me, I'd have given your father a loan there and then on the spot.' Arthur pressed his lips together and frowned before continuing. 'On this occasion, the answer was no.'

'And how much are we talking about?'

'I believe it was ten thousand pounds.'

Esme managed to contain the sigh and thanked Arnold before making her exit. Damn.

Chapter 17

BELLA

Spilling Some Tea

Every other Friday Bella's son, Jacob, went to his dad's for the weekend and on those days Esme always picked her own children up from school. Today was one of those days, so after the meeting with her sisters at the funeral parlour, Bella had the afternoon to herself. Under normal circumstances she might have phoned Ned to see what he was up to; today, however, she wasn't in the mood. Besides, she'd be rotten company as she knew she'd be distracted by thoughts about her dad. She immediately felt guilty for being so dismissive of Ned. Out of all of her friends, he was the one who was always there for her and who never said more than was needed. In the end, she spent the afternoon on something of a busman's holiday and cleaned her little cottage from top to bottom before getting changed for her regular Zumba class over at the village hall, where she usually met with Suzanne.

As the class got started there was still no sign of Suzanne, and five minutes into the first routine Bella had given up all hope of her turning up when in she bowled through the double doors. 'Sorry!' she called out to the instructor over the noise of the music before dumping her stuff on one of the outlying chairs and jumping straight into the routine next to Bella.

An hour later they were both puffing after a rigorous workout. 'I'm shattered,' declared Bella, taking a long drink from her water bottle. 'You OK?'

'Yeah, fine. Just got caught up with something and didn't realise the time.' Suzanne wiped her face with her towel. 'How are you? I heard your dad is still being held for questioning. Are *you* OK?'

Bella gave a resigned smile and shrugged. 'I think so – most of the time, if I don't dwell on it too much.'

'I don't know what to say,' confessed Suzanne as they walked out of the hall together.

'Don't worry. I know it's awkward for everyone. Most people are currently avoiding eye contact so they don't have to get into a conversation with me.' Bella thought about one of the mums from school she'd seen that morning who had practically sprinted away from the school gates rather than even acknowledge Bella was there.

Suzanne put an arm around her friend. 'Don't include me in that headcount. Most of the school mums are just fair-weather friends anyway.'

Bella gave a laugh. 'I'm beginning to find that out.' She hesitated but then decided there wasn't a better time than now. 'You don't fancy stopping in for a coffee, do you? I know it's short notice so don't worry if you're busy or you've got to get back, it's just Jacob's at his dad's this weekend and ... oh, I don't know ... I ...'

CHAPTER 17

'Say no more!' Suzanne held up her hand. 'Swap the coffee for wine and we'll call it a girls' night in. How does that sound?'

'You're on.'

Ten minutes later Bella was opening a bottle of wine and pouring two glasses while Suzanne gave her husband a quick call in the other room. Bella could hear her from the kitchen: 'I'm just stopping at Bella's for an hour ... yes, that's right, Bella Fairfax ... so what? She's a bit fed up ... of course I'm sure ... you can speak to her yourself if you want ... well, don't be so bloody suspicious.'

The call ended abruptly and Bella went through to the living room. 'Look, Suzanne, if it's going to cause problems for you, please don't stay on my behalf. I'll be fine.'

'Not at all,' said Suzanne. 'Jason's just being an arse.' She took her glass of wine and clinked it against Bella's. 'Here's to men who are arses.'

'I'll drink to that,' agreed Bella, sitting down on the sofa while Suzanne took the chair by the fireplace.

Suzanne took a sip of her wine and sighed as she sat back in the chair. 'Jase has always been the jealous type. At first I was flattered by it but over the years it's got unbearable.'

'Jacob's dad, Gavin, used to be like that,' said Bella. 'He never said anything outright but he was always checking up on what I was doing – where I was going, and who with. I've no idea why, it's not as if I ever gave him anything to be worried about. I was so in love with him, so in love.'

'And then he left you.'

Bella had spoken to Suzanne about her relationship with Gavin in the past but had never really gone into much detail about it. She wasn't one for oversharing, but this evening it felt natural to open up some more. 'Certainly did leave me,' she said. 'For someone he worked with. Turned out he'd been having an affair for about six months. I was the last to know. It was all so clichéd. Ha!'

'You don't sound very distraught about it now. Are you over it?' asked Suzanne.

'I wasn't, actually. Distraught, I mean. I was sad that our relationship had got to that stage, but it had been on the cards. After I had Jacob it was fine for a while, but we split up before Jacob was even two. It was for the best.'

'But it's been amicable, right?'

'More or less. I swore a bit, called him a few choice names. I told him he should've just finished with me rather than lie to me, but that was it.' They lapsed into a silence, which Bella broke first. 'Has it got to that point with Jason?' she asked in a soft tone.

Suzanne closed her eyes for a few seconds and then, opening them, sat forwards in her chair. 'I don't love Jason anymore but I don't know if I want to leave him.'

'It's not as easy as that, is it? You've got Archie to think of. Where would you go? What would you do for a home? What would you do for money?' said Bella. 'Unless you've already got somewhere to go or someone to go to.'

Suzanne shook her head and tears filled her eyes. 'I don't have any of those things,' she said, draining her wine. She reached over and refilled her glass, topping Bella's up at the same time. 'Our marriage has become more and more strained. We haven't had a physical relationship for at least six months. Sorry – TMI.'

'No, you're OK,' encouraged Bella. She really did feel sorry for Suzanne and although at the back of her mind she knew she might be on the brink of discovering whether or not Suzanne was having an affair with Dan Starling, her first and foremost thought was one of female solidarity. She didn't like to see her friend upset. 'Is there anything else?'

'God, I might as well tell you,' blurted out Suzanne, looking up to the ceiling. 'I'm not proud of what I've done and I didn't set out to do it, it just sort of happened.' Bella waited as Suzanne plucked up the courage to say what they both already knew. 'It's nothing serious or anything, and I don't know if that makes it worse or not. God, listen to me waffling on. You know what I'm going to say, right?'

'I think so.'

'I've been having an affair.' Suzanne drank her glass of wine down in one. 'There, I've said it. You don't look very shocked.'

Bella shrugged. 'It's not for me to be shocked. These things happen and usually for a reason.'

'He's not married so it's not as if he's doing the dirty – just me.' She gave a derisory laugh. 'Yeah, I'm the slut.'

'Stop! Don't say that.'

'You're very sweet, Bella. I'm very stupid, and that you can't deny.'

'Don't be putting yourself down. Is it someone local?'

'Sort of. I might as well tell you since it's practically over now, anyway – it's Dan. Dan Starling,' Suzanne said. 'I was so flattered by him. He's incredibly charming. I knew all that and, yet, I still fell for him. He was kind and understanding when I was upset about Archie being bullied. He said he didn't agree with how Max was handling it and he'd like to support me.'

'Dan seems to be very good at winning people over,' said Bella.

'I know. It's like he put this spell on me. Even though I knew what I was doing was wrong, I couldn't stop myself. He suggested we go for a drink to talk about Archie and one drink led to another, and then another, and before I knew it I was snogging him in the pub car park like a bloody teenager.' She shook her head. 'I just couldn't get enough of him. And, for a while, I thought he felt the same.'

'It's hard when you realise it's one-way,' said Bella. She really felt for her friend.

'I just felt so special and loved when I was with him. God, I sound pathetic.' Suzanne bowed her head and Bella was shocked to see her crying.

Bella put down her glass of wine and perched on the arm of Suzanne's chair to offer her some comfort. 'You'll get over this. It just feels bad at the time.'

'But it's not just that,' said Suzanne, mopping her face with a tissue Bella handed to her. 'When I said he put a spell on me, I meant it. I was totally at his mercy. I would do anything he said. Anything.'

Bella raised her eyebrows. 'Like what?'

'Like ... anything.'

'Like the More Than Vanilla club anything?' Bella asked.

'What?' Suzanne looked confused. 'Oh, nothing like that. He wasn't into anything kinky. No, what I mean is he asked me to do a favour for him and I did it. Now, I wish I hadn't. It was reckless.'

'What exactly did he ask you to do?'

'Look, this sounds bad and I know it is, but I just couldn't say no. I thought if I said no then he wouldn't want to see me again. I mean, how dumb is that for someone my age?' Suzanne paused. 'I'm only telling you because you're my friend and I know I can trust you not to judge me or to say anything to anyone. Promise?'

'What did you do?' asked Bella, avoiding making any promises she might not be able to keep.

'Dan is really ambitious. He loves his job as a teacher and he wants to progress. He doesn't just want to settle for Assistant Head Teacher, he wants to be Head Teacher,' said Suzanne. 'Anyway, he and Max didn't get on. Max thought Dan was being too friendly with the parents.'

'Yeah, I heard that. I also heard he went to the More Than Vanilla club, which is why I mentioned it.'

'He does, but it's for research. He's writing a crime book and has someone there who helps him with stuff.'

'Makes sense,' said Bella, wondering if it was a line Dan fed all the women in his life or whether there was actually some truth in it.

'Max saw some pictures on Dan's laptop when Dan was researching material for his book. Apparently Max was furious and wanted to have him disciplined or sacked. He said it was inappropriate and wouldn't listen to Dan's explanations. Anyway, Dan asked me to help him out … said it would help me, too.' Suzanne took a deep breath. 'He said we should get Max sacked. If Dan complained about him, it wouldn't be taken seriously – it would be seen as tit for tat because Max was threatening disciplinary action about the pictures – but if I complained, it would be taken seriously. He suggested I make a complaint of sexual harassment.'

'Oh, God, and did you?' asked Bella, keeping up the pretence that she had no idea about any of this.

'Yes. To my shame. I didn't want to but, as I say, I was under some sort of spell. I couldn't refuse Dan and so I wrote a letter to the board of governors. I was waiting to hear back from them but I was dreading it. I really was. I regretted doing it so much but Dan said I couldn't back out, it had gone too far.' Suzanne began to cry again.

'What will happen now?' asked Bella, although she thought she already knew the answer.

'As soon as I found out Max had been killed, I withdrew the complaint,' said Suzanne, wiping her nose. 'I wrote to the governors straight away and gave a copy to Mrs Bonham. That's when I saw you the other day.'

'Was it just the one letter?' asked Bella. 'Dan didn't try to get you to ... oh, I don't know ... bribe Max or anything? Send any threatening letters to him?'

Suzanne frowned. 'A blackmail letter. God, no! I wouldn't have done that. It was bad enough writing the formal letter – I can't imagine writing a blackmail one.'

'Not even if Dan asked you to?'

'He didn't, so it's all academic. Anyway, I've withdrawn my complaint. I can't go through with it and it's totally pointless now.'

'What has Dan said about that?'

'I've no idea. I was supposed to see him one evening. He invited me over and then, an hour later, he phoned to tell me not to bother. It was really strange. He was all over me coming out of school, giggling and saying he'd put clean sheets on the bed, and then I get the call to say it's all over.'

'And you've no idea why?'

'All I can think of is that I told him I'd sent the retraction letter to the board of governors. He wasn't very happy, but agreed that it was pointless to carry on with the allegation. I think, if I'm honest, he'd got bored with me and I'd served my purpose. Probably on to his next conquest by then. Poor cow, whoever she is.'

'I think you've had a lucky escape,' replied Bella, thinking about Isla and how she, too, had been fortunate enough to avoid getting involved with him.

Suzanne stood up. 'I'd better go. I don't want Jason getting his knickers in any more of a twist. I should really try to save my marriage.'

'Only if you think it's worth saving,' said Bella. 'You have to put yourself first.'

'I know.' Suzanne hugged her. 'What sort of a friend am I? I come here to cheer you up and end up telling you all my troubles. I'm sorry, Bella. Look, I'm sure everything will be OK with your dad, but give me a call tomorrow if you fancy meeting up for a coffee and I promise I won't bore you with my own problems.'

'You haven't bored me at all,' said Bella, telling the truth. 'It's been good to chat.' And that was even more truthful, Bella concluded, waving to Suzanne as she jogged off across the green towards her house. It had, in fact, been an excellent chat.

Chapter 18

ESME

Locking Horns

As was usual on a Saturday, Esme was up first. She relished the quietness of each new day and the chance to enjoy her morning cup of tea, either sitting in her kitchen looking out through the bifold doors onto the garden or, weather permitting, sitting on the terrace itself. Today, the weather was very much on her side.

The lawn stretched out over the entire length of the sixty-foot garden – an impressive size for a modern house – that shouldered the river. Esme usually found a sense of peace and happiness out here, but today it was missing. Even the bright yellow of the laburnum tree and the sweet scent of the wisteria that rambled over the summer house couldn't lift her spirits. Every time she thought of her parents she felt as though she were being punched in the heart. The idea of her dad having to spend another night in police custody accused of committing murder, and the fear that her mother was just a few days away

CHAPTER 18

from some sort of nervous breakdown, weighed heavily on Esme's mood. She hated the fact the police didn't seem to be looking for anyone else in connection with Max's death. It was as if they wanted to pin it on her dad so they could clear the case up as soon as possible. She knew from Conor that there was always pressure to solve high-profile cases, and the murder of the local head teacher definitely came under that category.

Esme sipped her tea, contemplating what she needed to do next. If she could just find out who had phoned her dad that day from the Applemere pay phone then he'd have an alibi. Well, maybe not an alibi, but it would at least give credence to his story that he was called away to make sure Aunt May was OK.

'Esme!' Conor's voice sounded out from within the house. It didn't have its usual friendly tone and she spun around in her seat as he approached the terrace. 'I've just had the bloody DCI on the phone. He's given me a right bollocking.'

'What for?'

'Because of you.'

Esme blinked, wondering if she'd missed some crucial part of the conversation. 'Me?'

'Yes.'

'I don't understand.'

'Because apparently you've been going around asking questions about Max Bartholomew's murder,' said Conor. He gave a deep sigh. 'You're doing exactly what I told you not to do.'

'Wait a minute,' snapped Esme. 'What you told me not to do? This isn't some draconian marriage from the forties where you tell me what I can and can't do.'

'You're being pedantic. You know what I mean.' Conor ran his hand down his face. 'The police went over to the bank to ask about your dad and were told you'd been in asking the same questions. You were also quizzing Fiona Bartholomew at the funeral.'

'I was doing no such thing,' said Esme. 'Well, maybe a little, but it was just in conversation – I wasn't exactly giving her the third degree.'

'It doesn't end there. Your sisters have been at it too.'

'I'm not responsible for their actions. I can't stop them asking questions.'

Conor narrowed his eyes and pressed his lips together before speaking. 'Look, Esme, I know you want nothing more than to prove your dad didn't kill Max, but you can't go interfering with police business. You've got to let them do their job.'

'I don't know what you mean.' Esme widened her eyes to suggest her innocence.

'You know exactly what I mean.' Conor sat down on the seat beside her and when he spoke, the anger was gone from his voice. 'Please don't get any more involved. There are procedures that need to be carried out so that all the evidence is gathered correctly and is admissible in the event of a court case. You could end up corrupting vital information.'

A robin landed in the beech tree and hopped onto the bird feeder, its wings fluttering every now and then as it pecked at the seeds, before it flew off into the bushes.

'I can't sit here and do nothing,' Esme said, still looking at the bird feeder as a couple of sparrows now helped themselves to breakfast. She could feel the tears gathering in her eyes at the thought of what might be to come. She turned to look at her husband. 'I'm desperate, Conor. I don't think I've ever felt this desperate in my life. We're all desperate.'

He reached over and placed his hand on her arm. 'You could

CHAPTER 18

just make matters worse.'

Esme pulled her arm away and stood up. 'You're not listening to me.'

'And you're not listening to me,' he snapped back at her. 'I'm getting it in the neck from the DCI. You running around playing Miss Bloody Marple is giving me a load of grief at the station – something I could do without, especially as I've still got to work with the team once all this is over.'

'Don't be so selfish.' She didn't know what else to say but was acutely aware that she was being just that herself. Picking up her cup, she marched back into the house. She hated arguing with Conor. They did it so rarely, but she was scared for her dad and she was hurt that her husband wasn't standing by her. Well, he'd just have to like it or lump it – right now, the most important thing to her was that a miscarriage of justice be avoided. She had to carry on, regardless of the consequences to Conor and to his job. But she was also aware that she was taking the strength of her marriage for granted. Her and Conor arguing and not coming to any sort of compromise just wasn't the way they worked. They'd always been a team. But, this time, she'd have to do things on her own and their relationship would somehow have to get through it.

She took a shower and by the time she was dressed and back downstairs Amelia and Dylan were loitering in the kitchen, with Conor standing over the hob tending to something he was cooking in the frying pan.

'Good morning, darlings,' said Esme, dropping a kiss on Amelia's head and ruffling Dylan's blond hair.

'Dad's making us pancakes,' enthused Amelia. 'I'm having chocolate sauce on mine.'

'I'm having maple syrup,' said Dylan with equal enthusiasm.

'Lucky you,' said Esme, revelling in her children's delight at the weekend treat. At least they still managed to lift her spirits, if only temporarily. 'You have swimming this morning,' she said to Dylan.

'Dad said he'd take me,' replied her son.

'Yeah, and he's going to take me for a milkshake while we wait,' said Amelia.

Esme raised her eyebrows. 'Is that so? Well, that sounds like a fantastic morning to me.' She glanced at Conor, who looked over his shoulder and made eye contact with her for the briefest of moments before returning his attention to the frying pan. Esme felt as though she was being left out of things that morning – but it did give her the ideal opportunity to do some more digging.

By nine thirty Conor and the children had left to drive over to the swimming pool at Great Midham and Esme was alone in the house. Before she'd even had time to think about what she was going to do, her phone rang. It was Bella.

'Oh, glad I've caught you,' began her sister. 'I've had something of a breakthrough. I met Suzanne at Zumba last night and she came back for a drink.'

Esme listened as Bella relayed the conversation to her. When Bella had finished talking, Esme blew out a long breath. 'Wow! So, it's Suzanne Edwards who's the Apple Runner and she's been having an affair with Dan Starling,' she summarised in a sentence. 'Let's see ... how does that fit in?'

'She absolutely denies sending the blackmail note,' said Bella. 'And I do actually believe her. There was no reason for her to lie about it – she'd already told me about writing to the governors. Have there been any developments with the police? Can you ask Conor?'

'Ah, probably not a good idea at the moment – we've had a bit of an argument,' confessed Esme.

'Oh no, that's not like you two.'

'The DCI isn't too impressed with us three asking questions and has told Conor to warn us off.'

'Really? We haven't done anything wrong,' said Bella. 'In fact, if it hadn't been for Ned and me, they wouldn't even know about the money or the letter. I take it Conor would rather we stopped.'

'Yep. But we're not going to.'

'Why don't you let Isla and me do the leg work?' suggested Bella. 'That way, you can tell Conor you're not doing anything now, and that will keep the peace between you two. I don't like it that you've fallen out.'

'We'll be OK,' said Esme. 'And no way am I stepping back. Conor and I will sort things out between us but at the moment that's not my priority. Dad is.'

'If you're sure.'

'I am.'

'OK, so back to the blackmail note, which is essentially what it is,' said Bella. 'If Suzanne didn't write it, then whoever did must have wanted it to look like it came from her, so they must have known about the letter to the board.'

'Who would know about that?'

'Mrs Bonham, anyone on the board of governors, Dan Starling. Can you think of anyone else?'

'Actually, there is someone,' said Esme. 'Tamsin Bartholomew. Remember I told you that when I took Fiona back after the wake Tamsin spoke to me? Well, she said that she and Max had fallen out. She didn't say what over – just that they didn't agree about something he wanted to do. Maybe she knew about the blackmail letter. And it would be perfectly acceptable to think that Fiona also knew.'

'Didn't you say they were having words at the Chapel of Rest?'

'Yes! That's right. I'd forgotten about that. Maybe they were talking about the accusation.' Esme tried to think back to the exact words of their conversation. 'It was something to do with what Max had done and Tamsin had fallen out with him over it but whatever it was, Tamsin didn't want her mother telling the police.'

'I feel like we're only ever getting half the details about anything. It's so frustrating.'

'I'm going to speak to Tamsin again today,' said Esme. 'I had no luck at the florists. The Flower House took the order for ten roses from Mrs Bonham and, as far as they were concerned, the bouquet was made up accordingly, but I checked at the graveyard and there were eight flowers in the bouquet, the one on its own, and I'm assuming the tenth rose from the order was the one left on the coffin.'

'It must be the Bonhams, then,' concluded Bella. 'Who else could it be, and why the single rose?'

'Oh, God, you don't think it's Mrs Bonham, do you? She adored Max, was so loyal to him. What if her feelings went further?'

'You're not thinking broadly enough,' said Bella. 'What if it's Pippa?'

'Oh no!' Esme put her hand to her mouth. 'That would tie in with why she's been so upset.'

'If that's what Tamsin and Max argued about, there's always the possibility they had an argument that went wrong,' ventured Bella.

'That's an awful thing to consider, but I suppose it's possible,' said Esme. 'But what about the money? How does that tie in?'

'I don't know. I must admit, I'm going around in circles with that one.'

Esme paced the kitchen, her phone pressed against her ear. 'OK, here's what we need to do. Isla needs to talk to Pippa and find out if she was having an affair with Max. If it's not Pippa then it's got to be Mrs Bonham. In that case, you'll need to talk to her. In the meantime, I'm going to see what I can get out of Tamsin. Hopefully we can start to put the pieces of this jigsaw together.'

'I don't like you going on your own,' said Bella. 'Not if Tamsin's capable of doing that to her own father.'

'She's more likely to open up if it's just me. Why don't you wait on the footbridge and I'll keep my phone on so you can hear what's being said? That way, if there's any trouble then you can come charging in like the cavalry.'

'Still not keen on you going alone, but I suppose it's that or nothing.'

'Good. Meet me at the bridge in twenty minutes.'

Chapter 19

ISLA

Still Waters Run Deep

'Mum's been looking forward to you coming,' said Isla as she let Heather Tindle into the house. 'She really enjoyed seeing you the other day.'

'I enjoy it, too. I don't mind my own company most of the time but it is nice to catch up with friends.' Heather smiled. 'Now, if you need to get off anywhere, I'll be here until lunchtime.'

'Perfect. Thanks ever so much, Heather.'

Isla made the older women a cup of tea before leaving them to chat. She was both grateful and sad about Heather having to come over – not that she seemed to mind, but Isla hated the idea that her mum didn't feel strong enough mentally to be left on her own. Their roles as mother and daughter had reversed over the last few days and it broke Isla's heart to watch her mum's usual enthusiasm and enjoyment of life seep away. Isla was thirteen when her mum had had her first breakdown and

CHAPTER 19

she looked back on it as a bewildering time. Not considered old enough by her dad to be told exactly what was happening, yet old enough to notice and make her own assumptions about her mother's state of mind, she had felt frightened. She'd had lots of unanswered questions – and what later turned out to be misunderstandings – about what was going on, with terms such as "crazy", "mad" and "fruit loop" bandied about in the playground by some of the kids at school, and for a long time Isla had resented her mother's mental-health decline. It had only been in recent years, as an adult, that she'd fully understood the situation, but by then it had been too late to talk about it with her mother – the moment had passed, and Marion was in good mental health. Until now. It was like watching a slow puncture as her mother's coping mechanism deflated further and further each day.

Isla was now heading towards the footbridge by the church, where she'd arranged to meet Pippa before she started work at the café that morning. As she passed The Flower House she glanced through the window and waved at Jackie, who was arranging the window display. Jackie waved back and then, in what appeared to be an afterthought, beckoned for Isla to come into the shop.

'I'm glad I saw you,' said Jackie, brushing down her bottle-green apron. 'Your sister, Esme, was asking me about some flowers at Max Bartholomew's funeral and I couldn't help her at the time, but since then I've spoken to Dale.' Isla nodded and waited for Jackie to get to the point and explain how her husband was key to this. Jackie continued. 'Can you tell Esme that on Monday, when Dale was in the shop, Pippa Bonham came in and asked to see the roses? Dale said she spent ages looking at them, which he thought was a bit odd but he didn't like to say anything. Anyway, he had another customer so didn't get the chance to ask her if everything was OK with the roses before he had to go out back to get his customer's order and when he returned, Pippa was gone.'

'Does seem a bit of a strange thing to do, but maybe Mrs Bonham asked her to check,' suggested Isla.

'I suppose it's possible, but I just thought I'd mention it,' said Jackie.

Isla took a moment to consider the scenario. 'When the roses came in from your supplier, did you count them to check they'd delivered the right number?'

Jackie looked a little put out at the question. 'Yes, of course,' she said.

'And when did you make up the bouquet?'

'Tuesday. We always do it the day before a funeral. I wasn't in on Tuesday, so it would've been Dale. Like I said to your sister, no one asked us to order a single rose so it must have come from one of the other florists.'

'OK, thanks. I'll let Esme know. Got to shoot off, I'm supposed to be meeting someone.' Isla left the shop, mulling over what Jackie had said. On its own it didn't seem like a very important piece of information but put it with what they suspected and it could be a very important clue. She phoned Esme and relayed the information. 'So, this is what could possibly have happened,' she said. 'Ten roses were ordered. Pippa goes in to look at them. While Dale's distracted, she slips two out and leaves the shop. The roses have already been checked, so no need for Dale to check them again before he makes them up into a bouquet. Jackie wasn't in the shop on Tuesday so she wouldn't have noticed either. The bouquet is brought round to the funeral parlour on the Wednesday and

CHAPTER 19

no one's noticed that two of the roses are missing.'

'So, Pippa sneaks in and puts one on the coffin and then discreetly lays the other next to the bouquet at the funeral,' concluded Esme. 'Well done, Isla. At last, we seem to be making progress. Did Bella tell you about Suzanne?'

'Yes, she phoned me this morning,' replied Isla.

'Actually, I'm just heading out the door to meet Bella and then I'm going to speak to Tamsin.'

'I won't keep you,' said Isla. 'I'm meeting Pippa now and I can see she's there already. I'll keep you posted. Bye.' As Isla approached her friend, the latter didn't look any happier than she had the last time they'd met. 'Hi, how are you?' asked Isla, leaning on the wooden rail in a mirror image of Pippa's pose.

'You know ... about the same,' said Pippa, leaning further over to gaze at the water streaming underneath the bridge.

The tidal river was fast-moving with plenty of undercurrents and, beautiful as it looked, when the tide was on its way out it was particularly dangerous. 'Have you thought about talking to someone?' suggested Isla, beginning to feel a real concern about Pippa's despondency. 'I mean a professional, like your GP.'

Pippa shook her head. 'Dr Taylor. He'd probably end up telling my parents.'

'He's not allowed to do that. Patient confidentiality. Whatever you say to him stays with him, like a priest.'

'Maybe I should go to confession instead,' replied Pippa. 'Perhaps I need to unburden myself.' She pushed herself upright and turned to rest her back against the wooden rail. 'Anyway, don't worry about me. I'll be OK. What did you want? What's with all the secrecy of meeting and not being able to talk over the phone? Is it to do with your dad?'

Isla bit her lip. 'It is, actually, but indirectly.'

'Now I'm even more intrigued.'

'Last week, at the funeral parlour, someone left a single white rose on Max's coffin,' said Isla, measuring her words so she could gauge the response. Currently there appeared to be no reaction from Pippa as she picked at her fingernail. 'Esme wondered who'd left it. She saw one just the same at the wake – it was the same type of rose as the ones in the bouquet your mum ordered.'

Isla paused and waited for the silence to force a response. Finally Pippa broke. 'Could be a coincidence.'

'It wouldn't have been taken from the bouquet at The Flower House when Dale served another customer and you were looking at the flowers, would it?'

Pippa gave a snort. 'There was me thinking I'd got away with it.' She looked at Isla. 'Yes, it was me. I'll wait while you join up the dots.'

Isla put her arm around her friend's shoulder. 'You and Max – you were having an affair.'

'Not an affair,' insisted Pippa. 'That makes it sound sordid, as if we were doing something wrong. We weren't. We were two consenting adults. Neither of us was married or in a relationship with anyone else. It was not an affair. It was a relationship. It was love. We were going to wait for him to retire and then move away to start afresh, somewhere no one knew us or would judge us.'

'Sorry, I didn't mean to be so clumsy,' said Isla. 'That's why you've been so cut up – because of ... what happened.'

Pippa let out a sob and Isla held her, stroking her back and trying to soothe her. 'I can't imagine how you must feel,' she said at last when Pippa pulled away to wipe her face. 'Does anyone know? Your parents?'

Pippa nodded. 'They know. They've known for a while. And Max's daughter.'

'Tamsin?'

'Yeah.'

'At least you have someone to talk to, people who understand why it's so hard for you.'

'I wish that was the case,' said Pippa. She blew her nose and wiped her face. 'Just because they knew, it didn't mean they approved. And now, I can't exactly go to any of them for support. Mum and Dad don't understand. And Tamsin – she's dealing with her own grief. I did go to see her but she didn't want to talk.'

'It must be difficult.'

'It is, for both of us. She was polite but she said she couldn't deal with what I was going through and although she didn't say it outright, I know she blames me for her falling out with Max and not reconciling with him before …' She broke off, unable to finish the sentence.

'I know you said Dan Starling and Suzanne Edwards were giving him grief,' said Isla, thinking back to their conversation in the café garden. 'Was there anyone else? What about Tamsin or her mother?'

Pippa looked startled for a moment, her eyes darting down and then up again. 'Erm, I wouldn't like to say, really.'

'What is it?' urged Isla, sensing that a revelation was on the tip of Pippa's tongue. 'My dad is being held. The police think he did it. I need to know if there's someone else who might have held a grudge. Please, Pippa.'

'OK, but I have no proof and I'm only guessing … but when I said Tamsin wasn't happy with Max, I mean she was furious.

She phoned him one evening when I was there and although I couldn't make out what she was saying, I could hear her shouting down the phone at him. He was trying to explain and when she wouldn't listen, they had a full-blown argument. About ten minutes later Fiona Bartholomew was on the phone to him telling him what she thought of him. Fiona still doesn't care, even though he's dead, but Tamsin feels really guilty. And so they both should.'

'Wow. I didn't realise, and I guess the police don't know this either ...'

'I don't know. They haven't been to see me. I was expecting them to but when I saw Tamsin, she said she hadn't told the police about us as she didn't want her dad's name to be dragged through the mud, with everyone talking about him and me. That suits me fine. And my mum and dad.'

'But isn't that withholding information?' asked Isla, thinking how this was actually a vital piece of information.

'You can't say anything,' said Pippa, grabbing Isla's arm. 'You *mustn't* say anything. There's no need to. You'd just be causing more pain for everyone. I've told you this as a friend and if you breathe a word, I'll just deny it and say you're making it up to get your father off the hook.'

Isla pulled her arm away, alarmed at Pippa's sudden change in demeanour. It was like a Jekyll-and-Hyde transformation. 'But, Pippa, I can't not tell the police. They need to know.'

Before Isla knew what was happening, Pippa had seized the collar of her shirt and pushed her against the railing, pinning her there with her body weight. 'Don't you dare! You keep your mouth shut.' She gave Isla another shove so she was bending backwards over the wooden rail.

Isla attempted to push her away, struggling with her, trying to twist from her grasp. 'Get off me!' she grunted as she summoned up as much strength as she could and pushed hard against Pippa's hands. She managed to catch Pippa off balance, making her stumble backwards and let go of Isla's clothing before banging into the handrail on the other side of the bridge and tumbling to the ground. 'What the hell are you doing?' shouted Isla. 'You're crazy!'

Pippa's face contorted with rage as she got to her feet. She pointed her finger at Isla. 'I wasn't joking. You say anything and you'll regret it.'

'What are you talking about? Are you actually threatening me?' Isla laughed at the ludicrous situation she found herself in. How had it got to her and her friend fighting on the footbridge?

Chapter 20

ESME

Blood is Thicker Than Water

Esme's house on the new estate was a stone's throw from the footbridge and as she crossed the main road to Church Lane on her way to meet Bella, she could see two figures on the bridge. She squinted and, to her horror, realised it was Isla and Pippa and they were wrestling with each other.

'Hey!' Esme yelled, breaking into a run. She shouted again but neither of the women turned around. By now, Isla had pushed Pippa away and they appeared to be arguing with each other. By the time Esme reached the bridge, Pippa was already stalking away. 'Isla, what the hell was that all about? Are you OK?'

'She just launched herself at me.' Isla sounded stunned.

'Why?' Esme held her sister's arms and, standing in front of her, looked her up and down to assess her condition. She didn't appear to have any physical marks, thanks goodness. 'Should I call the police?'

CHAPTER 20

'No. Not for that, anyway,' replied Isla, turning her gaze away from the departing form of her attacker. 'I'm fine, honest. Just a bit shook up. I don't think I've ever been in a fight.'

Esme brushed Isla's hair from her face. 'You once had a fight with Richard Kimmins when you were in Reception. I think it was over a red crayon.' She looked at her little sister with a wry smile.

'God, Richard Kimmins,' said Isla with a laugh. 'I did have it first, though.'

The two sisters laughed and Esme was relieved Isla seemed to be all right. Over Isla's shoulder she could see Bella cycling down the High Street towards them.

Bella hopped off her bike and leaned it against the railing before coming up onto the bridge. 'Hiya. I've just seen Pippa Bonham marching down the road. I called out to her but she just glared at me.' Bella stopped talking and looked from one sister to the other. 'OK, what have I missed?'

'Nothing much,' replied Isla with an exaggerated air of nonchalance. 'Just Pippa losing the bloody plot and trying to throw me off the bridge.'

'What?'

'Pretty much my response,' said Esme.

'In a nutshell, when I asked her about the rose, she confessed it was her and admitted to having a relationship with Max Bartholomew.'

'She admitted it. That's good,' said Esme. 'How did it descend into a fight?'

Isla went on to explain the chain of events. 'So, when I said she should go to the police, she got all aggressive and was shouting at me, saying I wasn't to tell them anything. Next thing I know, she's grabbed me and we've got into a tussle.'

'Seemed like more than a tussle from where I was,' remarked Esme.

'No wonder she looked mad as hell when I saw her,' said Bella. She turned to Esme. 'We need to let the police know.'

'We do,' agreed Esme, 'but not before I've had a chance to speak to Tamsin.'

'I don't know what all this is going to achieve,' said Isla.

'We need to know if what Pippa said is true,' explained Esme. 'Did Tamsin fall out with Max over the affair? Was Max really planning on leaving Applewick with Pippa?'

'Maybe that's what all the money in the drawer was for – a nest egg for their new life together,' suggested Bella.

'It's possible,' said Esme. She pursed her lips as she contemplated the whole situation. 'What I don't understand is how the police haven't been in touch with Pippa yet. Surely they would've looked at Max's phone records and seen lots of calls or texts to Pippa if the two of them were having an affair. How else would they have been able to arrange meeting up?'

'I suppose they could've met each time and then planned the next meeting,' said Bella.

'But who does that? If they were so in love, as Pippa claims, they would've been exchanging goodnight messages – miss you, love you, that type of thing.' Esme drummed the wooden handrail with her fingernails. 'Unless he had a different phone – one he used just for Pippa. One he didn't want anyone else to know about.'

'A burner phone,' said Isla.

'Exactly,' replied Esme. 'So, where would he have put that? Bells, did you see a mobile phone while you were tidying up?'

Bella thought back but shook her head. 'Nope. Nothing like that. Just a pen. No phone. Wait a minute – you know when I went back to the study with Ned and we found the money and the letter, I also noticed that the pen I'd found in the garden and then left on the desk was gone. Plus, there were a couple of bits of paper on the floor, which I assumed must have slipped off the desk – there's a draught from that old sash window – but what if someone had been back in, looking for that phone?'

'Wouldn't the police have already found it?' asked Isla.

'Not if it was hidden in a secret place, like …' She held her hands out, palms up, encouraging her sisters to finish the sentence.

'Like the drawer in the bureau,' supplied Esme.

'Precisely. And if Suzanne didn't write that blackmail note, maybe it was put there by whoever was looking for the phone – which must mean …' Again, she waited for a conclusion.

'Which must mean – whoever it was knew about the secret drawer,' finished Esme.

'Exactly. Go to the top of the class, girl,' said Bella. 'And who would know about the drawer? Someone like Tamsin. I'm sure she would've been told about it or discovered it at some point in her childhood – it's the sort of thing kids love.'

'Pippa might know as well,' put in Isla. 'Max might have told her about it to reassure her that the phone was being kept in a safe place.'

'And possibly Mrs Bonham,' said Esme. 'She'd worked with Max for years. Maybe he'd told her about it at one point.'

'The more we dig, the more questions we turf up,' remarked Bella. 'Questions and no answers.'

'Which is why I'm going over to speak to Tamsin right now,' replied Esme. 'I'm going to ring you and keep the call open like we arranged, Bella.' She recapped to Isla how she was going to put the phone in her pocket so Bella could hear what was being said. 'That way, if I need help, God forbid, you'll both be right there.' She took her phone from her bag and connected with Bella's phone. After they tested to make sure Bella could hear Esme with the phone in her pocket, the three sisters looked at each other. 'We're doing this for Dad, remember,' said Esme. 'Whatever happens, we need to find another suspect.'

Esme walked away from the bridge and across the car park to Riverside Drive, which ran parallel with the river, both meandering on towards the village of Appleside. She glanced back at her sisters and Bella gave her the thumbs-up sign.

Tamsin opened the door of the Airbnb with a surprised look. 'Esme, I wasn't expecting you. Is everything OK? If it's about the funeral bill, we're very happy with everything, we just haven't got around to sorting out the money yet.'

'No, it's nothing like that,' replied Esme, offering a friendly smile to allay Tamsin's apprehension. 'I'm not here on official business, as it were. It's more of a personal matter.'

Tamsin looked hesitant. 'Mum's not here but she'll probably be back soon. She's gone over to pick up the keys to Dad's place from Mrs Bonham – we've got to clear his stuff out. To be honest, neither of us fancies doing it.'

'I can imagine,' said Esme. 'It is actually you I wanted to speak to.' She looked over Tamsin's shoulder.

Tamsin took the hint and moved to one side. 'Do you want to come in?'

The Airbnb was a light and airy three-bedroom cottage with a spacious kitchen-diner at the rear of the property and a living room at the front that offered views of the river and the church opposite. Esme often recommended it to clients as somewhere for friends or relatives to stay if they were travelling to Applewick for a funeral. She followed Tamsin

CHAPTER 20

into the living room but declined a drink, opting for a glass of water instead. 'I'll get straight to the point,' she said.

'Please do, I'm intrigued.' Tamsin gestured to the chair by the window for Esme and took up a position on the adjacent sofa.

'It's a bit delicate and I hope you'll forgive me for being direct but there's no point in beating about the bush.' Esme realised her opening gambit was doing just that and the amused look on Tamsin's face told her she wasn't the only one to notice. 'As I'm sure you know, my dad is being held in custody in connection with the death of Max –'

'The murder,' interrupted Tamsin. 'The murder of my father.'

Esme met her gaze. 'Yes. The murder.' The words felt lumpy in her throat but she wasn't going to be made to feel ashamed or guilty. 'Obviously, my dad didn't kill your dad and I'm trying to prove that, even though the police seem to have made up their minds already.'

'Obviously,' said Tamsin. There was a tension in her voice that hadn't been there before.

'One of my sisters spoke to Pippa Bonham and she told us about her relationship with Max.' Esme scrutinised her face for a reaction but Tamsin remained motionless and expressionless. Esme continued. 'She said Max was going to move away with her. They were going to start a new life together.'

'That's what she said, is it?'

'She also said you weren't happy about it. Is that what you were referring to when you said you and your dad had fallen out? Was it over his relationship with Pippa?'

Tamsin eyed Esme for a few moments before letting out an impatient huff. 'What am I supposed to say to that? It's really none of your business, and how this will help your dad, I don't know … oh, wait, please don't say you're trying to shift the blame for my father's murder from your dad to me? Honestly, Esme, that's ridiculous.'

'I'm just trying to build up a complete picture, that's all. Pippa doesn't want the police involved but you know we have to tell them about their relationship.' Esme pressed on. 'I just wanted to know what the truth was. If I'm honest, I can't imagine it could possibly have been you who struck the blow, but the police do need to know about the whole situation.'

'I don't want my father's name dragged through the mud and everyone gossiping about him,' said Tamsin in a small voice, her tough exterior crumbling as she spoke. 'He doesn't deserve that. He was so well respected; I can't bear for him to be thought of as someone who had a silly infatuation with a young village girl.'

'The police do have to be told, though, but you know they will be very discreet.'

'He'd changed his mind,' said Tamsin, looking up at Esme. 'He phoned me to tell me that he'd spoken to Keith Bonham and had come to his senses.'

'What did Keith Bonham say to make your dad change his mind?' Esme's interest was piqued.

'Keith said, what if it were the other way around and it was him wanting to run away with me? Dad said it made him see things in a completely different way. It was like an epiphany. He said he realised then that what he was doing was ridiculous and he'd told Pippa so that afternoon.'

'That's not what Pippa's saying.'

'She wouldn't – it doesn't suit her narrative. She couldn't accept it. I feel sorry for her because I think she really was in

CHAPTER 20

love with Dad.' Tamsin shivered.

'Have you spoken to Keith or Pippa about it?' ventured Esme, hedging her bets and trying to steer the conversation.

'No,' replied Tamsin and then she hesitated. 'Actually, yes. Keith came to see me. It was all very awkward. He said Pippa had given Dad some money to look after, for when they went off together. Apparently, she'd emptied her savings account and Dad was looking after the cash for her.'

'What did you say to Keith?'

'I said I'd have a look. To be honest, I just wanted to get rid of him. I felt uncomfortable with him being there.'

'Was he threatening?'

'No, not threatening. He seemed just as uncomfortable as I did and said that Pippa didn't know he was here, that he was doing it for her as he didn't think it right that she should lose so much money. In fact, he asked me not to say anything to her about seeing him.'

'And you'd had no idea the money was there?'

'No. None at all. To be honest, it was the day after the funeral and I didn't feel up to rummaging around in Dad's things trying to find some money that may or may not belong to Pippa. And even if I did find it, I wasn't going to simply hand it over on their say-so. I just placated Keith and said I'd look so that he'd go away.'

'Poor you,' said Esme. She knew she wouldn't have liked to be confronted by Keith Bonham either. On the face of it, he came across as friendly enough, but he had a bit of a reputation in the village for his short fuse.

'It's all academic now, anyway. The police are holding the money as possible evidence,' said Tamsin. 'Not sure how Pippa feels about that if it is her money.

'You sound very patient with her. I don't know if I'd be like that if I was in your position.'

Tamsin gave a shrug. 'What's the point in being nasty to her? Despite what I think and the conversations I had with my father, after what's happened it would be petty.'

'You're being very gracious.'

'She's a nice enough girl but I can't say I wasn't pleased when Dad said he'd changed his mind.' She dipped her head. 'It's just a shame I didn't get the chance to tell him. You see, I was away for the weekend when he phoned to tell me about changing his mind so he explained it all in a voice message. After I'd listened to it, I thought I'd go over and see him in person but ... but I left it too late.'

Esme was just about to offer some comfort when she heard the door opening and Fiona calling out: 'I'm back! God, you won't believe how much junk your dad has in that house. Anyway, I thought ...' She stopped talking as she entered the room, seeing Esme there. 'Oh, sorry, I didn't realise we had a visitor.'

Esme rose from her chair. 'I just called by to make sure you were happy with everything last week,' she said, moving over to stand between mother and daughter to give Tamsin a chance to compose herself.

'We were very happy, thank you,' said Fiona, a note of caution in her voice.

'Tamsin and I were just saying it's a shame we didn't really meet up as children, given we're the same age,' blagged Esme. 'Anyway, I'm very glad you're happy with everything. I'll leave you to it.'

She hurried out of the house as soon as she could without it seeming like she was making a great escape and forced herself

CHAPTER 20

to wave from the end of the path.

'Well done.' Bella congratulated her sister as Esme arrived back at the bridge. 'Nicely executed.'

'What did you make of that?' asked Esme, taking her phone out of her pocket and ending the call.

'I had it on speaker phone so we could both hear,' said Bella. 'What do I think? I really don't know. It sounds as though Pippa has taken the ending of the relationship and then Max's death very, very badly. It's sent her over the edge, if grappling with Isla is anything to go by.'

'What do you think, Isla? You're very quiet,' said Esme.

'Why do you think Pippa doesn't want the police to be involved?' Isla asked. 'Surely she's got nothing to hide. If anyone didn't want the police involved, it should be Tamsin – and even she seemed resigned to the fact it was going to happen now. I don't get why Pippa was so adamant about it.'

'I need time to think this all through,' said Esme. She checked her watch. 'Oh, God, look at the time. Conor and the kids will be back. I need to get home – I'm in the doghouse as it is.' She gave both her sisters a hug. 'I'll speak to Conor about what we've found out so he can pass the information on to the police but in the meantime, get your thinking caps on. I feel we're on the verge of something important – quite what, I don't know, but it's there, we've just got to suss it out. Speak later. Love you both.' And off she dashed.

Chapter 21

BELLA

The Night Garden

Bella had planned for an evening in front of the TV catching up on the latest box set with a box of popcorn and a can of Diet Coke. Some weekends when Jacob was with his father Bella enjoyed the solitude, but tonight it was bringing her none of the usual respite and she found herself missing her son deeply. He may only be four years old but just one cuddle from him, or a cheeky grin, had amazing restorative powers and made Bella feel as if she could take on the world. She wished he was here now. On top of missing her son, Bella couldn't stop thinking about her dad and the fact that it was less than twenty-four hours now until the police must either charge or release him. The uncertainty was making her feel restless and she couldn't settle or concentrate on anything.

So, when her phone buzzed and she saw it was Ned calling, she felt her spirits lift a little.

'What you up to?' asked Ned, getting straight to the nub of

CHAPTER 21

the conversation.

'Nothing. B. O. R. E. D.' Bella muted the TV.

'Perfect! I'm about to resolve all that for you.'

'You are?'

'Yep. Get your coat on, we're going down the pub.'

'The Horse and Plough?'

'Yeah. I know it's not the most salubrious of establishments, but I don't fancy driving or shelling out for a taxi.'

'OK,' agreed Bella, figuring beggars can't be choosers. 'How long will you be?'

'About two seconds.' With that, there was a rap at the front door.

Bella laughed, switched off the TV and got up to open the door. 'I admire your confidence in my acceptance,' she said, stepping aside so Ned could come in.

'I wasn't taking no for an answer,' replied Ned. 'I thought you could do with cheering up.'

Bella slipped her phone into her bag, which she slung across her shoulder, and then grabbed her jacket from the coat peg. 'Can we just sit in the saloon bar at the back, though? I don't fancy sitting in the main bar and either having everyone stare at me or someone ask questions about Dad.'

The saloon bar of the Horse and Plough was busy enough that they could slip in unnoticed but not so busy that they couldn't grab a table in the corner towards the back. Ned went up to the bar and got their drinks.

'You don't need to hide away,' he said, placing the two bottles of lager on the table.

'I know, I'm just not in the mood for other people tonight,' admitted Bella. She took a swig from the bottle. 'Present company excepted, of course.'

'Naturally.' Ned tipped his bottle towards her in acknowledgement before taking several gulps. 'That's better. I've been cutting down some massive leylandii today. It was hard going on my own.'

'Where was that?'

'Over at Appledown. It didn't help that I had the next-door neighbour coming out and complaining.'

'About what?'

'Oh, disturbing the birds in her garden – said some were nesting and I could shock them all to death.' Ned sighed and rolled his eyes before taking another slug of lager. 'She was also going on about the hedgehogs.'

'Oh dear, poor you,' said Bella.

'I'm only doing my job. It looked like she had a small animal sanctuary going on in her garden – chickens, rabbit pens, a goat. Just as well it was a big garden – about a hundred feet, I'd say. She went inside but I could see her watching me from her upstairs bedroom window with a pair of binoculars.'

'Binoculars!'

'Yeah, I guess she uses them to watch the wildlife in her garden,' said Ned. Bella paused, beer bottle midway to her mouth, as a thought struck her. Ned cocked his head to one side and looked at her. 'You OK?'

Bella held up a finger to stop him interrupting her train of thought as the idea crashed around her brain so fast that it was a job to pin it down; finally, she wrestled it into submission. She put the bottle down on the table. 'Sorry, Ned. I've got to go.'

'What? We've only just got here.'

Bella was already out of her seat. 'I've got to do something.'

Ned rose, taking a final gulp from his bottle, and hurried

CHAPTER 21

along behind her as Bella burst out onto the street, pulling on her jacket.

'Can you please tell me what's going on?' pleaded Ned.

Bella was by now striding along the High Street towards the Old School House. 'I don't know why I didn't think of this before,' she was saying out loud but not necessarily to Ned. 'What with everything that happened at the house, I totally forgot about it.'

'Bella! Stop!' Ned caught her arm and brought her to a halt. 'What are you going on about?'

'You talking about the crazy neighbour, the animals she has, the binoculars she uses to watch the garden made me think of Max Bartholomew's garden and the bird house you spotted the other day. The one with the camera in it.'

'And?'

Bella was walking off again. 'And – it may give us the evidence we've been looking for to prove that Dad didn't kill Max.'

'You're going to have to fill me in on that thought process.'

'The CCTV at the Old School House only showed the front door. The rear camera was out of action. What if whoever killed Max came in through the back garden? If that camera in the bird house is one of those that records when there's movement, what if it captured on film someone coming in that night?'

'Bloody hell, Bells,' said Ned. 'And that's where you're going? To get the camera?'

'Of course.'

'In that case, I'm coming with you.'

They headed up to the top of the High Street and turned onto Lantern Road, taking the track that led to the back of the Old School House. Bella lifted the latch on the gate but when she tried to push it open, it wouldn't budge. 'The bolt must be across on the other side,' she said in a low voice to Ned. 'Maybe Fiona or Tamsin bolted it when they were here earlier.'

'I'll hop over,' said Ned, assessing the six-foot-high stone wall. There was no way to lean over the gate to unbolt it as the wall extended into an arch over the top of it. 'Give us a leg-up.'

Bella cupped her hands together and, leaning against the wall for support with her knees slightly bent, braced herself for the weight. Thankfully Ned was athletic and nimble, and on the second attempt managed to hoist himself up and over the wall. He unbolted the gate. 'I hope they haven't had the CCTV fixed in the meantime,' he whispered as Bella slipped in through the gateway.

She nipped across the lawn and, with the aid of the moonlight, was able to locate the little bird house and extract the camera. She dropped it into her bag and zipped the bag back up. 'Got it,' she said. 'How are we going to relock the gate and get out?'

'I'll bolt it once you're out and then use the wheelie bin as a hop-up.'

A few seconds later, Ned was jumping back over the wall and landing on the ground with a gentle thud.

'Thanks, Ned,' said Bella with warmth. 'I wouldn't have been able to do all that on my own.'

'You know what we've done is basically stealing,' said Ned as they hurried back out onto Lantern Road and rounded the corner onto the High Street.

'I'll put it back if there's nothing on it,' said Bella. 'We'll go back to mine now and look at it.'

Within a few minutes they were sitting in Bella's living room, the camera placed on the centre of the coffee table while they took a moment to eye it up. 'So, are you going to look or do you want me to?' asked Ned at last.

Bella wiped her palms down her trousers. 'I'm a bit nervous. A bit excited and a bit like I don't know if I want to do this,' she admitted. 'What if there's nothing there and I've built this whole thing up and it's just a bloody hedgehog or a fox?'

'What if it's not?'

'OK, let's see,' said Bella. She picked up the camera and turned it over to inspect the back. 'Do you know anything about these?'

'Not really, but it looks like the whole back opens on these hinges here.' Ned pointed to the side of the device. 'There's probably a release catch or a pressure point on the right-hand side.'

'Ah, here we go,' said Bella, sliding across a small catch. She eased the back of the camera open. On the inside of the door was a screen with buttons marked up for play, fast-forward and rewind, while the other side just looked like the back of a normal digital camera. Bella pressed a few buttons but nothing happened.

'It's probably dead,' said Ned. 'What sort of charger does it take?'

Another inspection revealed a standard USB port. 'I'm sure it's the same as my e-reader – I've got a cable upstairs somewhere.' Bella left the camera with Ned and nipped up to her bedroom, returning in less than a minute with the charging lead and plug. It was the right fit and she plugged it in. Within a few seconds a little red LED light began flashing. 'I guess it's charging.'

No amount of staring at the camera was going to make it charge faster, Bella finally conceded, and went to the fridge, hooking out a bottle of wine. She poured each of them a glass and switched on the TV to distract herself from the camera. Then she sat down on the sofa next to Ned and tried to concentrate on whatever programme it was blaring out. Neither of them felt the need to make small talk and Bella was glad they could sit silently in each other's company without any self-consciousness. Her thoughts turned to her father and the looming deadline of the following day. Would the police formally charge him or not? She looked over at the camera, which was still flashing red. 'Come on,' she urged, sitting forward on the edge of the cushion, her fingers drumming on her glass.

Ned moved forwards and put an arm around her. 'Keep calm,' he said, pulling her towards him and kissing her on the head. 'Give it another five minutes and I reckon it will be charged enough for us to look at.'

Ned's guess proved to be right and a few minutes later the light on the camera turned amber, showing it was charged enough for them to look at it as long as they kept it plugged in. 'Right, here goes,' said Bella, flicking on the camera and fiddling around with the date selection. 'Thank goodness this automatically records the date and time.'

Bella pressed play, Ned peered over her shoulder, and together they studied the footage in front of them. 'It only records when there's been movement,' said Ned, 'so we won't have to trawl through hours of footage. Oh, wait, here's the first one.'

'It's a mouse! Did you see that? It scurried across the path there and under the bin.'

'Flick to the next clip.'

It was the mouse again. The clip after that was a cat, and

the next one the same cat walking back the other way. It was the fifth clip that made Bella's breath catch in her throat. Someone had hopped over the wall, just as Ned had done earlier. They were wearing what looked like a white pair of trainers, although it was hard to see in the grainy black-and-white image. Bella gripped Ned's arm. 'Oh, God, there was someone!'

'Shame we can only see their feet,' remarked Ned.

Bella held on to Ned's arm as they watched the screen intently. The person could only be seen up to their thighs but Bella was pretty certain it was a male. The intruder walked along the garden path and disappeared from sight. 'They're going into the house,' said Bella in a whisper.

After that, the clip ended.

'Play the next one,' urged Ned.

This time the same person was walking back down the path. They came to a stop at the corner of the shed, shot off across the grass and then came back carrying a step ladder, before going back towards the house again.

'What are they doing?' asked Bella. 'What would they want a step ladder for?' She checked the time on the clock: 10:15 p.m. The camera kept running for another minute before it stopped through lack of motion. Bella hurriedly moved it along to the next clip: 10:23 p.m. The person came back down the path and replaced the step ladder. They moved quickly and seemed to have a sense of urgency as they headed down the path towards the back gate, where they stopped for a moment before hopping up onto the wheelie bin and out of sight of the camera. 'They must've gone over the wall,' said Bella. She sat back, taking it all in. 'So, when someone told the police they'd seen Dad walking from the track and onto Lantern Road that night between ten and ten thirty, it wasn't actually Dad but this person, here, on the tape. This person must look a bit like Dad, I guess.'

'Play it again from the start,' said Ned. 'See if we can spot anything that might help identify who it is. Didn't you say you'd found a pen up by the bin? Maybe this was when it was dropped.'

'By the killer?'

'Yeah. Maybe it wasn't Max's pen after all.'

'Oh, God, and I put it in the study and then it disappeared. The killer came back for it.' Bella fumbled with the camera and found the first scene again. She and Ned looked even more closely the second time.

'I can't see those trainers clearly,' said Ned, 'but they look like Adidas Gazelles.'

'How can you tell?'

'You know I love my trainers,' said Ned. 'They're quite common ones, but the stripes down the sides – I can just make them out. And I definitely think it's a bloke.'

'Yeah, me too.' They watched the footage again, pausing and replaying the last scene – the intruder climbing onto the bin. 'I can't see if he's dropped anything or not.'

'Wait! There!' Ned took the camera and played the clip back. 'Just here, look! See that?'

Bella squinted and she could just make out something catch the light of the camera as it hit the path and then rolled away. 'The pen!'

'Yep.'

'And the step ladder – what if they went back to tamper with the CCTV covering the back garden?' said Bella. 'So they could dispose of any evidence showing they were there.'

'What about the recording inside, though?'

CHAPTER 21

'They must've taken that. They couldn't just break the camera – they'd have to take the tape as well,' said Bella. She looked up at Ned. 'I think we've just seen the murderer.'

Ned nodded back at her, looking stunned. 'I think you're right.'

Bella checked her watch. 'It's too late to ring Esme and Conor. I'll have to tell them in the morning.'

'What are you going to do with the tape in the meantime?'

'I need to take it over to Great Midham Police Station.'

'I can't drive, I've had too much to drink.'

Bella was already reaching for her phone. 'I'll order a taxi. This can't wait until the morning. This could get my dad released. It's vital evidence.'

Chapter 22

ISLA

A Little Bird Told Me

'Did Bella speak to you?' asked Isla as she opened the door to her eldest sister on Sunday morning. She glanced back over her shoulder to make sure her mum wasn't within earshot.

'About the camera?' Esme nodded. 'She phoned me first thing this morning. It's fantastic, isn't it? I just hope the police take it seriously.'

'They can't ignore it, and I don't see how they can charge Dad now they have it,' replied Isla in a whisper.

'Ah, there you are,' came their mother's voice as she walked down the hallway. 'Any news?' Marion looked pale and drained, her cheeks more hollow than usual, Isla thought, and the dark circles under her eyes a testament to her late night as she'd got herself more and more distressed over their father's situation. In the end Isla had been quite stern with Marion and insisted she took her sleeping tablet.

'No news,' said Esme, going over to her mum and giving her

CHAPTER 22

a hug.

'We'll find out today if they're going to charge him,' said Marion, stating what they all already know.

'I think the longer they leave it, the more difficult it must be for them to find enough evidence,' reassured Isla. She'd said this over and over again to her mother last night and this morning but Marion just didn't appear to be taking it in. Isla sighed to herself. She knew it wasn't her mother's fault she was "always living on her nerves", as Heather had put it, but she sometimes wished her mum could've been the carefree and optimistic type. Growing up, Isla had been acutely aware that Marion was more fragile than her friends' mothers, that everyone needed to handle her with care, and she'd been constantly reminded not to upset her mother. But she wished – more for her mother's sake than her own – that Marion didn't have to be like this. It was the burden of worry her mother constantly carried around with her that really got to Isla. She had small pockets of memory of how life was before her mother became ill. She could recall running around, full of life and fun; holidays by the seaside with her mum looking glamorous in her bikini and big round sunglasses; how her mum used to throw her head back and laugh at a joke her father had told; how she'd scooped Isla up in her arms and spun her around. When Isla looked back on those days, it was like watching an old cine film from another lifetime. It was heartbreaking to realise how much her mother had been affected by poor mental health.

'Hey, you OK?' It was Esme's voice, snapping her from her thoughts.

'Yeah, sure. So, Mum's going to have dinner with you and you'll bring her back later?' asked Isla, checking the arrangements. Esme had said she wanted to be with her mum when they found out whether their dad was being charged or not – she didn't want Marion to be on her own if it was bad news. Isla was grateful for her sister's forethought. She wasn't sure if she was emotionally equipped to be of any use to her mum if things reached crisis point. Esme was so much better at dealing with things in an emergency.

'Are you sure you don't want to come too?' asked Esme. 'You know you're more than welcome.'

Isla shook her head. 'No, I'm fine, thanks. I thought I might go for a run this afternoon and as appealing as a Sunday roast is, there's no way I'd be able to move after that. And then I'll just chill out afterwards.'

It wasn't until after they'd gone that Isla wondered whether she'd made the right decision. She suddenly felt very alone in the family house. She thought back to when they were all living at home and there was always something going on – music coming from one of the rooms, someone calling to someone else, their mother busy in the kitchen and their father dodging out of the way of one of his daughters, who could never walk anywhere, he was always complaining half-heartedly. They all knew Frank adored having his daughters at home and loved the hustle and bustle that came with a female-dominated household.

In those days Marion worked with Frank a lot as he built up the business and they had the luxury of a cleaner. Babs would come in twice a week and tease the girls about the state of their bedrooms, saying "she wasn't paid enough to venture into their bombsites" – not that it was in her remit, anyway. Babs was there to clean the downstairs of the house and the bathrooms. Isla smiled at the memory. She'd been fond of

CHAPTER 22

Babs, who sometimes used to bring the girls sweets and, on her coffee breaks, tell them stories of her childhood back in Scotland. Babs had also babysat for them on occasion, staying overnight if their parents were away.

Babs was in her late sixties when she'd started working for the family and had eventually decided to hang up her duster when she hit seventy. The Fairfaxes had thrown her a lavish seventieth-birthday-cum-retirement party. That was some years ago now and, since then, Babs had moved into the village's retirement complex, near the green. The sheltered accommodation meant she could be independent but with the knowledge someone was on hand should she need it.

On a whim, Isla decided to go and pay Babs a visit – which wasn't particularly unusual as the family often went to see her – and twenty minutes later she was sitting in Babs's living room bringing her up to date with everything that was going on.

'I heard your father had been arrested,' said Babs. 'Awful affair. The police have certainly got that wrong.'

'I know. It's just trying to convince them of that. We're hoping they'll release him this afternoon.'

Babs frowned. 'It's a shame whoever phoned him about your Aunt May can't be found,' she mused. Babs may have been in sheltered accommodation but that was only for the company, as far as she was concerned, and her mind was as agile as it had always been.

'I know Dad's not making it up.' Isla bit into a shortcake biscuit. 'The police say the call was made from a pay phone in Applemere.'

'Maybe it was just someone who was concerned about your aunt.'

'I don't know who that would be – it's not as if she goes out anywhere. She doesn't live in a place like this, she's still in her own home.'

'A friend?'

'I don't think so.'

'Who else does she see? Her GP would surely have introduced themselves, as would someone from social services,' reasoned Babs. 'What about a carer? Or her meals on wheels?'

Isla jumped to her feet. 'Babs, you're a genius!' she declared. 'Why didn't we think of that before? I need to check this out as soon as possible so I can let them know at the police station.'

'You'd better get off, then,' said Babs with a chuckle.

Isla said her goodbyes and thanked Babs, giving her a huge hug before heading back home. As she walked, she puzzled over how she could find out who the carers were and which one might have phoned her dad. What she really needed to do was go over to Aunt May's and have a look in the book where the care staff recorded their visits. Her immediate problem, though, was in getting over to Applemere. Isla was loath to fork out on a taxi as she really didn't have much spare cash hanging around. The bus, of course, would be a lot cheaper. She headed over to the bus stop on the corner of the green and ran her finger down the timetable – digital timetable boards hadn't yet come to the little village of Applewick.

As she was trying to work out the Sunday bus service, Isla became aware of a car pulling up alongside her.

'You'll be lucky!' the unmistakable voice of Dan Starling called out.

She turned around and smiled at him. 'Tell me about it.'

'Where are you going?'

'Oh, erm, I'm just looking,' said Isla, unsure whether she

should confide in Dan or not. She'd made a promise to herself to give him a wide berth after their last encounter, when he'd made it clear how he felt about their ... she struggled to find the appropriate word for it ... their friendship was maybe the most accurate thing she could call it.

Dan gave her a sceptical look. 'Have you really got nothing better to do with your day than look at bus timetables? That's got to be up there with stamp collecting. I must admit, I had you pegged as slightly more rock 'n' roll than that.'

She knew he was teasing her but it rankled all the same and she found herself rising to the bait. 'Actually, I'm trying to get to Great Midham to find out some important information to do with my dad.' She sounded pompous even to herself and judging by the expression of amusement now creeping across Dan's face, he thought the same.

He leaned further across the inside of the car and pushed open the passenger door. 'Best you get in so I can give you a lift. You'll be there all day waiting for a bus.'

Isla eyed the passenger seat. She would've liked nothing more than to jump in the car with Dan but her head was valiant in its efforts to battle with her heart. Getting in the car with Dan would be a bad idea. Being in such close proximity to a man she had to admit she still had a super-crush on was not a good idea. 'It's OK. I'll wait for a bus.'

To her surprise, Dan looked hurt by her rejection, but he shrugged. 'OK. It's up to you. Catch you later.' He pulled away and Isla watched as he drove up the High Street and then pulled into the school car park. It seemed an odd thing to do on a Sunday but she assumed he was getting something organised for the start of the new week. She sat down on the bench. The bus was due in about twenty minutes so it wasn't worth going home or even popping into Bella's. She knew Jacob was with his dad so Bella might be having a lazy morning and Isla didn't want to disturb her.

Twenty minutes came and went and still no sign of the bus. Isla checked her watch several times as the minutes ticked by and cursed the rural and somewhat unreliable Sunday bus service.

Just as she was about to give up and go begging Ned for a lift, Dan Starling's blue BMW came down the road towards her, his errand presumably completed. She sunk back into the bench, hoping he wouldn't notice her but resigned to the fact that he surely couldn't miss her.

Yep. Here he was now, pulling up kerbside.

This time, instead of lowering the window he stepped out and called to her from over the roof of the car. 'Why don't you stop being so stubborn and just get in? I'm on my way home now and although I don't confess to being a user of public transport, I feel confident in predicting that your bus isn't going to show up.' He rested one hand on the rooftop. 'Come on, you know you want to.' Then he gave her that cheeky grin of his that she knew she couldn't resist.

With a sigh, Isla got up from the bench. 'My mum warned me about accepting lifts from strangers,' she said.

'I'm not a stranger, just strange,' quipped Dan. 'Chop-chop, in you get.'

'Only because I have no other option,' she clarified.

It was a beautiful day to be out for a drive and even though there was a serious reason for her journey, Isla rested her head back and gazed out of the window at the passing scenery as they left the village and the streets and houses faded into open fields and hedgerows.

CHAPTER 22

'What's this mission you're on, then?' asked Dan as he navigated the car around a sharp right-hand bend.

'I need to check something with my aunt. Technically, she's my great aunt, but we don't bother with the great bit. Anyway, I need to see who her carer was the day Max was killed.' Isla didn't see the point in not telling Dan the truth. Even though her sisters may not be convinced, she was sure Dan had nothing to do with Max's murder. 'Someone rang my dad to tell him my aunt wasn't well and he went over to see her on the night of the murder.'

'Ah, an alibi.'

'Yep. I think it may have been one of her carers. I just need to find out who and then get them to tell the police they rang my dad.'

'Does it get him off the hook?'

'Not exactly, but it adds credibility to his story of that being where he was. At the moment no one knows who rang because the call was made from a pay phone in Applemere.'

'So, the mystery caller, who you think is the carer, probably lives in Applemere and called your dad on their way home.'

'Yes, so it's quite handy you live in Applemere as you can drop me at the carer's house – assuming I can find them, that is,' said Isla.

They were soon pulling up outside Isla's aunt's house in Great Midham. 'I won't be long but if you need to get off, I can get a bus or phone someone.'

'Don't be daft,' said Dan. 'I'll wait for you. Text me if you need me for anything.'

Aunt May was pleased to see Isla, although Isla wasn't convinced she knew who she was as Aunt May kept calling her Marion. However, it seemed petty to correct the elderly lady.

'Shall I make us a cup of tea?' suggested Isla and, leaving Aunt May in the living room, she went through to the kitchen, where the report book that the carers filled in was kept. As she waited for the kettle to boil, Isla flipped through the pages, coming to rest on the date Max was killed. The book required a signature and printed name for each visit and Isla saw that Jessie Washington was the carer who'd been out to Aunt May that day and, looking back through the book, that she'd been five out of the preceding seven days and quite a few times before that. She was obviously a regular member of staff from the agency; now all Isla had to do was to find out where she lived.

She took out her phone and sent a message to Dan.

Can you look up the name Jessie Washington and see if you can find out if she lives in Applemere? Thanks.

As she made the tea, she got a reply almost straight away.

I can do better than that. I actually know her. I even have her number!

Isla couldn't believe her luck. How amazing was that? Her elation took a dip, though, as she guessed Jessie Washington was one of Dan's conquests. It didn't surprise her that he knew her – no woman escaped his notice or his charms. She sighed and reminded herself of the reasons why she shouldn't have anything to do with Dan.

Having spent a respectable amount of time with Aunt May and made sure she had everything she needed, Isla returned to

CHAPTER 22

Dan's car.

He grinned at her when she got in. 'How cool is that?'

'I have to admit, it is pretty cool,' said Isla, forcing a smile. She was grateful, just a little disappointed for her own reasons. 'Don't tell me she's one of your special friends.'

Dan started the engine. 'And you'd have a problem with that?'

'No. Not at all,' fired back Isla, avoiding looking at him even though she could feel his gaze on her.

'So, it wouldn't matter that she comes over to my house every week?'

'Not my business.' God, nothing like rubbing her nose in it.

'That she has her own key ...'

'Like I said, none of my business. I don't know why you think I should be bothered,' retorted Isla, aware of how starchy she sounded. She did look across at him this time, scowling as she did so, which made Dan laugh.

'You are such a sweetheart, Isla.' His face grew serious and he ran his forefinger down the side of her cheek. 'She's old enough to be my mother.' Isla started to speak but Dan put his finger to her lips. 'She's my cleaner.'

Isla knew her face had flushed red as the heat rushed up her neck. 'Great,' she replied. 'That's good.' She didn't know what else to say. Slapping him and yelling at him for winding her up was not a thought she should act out.

With his hands now back on the wheel, Dan steered the car away from Aunt May's house and out of Great Midham. 'I've already spoken to her on the phone and she's more than happy to talk to you.'

'She is? Oh, thank you, Dan. That's brilliant,' replied Isla, regaining her composure.

'You can ring her from my phone, if you like. Unless, of course, you particularly need to see her. I mean, you might want to check her out, to make sure I'm not lying about her age.'

'I'm ignoring that remark,' said Isla. 'Let's ring her now.'

Dan tapped his hands-free set and *Jessie the Cleaner* flashed up on the screen. He pressed the call button. Isla couldn't help feeling a sense of relief that Jessie was listed as the cleaner.

'Hello, Dan!' came a woman's voice. She didn't sound young, which Isla's found reassuring.

'Hi, Jessie. I've got Isla Fairfax in the car with me.'

'Jolly good.'

'Hello, Jessie,' said Isla. 'Thanks for letting me phone you.'

'Oh, no problem. Dan tells me you're May Fairfax's niece. What can I do for you?'

'My dad received a phone call the Monday before last about Aunt May and the caller told him she wasn't too well. He thought it was a neighbour, but since none of the neighbours say it was them, I'm trying to find out who did ring him.'

'It was me,' said Jessie. 'I'm not supposed to ring families directly, so I didn't give my name. I'm supposed to go through the agency but they're not very good at relaying information. I was concerned about May. She's seemed more confused lately and I'm not sure she can live on her own for much longer. That particular day, she was very confused and I phoned your dad to tell him. I thought she might have a UTI – you know, a water infection. It can make the elderly more confused. Anyway, he was very good and said he'd go over straight away to see her. I reported the suspected UTI to my boss, who said she was arranging for a nurse to call out. And that was that.'

'Where did you call my dad from?'

CHAPTER 22

'The phone box near the station. My mobile died. Does it really matter?'

Isla hesitated but Dan gave her an encouraging nod. 'I expect you heard about the murder at Applewick, of the head teacher.'

'Oh, yes, terrible business, that.'

'Well, my dad, Frank, has been arrested for his murder.'

'What?' exclaimed Jessie.

'The police don't believe he got that call from you; they think he's making it up. Would you be prepared to give a statement to the police? Please.'

There was a pause at the other end of the phone.

'If you could, Jessie, it would mean a lot,' added Dan. 'It might stop an innocent man being charged with murder.'

'Oh, all right,' said Jessie with a certain amount of reluctance. 'I don't want this getting back to my work, though. They'll fire me for breaking the rules and I need the money. I don't do two jobs for the love of it, you know that.'

'Thank you, Jessie,' said Isla. 'Thank you so much.'

'Yeah, thank you, Jessie, you're a darling,' said Dan. 'I'll see you right.'

The call ended and Isla could hardly contain her excitement as she bounced in the passenger seat. 'Oh, thank you so much, Dan. You don't know how happy I am. I could bloody kiss you!' She clasped her hand over her mouth.

Dan smiled at her. 'Now, there's a thought.'

He drove her all the way back to Applewick, dropping her off at Esme's house.

'I can't wait to tell Esme the good news,' said Isla. In a rush of emotion she leaned over and hugged Dan, for once taking him by surprise, before hopping out of the car and running up the drive to her sister's house.

Chapter 23

ESME

Esme Puts Her Foot Down

'Oh, my God, Isla, you are bloody brilliant!' squealed Esme and then, remembering their mum was just in the living room, she lowered her voice to a whisper as she stood in the kitchen with her sister. 'I can't believe you found all that out, and so quickly.'

'If I hadn't been with Dan, I'm not sure I'd be here telling you the good news,' confessed Isla.

'I won't ask you right now why you were with him,' replied Esme, logging that question in the back of her mind for a more appropriate time, 'but I'm so glad you were. What with that, and what Bella found on the camera last night, the police probably now have their doubts. They can't possibly charge Dad.'

'What's that?' It was Conor coming into the kitchen. 'You two are looking very pleased with yourselves.'

Esme and Conor weren't quite back on the usual good terms

of their marriage but they'd called an unspoken truce and were at least now getting along without arguing.

'Isla's found out who called Dad from the Applemere pay phone,' announced Esme, unable to keep the air of triumph out of her voice.

'What? Have you? How did you manage that? Who was it?' Conor put his cup down on the table.

'That's a lot of questions,' said Isla with a grin. She explained to her brother-in-law the chain of events.

'So, now we can give that information to the police and they can let Dad go,' finished off Esme.

She was hoping for a cheer or at least a "yes!" of congratulation from Conor but he seemed underwhelmed by the revelation.

'That's good news, right?' asked Isla, who had obviously also picked up on his lack of reaction.

'Well, yes, it is. On the face of it,' replied Conor. 'And it does give more weight to your dad's version of events.'

'But what?' demand Esme, sensing his hesitation.

'But it has to tie in with the timeline. Technically speaking, he could still have come back to Applewick and committed the offence.'

'Oh, don't be so ridiculous,' scoffed Esme, the shine of the excitement dulled.

'If this woman gives a statement, it still doesn't account for what he did after the phone call. Did he go back to Max's or did he go to Aunt May's? Unfortunately, Aunt May isn't a credible witness.'

'But surely the film that Bella found will back this up,' said Isla.

Conor looked decidedly uncomfortable.

'What is it?' asked Esme.

'It depends what's on the film. If it doesn't show the face, then who's to say it wasn't your dad?'

'Because Bella said the person in the film was wearing trainers. When have you ever known Dad to wear trainers?' snapped Esme, her frustrations bubbling over. 'He always wears brogues. You know that.'

'The police might argue that your dad wore trainers that night for the very reason you just stated – to make people think it couldn't be him.'

'Can't you phone the station and find anything out?' asked Esme. She glanced towards the living room, where she could hear Amelia talking to Marion. 'They've got to let him go this afternoon, surely. What would you do if it was you?'

'If I was holding your dad? To be honest, I don't know,' confessed Conor. 'I'm just trying to prepare you for the worst.'

'Don't say anything to Mum,' said Esme, her disappointment so huge that she couldn't even bring herself to acknowledge what Conor had just said.

Isla ended up staying for the afternoon and Esme was glad she was there. Conor had gone off to Great Midham Police Station to hand over the new information, but he hadn't been able to find anything else out while he was there and so had come back home an hour ago. Esme gave Bella a call and invited her over too. She wanted the three of them to take the news together and to shoulder the fallout together; that's what they did, her and her sisters, they did everything together.

The closer it got to five o'clock, the less hopeful Esme became of good news from the police station about her father. The strain of the waiting was clearly also getting to Marion, who was currently at the bottom of the garden looking out across the river.

'How is she today?' asked Bella, joining Esme at the bifold doors.

'On edge. Trying to put on a brave face for the kids, but as soon as she's on her own, the worry is there,' said Esme. 'This is an agony like no other.' She looked at her watch for what must have been the hundredth time. 'It's nearly five o'clock. Surely they know by now whether they're releasing Dad.'

'Maybe they're looking at all the evidence and checking up on things.' Bella slipped her hand through the crook of Esme's arm and rested her head on her shoulder. 'And even if it's bad news, I'm not giving up.'

'Fighting talk.' Esme smiled. 'And you were the one who wasn't keen to investigate it originally.'

'I had faith in the police, but I'll admit, I kind of felt I should be more proactive, seeing as you and Isla were so for it. I mean, I didn't want to be left out.' She gave a wry smile. 'I'm glad now that I did get on board as the police have done nothing to convince me they've got a handle on this.'

Isla joined them, standing on the other side of Esme and also linking arms with her. 'I can't bear this waiting,' she said.

The sound of Conor's mobile phone ringing out made all three women jump and they spun around as Conor, who was sitting at the breakfast bar, answered the call. Esme held her sisters' hands as they stood in silence, transfixed on Conor, trying to get any clue from his side of the conversation as to what was happening.

'Yes ... I see ... Yep ... Yep ... Right ... Thanks for letting me know ... Of course ... Thanks again. Bye.' Conor put his phone down and rested his hands on the countertop, his elbows locked, his head bowed.

'Conor?' ventured Esme, aware of the fear in her voice.

Her husband looked up at her and his expression was grim. He pushed himself up from the bar stool, his hands going to his hips, and blew out a breath. 'Not good news. They've just charged your dad with murder. I'm sorry.'

After a stunned silence of roughly three seconds, all hell broke loose.

Isla sprang forward, gripping the chair in front of her. 'It can't be true. They've got this wrong. Haven't they looked at the evidence?'

Bella swore, several times over, her cries at the injustice of it even louder than Isla's, while Esme just stared at her husband in utter disbelief. Then she turned to look at her mother, still standing at the bottom of the garden. How on earth were they going to tell her – and, more to the point, how was she going to take the news? She looked around at her sisters. She felt shell-shocked. Even though she'd been trying to prepare herself for this, she hadn't truly expected it.

Something inside her kicked into gear. This was no good. This wasn't going to help the matter. In fact, it made her even more determined to get to the truth. How, though, she had no idea. She clapped her hands together several times like a schoolteacher and her siblings obliged like good pupils, lapsing into silence – much to the relief of Conor, if his face was anything to go by.

'Right, listen up,' she said, with a confidence that belied her true feelings. 'I think we can all agree the police have got this wrong but getting het up about it isn't going to change anything. We need to get the facts. I'll speak to the solicitors to find out exactly what evidence the police have and why they're not looking at the evidence we've provided them with. We also need to keep calm heads. Going into panic-and-outrage mode won't actually achieve anything. Once we've got all our information together, then we can work out what to do next.'

'Esme,' said Conor in a warning voice. 'Don't get involved. You've done enough.'

'Clearly we haven't done enough,' retorted Esme. 'If we had, our dad wouldn't be charged with murder. If we'd done enough, he'd be walking through that door any minute now. If we'd done enough, I wouldn't be having to face my mother to break the news to her. We haven't done enough and we need to do more.' She could feel the emotion rising in her throat, trying to choke her words, but she refused to give in to it.

'Leave it to the police,' said Conor gently.

'No! I won't. They don't want to find the real killer. They have no intention of looking for someone else. We ...' She gestured towards her sisters. '... We are the only ones who can help Dad now. And I'll do it with or without your blessing.' She glared at her husband, daring him to challenge her. He held her gaze, but finally broke his away. Esme gave a satisfied huff. 'Now, if you'll excuse me, I've got to somehow tell Mum.'

With that, she spun around and strode out of the kitchen and across the terrace, not adjusting her gait or body language to anything less aggressive until she was halfway down the garden.

Her sisters fell into step, one on either side, and a wave of gratitude that they were there washed over her as she looked at the waif-like figure of their mother at the water's edge. Her poor mum. Her darling mum. Esme hoped to God that Marion would be able to dig a little deeper and find some more reserves. The thought of her mother relapsing even further chilled her and at the same time ignited an inner strength within her.

It wasn't the first time she'd had to step up when her mum couldn't, and this time Esme had an even greater challenge than having to parent two siblings. This time, she had a killer to find. She didn't know how they were going to do it but she wasn't giving up, and she knew she had Bella and Isla in her corner.

Chapter 24

BELLA

The Writing is on the ... Paper

Bella had been reluctant to leave her mother that night but everyone had been surprised at just how well Marion had taken the news that Frank was officially being charged. Yes, there had been tears, but they'd been controlled and minimal. 'I knew this would happen,' was all she'd said. Esme had wanted Marion to stay with her for the night but she'd insisted on going home, saying she'd be better off in her own place, so Esme had driven Marion and Isla home, dropping Bella off on the way.

Bella climbed out of the car, pausing to whisper to Esme. 'Tell Isla to keep an eye on the sleeping tablets, just in case.' She gave a pointed look to Esme, who nodded in understanding.

She watched Esme drive off past the school and around the bend that went on to Lantern Road and down to the family home. Then she turned and was just opening her front door when she saw a car pulling up. It was Ned's unmistakable

Morris Minor van.

Ned got out of his van. 'Hey, I was just thinking of you. Any news on your dad?'

Bella tried to speak but found that the words clumped in her throat and tears sprang to her eyes. 'It's bad news,' she managed to splutter out.

In a couple of strides, Ned was in front of her and enveloping her in his arms. He smelt faintly of woodsmoke but Bella didn't mind – in fact, she found it comforting.

'Come on, let's get you inside,' said Ned in a soft voice. He took the key from her and, with one hand still around her shoulders, opened the door and guided her in, then sat her down on the sofa. 'Where's the little fella?'

'He's staying with his dad tonight. I'd already arranged it, just in case Mum needed me.'

'I take it she doesn't.'

'No. Amazingly she's taken it far better than any of us expected, although her stoic front is a bit of a worry.'

'Is she with Esme?' asked Ned, going into the kitchen and returning with a piece of kitchen roll, which he handed to Bella.

'No. Mum insisted on going home, so Isla's with her.' Bella wiped her face with the rudimental, not to mention rough, tissue. 'I don't know why, but I feel uneasy about her tonight.'

Ned sat down next to her. 'Don't be. I'm sure she'll be OK. What's the plan now?'

'Right this minute?' asked Bella, getting to her feet and taking her turn to go to the kitchen. She hooked a bottle of wine from the fridge and nabbed two glasses from the cupboard. She returned to the sofa with them, passing a glass to Ned as she sat down. 'My plan is to have a drink. And I insist you join me.'

CHAPTER 24

'I'm only partaking to keep you company.'

'I don't want to think about any of it right now,' said Bella. 'So, conversations involving my dad are strictly off limits.'

'Understood.'

Two hours later and the bottle of wine empty, Bella lolled back on the sofa. 'I'm probably going to regret this in the morning.'

'Me too,' said Ned. 'I've got to climb up a bloody tree tomorrow and lop off some branches.'

'I don't envy you that.'

'Why don't you get off to bed?' suggested Ned. 'I'll see myself out.'

'You'll do nothing of the sort,' said Bella. 'You can't drive – you've had too much to drink.'

'I can walk.'

'That's silly, because then your car will be in the wrong place in the morning.'

'And in the morning, I'll walk back for it.' Ned stood up and pulled Bella to her feet. 'Go on, get some sleep. I'll speak to you tomorrow, no doubt.' He picked up his jacket and slipped his arms into the sleeves before shrugging it over his shoulders.

'Thanks for your company tonight,' said Bella, giving him a hug. 'I do appreciate it.' She followed him to the front door. 'The neighbours are, of course, going to think you stayed the night.'

'Who gives a fu–' Ned stopped the expletive from fully forming. 'Now, lock the door and go to bed!'

Bella did as she was told and staggered upstairs. She was so tired, not just physically but mentally, too. She had needed that down time tonight, even though she'd been aware of the little niggling feeling of guilt for actively stopping herself thinking about her dad.

As she brushed her teeth, she chided herself for being so selfish and resolved to do whatever it took tomorrow to find out who killed Max. She climbed into bed with a head full of jumbled thoughts about all the possible suspects and their motives, none of which she could make any sense of, and with them swirling around in her head, she fell into a troubled sleep.

When Bella awoke in the morning it took her a few seconds to work out why she had a headache and a parched mouth.

'Oh, God,' she groaned as she remembered the drinking session she and Ned had embarked on. Her next thought was of her dad and, this time, instead of a groan she let out a small whimper. Her poor dad, now facing a murder charge. Sod the headache, she needed to get her backside into gear and do something to help him.

It was strange not having to take Jacob to school that morning but Bella was grateful her ex had been understanding. She had to admit, things between her and Gavin had improved in the last couple of years and she put this down to his new girlfriend, who seemed to be able to bring out the best in him – unlike her, who'd had the opposite effect. She pushed the thought from her mind. She was long over her breakup with Gavin but, all the same, it did hurt sometimes to think she'd failed on the relationship front.

Bella took her bike out through the back gate and cycled down to the vicarage for her usual Monday-morning cleaning job. There was a van parked in the driveway, which Bella recognised as Keith Bonham's. She wondered why he was here; the house was usually empty on Monday mornings.

Jemima, the vicar's wife, opened the door to her. 'Hello,

CHAPTER 24

Bella. I expect you're surprised to see me. Something's gone wrong with the computer and Keith Bonham is here having a look at it. He's in the study, so maybe if you leave that room till last?'

Jemima was in her early forties and her teenage children went to the local secondary school over at Great Midham. Although Bella didn't class her as a mum friend, the two women got on well together and it made Monday-morning cleaning that much more pleasant on the odd occasion when Jemima was at home.

'Sure, no problem,' replied Bella.

'If you need anything, I'll be in the kitchen,' said Jemima. 'Simon's just left – he's gone over to see a parishioner in Appledown – and once Keith's done, I'm off to the hospital; it's my day at the café there.' Jemima was part of the Friends of Great Midham Hospital group and volunteered there a couple of times a week as well as doing a stint at Applewick Residential Home for the elderly.

'OK, I'll do the living room first,' said Bella, grateful Jemima hadn't asked about her father, and set about her work, listening to her music with her earbuds in.

The time went quickly and despite her headache, Bella got all the rooms done. With only the study left to clean now, she went to see if Keith had finished and found him in the kitchen with Jemima.

'I was just checking it's OK to get on with the study,' said Bella, poking her head around the door.

'Yeah, all done,' said Keith.

'Why don't you have a coffee before you do that?' suggested Jemima, putting down a cup. 'I was just coming to find you.'

Bella wanted to get finished so she could go and see Esme

but she didn't like to appear rude, especially as Jemima had already gone to the trouble of making her a drink. Not only that – a coffee would be a welcome way to finally see off her headache and hangover. 'Thank you,' she said, going into the kitchen and taking a seat at the breakfast bar where Jemima had placed her coffee.

'So, that's all done,' Keith said, picking up his conversation with Jemima. 'I just need you to sign here.'

Jemima looked around the kitchen. 'Have you got a pen?'

'No, I think I left mine at home,' replied Keith, making a show of patting his pockets.

'Oh, look!' said Jemima with a laugh. She pointed to Keith's shirt pocket. 'You've got a pen right there. May I?'

Keith gave something akin to a laugh. 'Oh, so I have. I don't know if it works,' he added.

Jemima plucked the pen from his pocket before he had time to protest further. 'Ooh, nice,' she remarked, inspecting it. 'You wouldn't want to lose this one – not your average pen. Now, where do you want me to sign?'

Bella nearly choked on her coffee when she saw the pen Jemima was holding. It was a silver Paper Mate, just like the one she'd found at the Old School House. She managed to gulp down the mouthful of hot liquid. 'That is a nice pen,' she said. 'Too nice to be taking to work.'

Keith looked uncomfortable. 'Yes. I ... err ... I forgot I had it with me.'

Jemima squiggled her signature and looked again at the pen. 'Twenty-five years of dedicated service,' she read out as she turned it over to see the inscription. 'Nice present.'

'Yes. I got it last year.' He whisked the pen off her and pushed it back into his pocket before giving Jemima one copy of the invoice and filing the other in his briefcase.

'You OK, Bella?' asked Jemima with a concerned look as Bella struggled to contain her cough.

'Sorry. Coffee went down the wrong way,' she managed to reply. By this time Keith, on the other side of the breakfast bar, was picking up his case and saying his goodbyes. Hoping to appear casual, Bella tracked him as he walked around to her side of the counter on his way to the door. Would he be wearing trainers like the ones in the video footage? She glanced down to his footwear and felt her heart sink when she saw his black lace-up shoes. Her mouth went into gear long before her brain and she heard herself saying, 'My feet are killing me. I wish I'd worn my trainers. How do you manage all day in formal shoes, Keith?' She wanted to clamp her hand over her mouth to stop the random thoughts evolving into spoken content.

Keith paused and gave her an odd look. 'Shoes?' He looked down at his feet and back up at Bella with an expression pitched somewhere between bewilderment and caution. 'I always wear these for work. They're very comfortable. Had them years.'

'You don't ever wear trainers, then?' Bella hoped it sounded as natural as she'd intended.

Keith exchanged a look with Jemima that clearly noted the oddness of the conversation. 'Sometimes, but not for work.'

'You should try the shoe shop in the square at Great Midham,' chimed in Jemima, looking at Bella. 'They do nice shoes there. I can give you a lift over one day, if you like. I know the owner – he's very helpful, and I might be able to get you a discount.'

'Oh, yes, OK. Thanks,' said Bella, marvelling at her ability to get herself into such situations.

'Right, well, I'll get off,' said Keith and made his way out of the kitchen with Jemima following, thanking him for coming out at such short notice.

Bella tipped the rest of her coffee down the sink and put the cup in the dishwasher. As she dusted and polished, she kept replaying in her head the scene where Jemima used the pen. There was no doubt in Bella's mind that it was the pen she'd found in Max's garden – the same pen that had been dropped and the very same pen that had disappeared from Max's desk. It had to be Keith's – which meant that the man captured on the wildlife camera the night of Max's murder must also have been Keith. She shuddered at the implication. Keith was Max's killer! Had she just solved the murder?

After a hurried goodbye to Jemima and vague promises to call her when she wanted to go shoe shopping, Bella hopped on her bike and sped over the footbridge and down towards the old Wesleyan chapel and Fairfax Funeral Parlour.

She burst through the doors and into the office, skidding to a halt in front of Esme's desk. 'I know who did it,' she gasped, trying to catch her breath. 'I know who killed Max Bartholomew!'

Chapter 25

ESME

A Step Too Far

Esme nearly jumped out of her skin when her sister hurtled into the office and blurted out that she knew who'd killed Max. Still holding the receiver of the phone she'd been using, Esme took a moment to appraise her sister. Bella held her gaze, her eyes flooded with adrenalin.

'Hello? Esme? You there?' It was the solicitor's voice on the other end of the line.

'I'll call you back later,' said Esme. 'Something important has come up.' It did cross her mind as she replaced the receiver that the solicitor would wonder what on earth could be more important than her father's murder charge, but she knew from Bella's face that she wasn't joking. 'Say that again,' she said to Bella. 'Only this time, more slowly.'

'I know who killed Max,' repeated Bella. She sat down in the chair used for client meetings, her breathing ragged from her exertion. 'I was at the vicarage, cleaning, and Keith Bonham was there. He was fixing the vicar's computer. Anyway, he needed Jemima to sign for the repair and he used his silver Paper Mate pen – the exact same one that I found at the Old School House ... the exact same one that I saw being dropped in the garden on the wildlife camera.'

'Are you sure it was the same pen?' asked Esme. She could feel the anticipation rising in her.

'Yes. Jemima said what a fancy pen it was and then went on to read out the inscription. It said, "twenty-five years of dedicated service".'

Esme took a moment to compose herself so she could think logically despite the excitement bubbling away inside her. 'OK, but before we go through this, I've got some good news.'

'Good news?' Esme and Bella both looked to the door as in walked Isla. 'Sounds like I got here at just the right time.'

'I've been speaking to the solicitor and Dad has been granted bail,' said Esme.

'Oh, thank God for that!' cried Bella. 'That means he can come home.'

'Oh, Mum will be so relieved,' said Isla. 'What does it mean in regard to Dad being guilty, though?'

'Basically, it just means the CPS don't think Dad is likely to run off or to cause harm to himself or anyone else. They don't think he's a threat,' explained Esme. 'I've got to go and pick him up at one o'clock.'

'I'm so happy, I could cry,' said Isla.

'Bella thinks she knows who killed Max,' added Esme and brought Isla up to speed.

'So, you think the man on the wildlife camera is Keith?' asked Isla. 'Have you got any other proof? What about his trainers? Ned said they were a specific brand.'

CHAPTER 25

'Keith was wearing work shoes today,' admitted Bella. 'But that doesn't mean he hasn't got trainers or that it wasn't him.'

'And his motive?' pressed Isla.

'Pippa,' said both Esme and Bella at the same time.

Esme put her hand out in a you-first gesture. 'Bella, do you want to explain?'

'I haven't quite fitted everything together,' admitted Bella, 'but here's my theory: Keith Bonham found out that Pippa and Max were in a relationship. He wouldn't like that. Keith went to school with Max – it's not something he'd approve of or be able to deal with, not least because of the huge age gap between Max and Pippa. Keith must have gone around to Max's place with the intention of doing some sort of harm, otherwise he wouldn't have gone to all the trouble of sneaking in over the back wall. Whether he meant to kill Max or not, we don't know, but he definitely had something in mind, and it was premeditated.

'Sounds plausible so far,' encouraged Esme.

'So, Keith went in through the back door because he didn't want to be caught on CCTV at the front door. Poor Dad just happened to be in the wrong place at the wrong time. It was all very convenient for Keith to have a ready-made prime suspect.'

'How did Keith know the CCTV at the back of the property wasn't working?' asked Isla. 'And how did he get into the house?'

'Who's to say it wasn't working?' suggested Esme, already cottoning on to Bella's theory. Bella nodded and Esme continued. 'What if it was working? What if, after killing Max, Keith broke the camera in some way and erased the footage?'

'Exactly,' said Bella. 'He is an IT expert – he'd know how to do that. He obviously didn't know about the wildlife camera.'

'It's not solid proof, though,' said Isla. 'Don't get me wrong, I want to believe it as much as you two, but we're only guessing what happened. And we don't know it was definitely Keith. For a start, how did he get inside the Old School House?'

'Keys,' said Bella. 'Mrs Bonham has a set of spare keys. She even lent them to me so I could do the cleaning.'

'Yes!' exclaimed Isla. 'Of course. And he could easily have used the keys again to go back and get his pen. He must've realised he'd dropped it somewhere.'

Esme considered everything Bella was saying. 'There are still some loose ends, though,' she said at last when she realised her sisters were looking at her. 'We obviously need to prove it was Keith. We need something concrete that will prove he was there. Like his shoes – or, rather, those particular trainers. And the mobile phone that's missing – we need to find that. My guess is that's what he was looking for when he came back to get the pen – that's why there were some papers on the floor when you went to get the rug and discovered the money.'

'What about the money?' asked Isla. 'We still don't know where that came from or if it's anything to do with the murder. Or if it's something to do with the blackmail letter – and that in itself is a mystery as Suzanne said she didn't write it.'

The three sisters lapsed into silence as they considered all the scenarios.

'I don't know how that fits in,' confessed Esme after a while. 'If Keith was going to blackmail Max then surely he would've made sure he had the money before killing him – but in that case, why kill him at all? Why not continue to blackmail him? And if the money was something to do with Suzanne, why was it still in the desk?'

'Maybe Keith thought he'd find the money himself but

CHAPTER 25

because it was in the secret drawer he never did. Or maybe if Max was being blackmailed by Suzanne, he hadn't given it to her yet,' suggested Bella. 'Perhaps the money and blackmail letter are nothing to do with Keith.'

Esme walked over to the window and looked out at the car park. It wasn't so bright today and there had been a shift in the weather, with a feeling of rain on the way even though the clouds weren't particularly grey. The shrubs and Red Robin bushes in the borders of the car park were bobbing away – the breeze was definitely picking up. She turned to face her sisters. 'I think someone wanted the blackmail letter to be found,' she said, looking at Bella.

'You mean the note was forged to throw the police off the scent?' asked Isla.

'Or it was from someone who wanted to drop Max in even more hot water,' said Bella. 'Someone like Dan.'

Isla shook her head. 'I know you don't like him, but he wouldn't stoop that low.'

'He didn't mind coercing Suzanne into making a complaint,' said Esme. She spoke softly, aware that her sister still had feelings for the man despite him proving to be a complete shit. 'Anyway, it doesn't matter right now. I don't think it's an important piece of the puzzle. What we've got to do is to prove our theory about Keith.'

'How are we going to do that?' asked Isla, still looking unhappy about the allegation made against Dan.

'I'm not sure yet, but I'm working on it,' said Esme. She looked at her sisters. 'There's something else you should know.'

'What?' demanded Bella.

'I spoke to the solicitor just now and he said the videotape of Max's back garden hasn't found its way to CID yet.'

'You're joking!' cried Bella. 'That bloody idiot policeman on the front desk. I knew I shouldn't have given it to him. I should have waited until the morning and handed it directly to Marsh.'

'They're looking for it now,' said Esme. 'I couldn't believe it when the solicitor told me. But, like he said, it can't have gone out of the building so they will find it. You do have a receipt, don't you, Bella?'

'Yes, it's at home, but it doesn't matter, does it? If they can't find the tape, it means nothing.' Bella scowled and Esme knew this wasn't directed at her but at the incompetence of the police at the station and also her own decision to drop the videotape off at the desk.

'Don't worry, Bells, it will turn up,' she attempted to reassure her sister.

'I need to go,' said Bella, picking up her bag and hooking it onto her shoulder. 'I'll call over to see Dad later. Will you be there?'

'Yes. I'll meet you there after school pick-up. You're getting the kids, right?'

'Sure.' Bella left without saying goodbye.

'She's just cross with herself,' remarked Esme as Isla looked on, concerned. 'She shouldn't blame herself, it's not her fault.'

'You sound very confident it will be OK,' replied Isla.

Esme smiled. 'I have no doubt.' It was, of course, a complete lie – she didn't feel confident at all – but putting her little sister's mind at rest seemed the best way forward. They could all worry and beat themselves up about it if and when the tape truly was lost.

'I've got to go as well,' said Isla. 'I promised Mick I'd do the lunchtime shift at the pub.'

Esme followed her sister as far as the main entrance of the funeral parlour and leaned against the door frame as Isla crossed the road and went into the Horse and Plough. Then she pushed herself upright and was just turning to go back inside when she saw the blue van of Keith Bonham coming along.

He looked directly at her as he sped past and although Esme put her hand up in acknowledgement, Keith just looked away and appeared to drive even faster. It was a ridiculous speed to be travelling at through the village and Esme watched him as he reached the end of the High Street and turned right onto Great Midham Road, disappearing from sight. Where on earth was he going in such a hurry? And why the glare?

Esme considered Keith Bonham's expression – was it just a glare? Or was there fear, too?

Without any real thought about what she was doing, Esme nipped back into the office and grabbed her bag and keys. She locked the door and hurried along the High Street towards the footbridge.

Once over the bridge, she carried on along on the river footpath, past the church and the graveyard and on towards Orchard Cottages. She slowed her pace as she reached the first of the cottages, where the Bonhams lived. She was relieved that there was ample foliage on the path to keep her hidden from view, and as she peered over the stone wall and through the trees of the apple orchard, she could see the rear of the Bonhams' house, with Keith's van parked at the end of the drive. A hedge running the length of the orchard partially hid the back garden of the cottage but Esme could see smoke rising from the other side, and the distinct smell of petrol or a similar accelerant invaded her nostrils. The wall to the orchard was low and Esme took the snap decision to climb over; then, running at a crouch – which made her feel slightly ridiculous, as if she were in some sort of special-ops movie – she legged it over to the hedge. It was too dense to see through properly so she kept in close to it until she reached the far end of the garden, where Keith's van was parked. Using the van as a shield, she peered around the tailgate.

The Bonhams obviously valued their privacy because another hedge was now partially blocking her view. Esme could see an incinerator, which was the root of the smoke, but from where she was hiding, she couldn't see Keith. She needed to get closer before he reappeared or came back out to his van – she could hardly say she was inspecting his tyres to explain what she was doing there.

A shed was opposite her, just inside the perimeter of the garden, and there looked to be enough of a gap between that and the garage for her to squeeze through. Checking there was no one about, Esme darted across the drive, the gravel scrunching beneath her feet, causing her to lose friction and nearly fall over, but she managed to stay upright and nip between the two outbuildings.

Her heart was hammering in her chest, not just after the burst of energy but from nerves and adrenalin. There really was no way out of this if Keith spotted her now. The pebbledash of the garage wall scratched her back through the soft fabric of her blouse and she winced as one particularly sharp pieced clawed her. She shuffled along to the end of the shed and was relieved to see a wider gap between the shed and the neighbour's boundary hedge. The shed had a window on each side and double front doors with six panels of glass in each one – it was probably more of a summer house than a shed, and it gave Esme a clear view of the garden through its windows. She could see the incinerator without being seen. Perfect.

She didn't have long to wait before Keith emerged from the house and headed down the path towards the incinerator. Esme squinted to get a better idea of what he was carrying. She stifled a gasp as she realised he was holding a pair of trainers. She couldn't tell the make but they had three blue stripes along the side. She knew exactly what he was going to do and her heart plummeted. If he burned those trainers then there would be no direct proof that it was him on the wildlife camera the night of the murder.

Esme snatched her phone from her bag and, making sure it was on silent, zoomed in on Keith as he approached the incinerator. She took several shots, capturing him as he got closer and closer. She focused in on the trainers in his arms and then repeatedly hit the camera button, taking a barrage of pictures as he lifted the lid and dropped the trainers into the flames that were reaching up and out of the container.

Keith replaced the lid and took a step back before looking up and, it seemed, straight at Esme. She dived back out of sight and crouched as low as possible, praying he hadn't seen her. She held her breath as she listened, trying to deduce where he was.

The shed door opened suddenly and Esme had to stifle a yelp of surprise. She swallowed hard, her mouth dry and her lips sticking together. She was glad her phone automatically uploaded pictures to the online storage cloud – at least she knew those images were secure now.

Esme could hear Keith opening what sounded like a metal drawer and rummaging around through some tools. She desperately wanted to see what he was doing but didn't dare look in case he saw her; she suspected that whatever it was related to the murder in some way and she knew she had to find out. Stealing herself, and using the thought of her father being locked away for life as motivation, she turned her phone to its video setting, flipped the camera onto selfie mode and pressed record. Inch by inch, she shuffled the camera up the side of the shed until it reached the window ledge. She took a deep breath, willing her hand to keep steady, and moved the camera a bit higher so that it peeked over the ledge. From where she was below, she could just see the screen and what the phone was recording.

Keith had something on the bench in front of him and was raising his hand, in which he held a wooden mallet. He brought it crashing down on the object. As the camera found its focus Esme could see the object more clearly, just before Keith smashed it for a second time – it was a mobile phone. He then collected up the pieces and left the shed. Esme took her chance and watched him through the window. He went over to the incinerator and threw what was left of the phone into it.

He stood looking at the roaring flames for a few minutes before replacing the lid and going back up to the house. Esme stayed where she was, not daring to move from her hiding spot just yet. She was glad she'd decided to stay put because Keith came out of the house once again, this time locking the door behind him, and strode down the garden, past the burning incinerator, to the parking area. Esme listened as the van's engine came to life and then Keith was reversing out of his spot and driving away down the lane from the cottages to the main road.

Esme's whole body relaxed and she exhaled, then drew in several long, deep breaths. She was confident no one was home

CHAPTER 25

or Keith wouldn't have locked the door.

Taking one last look about, she ran across the lawn and used the poker that was lying beside the incinerator to hook the handle of the lid and remove it. The flames had died down somewhat and smoke billowed out into the air. Esme coughed as the fumes caught in her throat. Using the poker again, she delved into the incinerator and fished out the remains of a trainer. She dropped it onto the grass and then smothered it with the tin lid.

When she lifted the lid, the trainer was still smouldering. She hadn't thought much further than this. There was no way she'd be able to take the trainer with her as it was far too hot to handle and might even disintegrate. Anyway, how would she prove where she'd found it if she moved it? Would the photographs be evidence enough, or would they be inadmissible because of her interference? She needed to get the police down here and quickly.

She was just about to call Conor when she had a sudden awareness that she was being watched. She looked up and there was Pippa on the edge of the lawn by the garage.

'What the hell are you doing?' the young woman demanded.

Chapter 26

ESME

Close But Not Close Enough

'Oh, Pippa!' cried Esme, relieved it wasn't Keith who'd come back. 'Thank goodness it's you.'

Pippa frowned and then made her way across the garden to come to stand beside Esme. 'Like I said, what are you doing?' She looked down at the smouldering trainer.

'Have you got a bucket or something I can put this in?' asked Esme. 'I'll explain, I just need to preserve this.'

'OK,' said Pippa slowly. 'There's one in the shed, I'll get it.'

As Pippa went off to get the bucket, Esme ran towards the house and turned on the hosepipe, reeling it out towards the shoe to give it a soaking. 'That should do it,' she said to Pippa, who by now had returned with a bucket. Esme picked up the shoe and dropped it inside.

'Can you please tell me what's going on?' asked Pippa.

Esme paused and took a moment to look at the poor girl. How on earth was she going to tell Pippa her father had killed

CHAPTER 26

Max? And, more to the point, how would she react – especially after the way she'd attacked Isla the other day? She picked her words carefully. 'It's really important that the police get to see this shoe,' she began. 'It could help them with a case they're working on.'

'You're talking to me like I'm a child,' snapped Pippa.

Esme shifted uneasily on her feet. 'Do you know who this shoe belongs to?'

Pippa shrugged. 'My dad, I guess. You're still not telling me what's going on.'

'I think maybe we should wait for the police to get here,' said Esme at last. 'It's probably best if they talk to you.' She took her phone from her pocket, where she'd popped it while dealing with the trainer, and went to locate Conor's name.

'I don't think there's any need for that,' said Pippa.

There was a coldness in her voice that made Esme freeze, her finger hovering over her husband's name. She looked up at Pippa, whose face was relaxed apart from her eyes – they were staring with laser-like intensity at Esme. The glint of something shiny in Pippa's hand caught Esme's attention and when she looked down, she almost dropped her phone in shock. There in the young woman's hand was a Stanley knife with an inch-long blade protruding from the end.

'What are you doing?' Esme stammered.

'Shut up,' commanded Pippa. 'Now, you do what I say, without making a scene. If you scream or shout out, I won't hesitate to use this. And don't think I won't. You know what they say about once you get the taste for blood.'

Esme gulped at the words. She wasn't sure whether or not she believed what Pippa was saying. Was that because she didn't want to believe her? Had they got it wrong about who

245

had killed Max? Too many thoughts swamped her mind and she couldn't think straight. 'Don't do anything silly, now.' Esme heard herself speaking in a much calmer voice than the speed of her beating heart would suggest was possible.

'Don't *you* do anything silly,' countered Pippa. 'Now, drop your phone onto the grass and kick it over to me.'

Esme hesitated. She didn't want to let go of the phone – it was her only lifeline. 'You really don't have to do this,' she said, hoping to buy some time to at least think of a strategy to get herself out of this situation without coming to any harm.

'I told you before ... shut up,' snapped Pippa.

Before Esme knew what was happening, Pippa had closed the space between them and snatched the phone from her hands, shoving it into her jeans pocket, before taking a few steps away. Esme wondered whether she could wrestle the knife from Pippa but wasn't sure she was up to a fight with her – not yet, anyway. Esme needed to keep her cool and wait for the right moment. She had no idea what Pippa had got planned for her but somehow she didn't think it was going to end in a girly chat over tea and cake.

'You know I can help you,' said Esme. 'We can end this calmly without anyone getting hurt and I can make sure Conor knows you've been cooperative and weren't really trying to harm me. We can explain how you've been so distraught over Max's death that you weren't thinking straight; how it was your father who killed Max and what a terrible effect that's had on you while you've been struggling to deal with the grief of losing the love of your life.' Esme was aware she was now gabbling on and from the look of amusement on Pippa's face, she knew it too.

'That's very kind of you, Esme,' said Pippa, 'but we both know that's not going to happen.'

CHAPTER 26

Esme weighed up her options. She could do as Pippa said and go along with her until there was an opportunity to escape somehow, or she could make a break for it now. She could try to dart around the side of Pippa and run down the driveway and out onto the main road, or she could run back through the orchard – which was by far the quicker way into the village, where she might be able to find help.

'Honestly, Pippa, it's the best way. You don't have to do anything silly that will make things worse for you.'

'Ah, if only that were true,' said Pippa, still sounding very amused, before making a move towards Esme again. But she lurched to one side as she stepped into a dip in the ground.

Esme took her chance and sprinted to Pippa's right, giving her a wide berth. She just needed to get past her and out onto the lane. She ran as fast as she could and in her peripheral vision was aware of Pippa moving towards her at speed, the stumble having been nothing more than uneven footing. And then Esme felt the full-body smash of Pippa as she was shoulder-charged and sent flying to the ground, her hands, knees and elbows scuffing into the gravel bed of the parking area.

Ignoring the pain that shot through her shoulder and the grazing on her skin from the gravel, Esme tried to get to her feet but Pippa shoved her to the ground, grabbing a handful of Esme's hair and pushing hard into the back of her neck. Esme's face was embedded in the small stones and then she saw the blade of the Stanley knife in front of her eyes.

'Stay still!' Pippa hissed into her ear.

Esme could feel the warmth of Pippa's breath on her face. 'OK, OK, I'm sorry.' Esme needed to buy some more time.

'Now, get up, nice and slowly,' ordered Pippa, still clenching

Esme's hair in her fist. She yanked Esme's head back, forcing her spine into an arch. 'Over to the garage.'

Esme staggered towards the side door of the garage, which Pippa made her open before frogmarching her inside. It was dark inside the garage, with the only light coming from the open door. As Esme's eyes became accustomed to the dark, the far side of the wall came into focus. It was lined with shelving units full of plastic boxes, all labelled up with the names of various computer components. The near side had several upright toolboxes. Dotted around was the usual garden paraphernalia – spare fold-out chairs, a lawnmower and some outdoor games that probably hadn't seen the light of day since Pippa was a child. The garage obviously wasn't used for keeping vehicles in. Esme glanced to the up-and-over garage door with a rope handle hanging down that enabled the door to be lifted from the inside. It wasn't an option for escape – it would take too long to get the door open, even if she could free herself from Pippa's grasp.

'This way,' said Pippa, pulling Esme to the side.

Pippa pulled a box down from the shelf and tried to open the lid but with one hand still holding Esme's hair and the knife in the other, it was proving difficult. Pippa put the knife on the workbench so she could remove the lid. Without stopping to think, Esme held on to her own hair and spun around, causing Pippa's arm to be wrenched over. Pippa cried out in surprise and pain, releasing Esme's hair. Esme pushed Pippa away and ran towards the open side door but, again, Pippa was too quick and had now managed to grab Esme's jacket, slowing her escape. The two women grappled with each other in the garage, Esme desperately trying to get away. She shrugged her jacket from her shoulders and just as she thought she was

CHAPTER 26

going to make it, something hard smashed into the side of her head and she blacked out.

Chapter 27

BELLA

A Missing Sister

The mood was sombre when Bella arrived at her parents' house after school with Jacob, Amelia and Dylan. Although her dad was home, there was no reason to celebrate. This was just the beginning of trying to prove him innocent.

She hugged her dad tightly, not really knowing what to say, and was overcome with emotion as he returned the embrace.

'Ah, there, there, Bells,' he said. 'Don't be crying. It's going to be OK. Come on, sweetheart.'

'Sorry, I can't help it,' Bella managed to say when she eventually got her emotions under control. 'I'm just so glad to see you.'

She dried her eyes with a tissue from her bag and, with her father's arm around her shoulder, walked through to the living room to join her mother and Isla. The French doors were open and the children were already playing outside. Her father had built a den at the end of the garden from willow-tree branches

CHAPTER 27

and had installed a big wooden climbing frame, complete with slide, swings, and a castle at the top. Jacob was adept at keeping up with his cousins, his fearless attitude sometimes leaving Bella's heart in her mouth.

'Sit down here,' said Frank, guiding her towards the chair near the French doors.

'Do you want a drink?' asked Isla. She didn't wait for an answer but got up and made eye contact with Bella, then paused in the doorway with her hand on the side of the door, tapping it three times with her forefinger. 'I'll make some tea.'

Bella didn't miss the unspoken gesture. It was the code she and Isla had used when they were teenagers living at home and it meant that one of them had something important to say to the other out of earshot of their parents. 'I'll give you a hand. I need to nip to the loo anyway.' She got to her feet and hurried after her sister, who was waiting in the kitchen. 'What's up? And where's Esme?'

'I was going to ask you that,' replied Isla. 'I thought she would've got here earlier, but then I thought maybe she was coming with you.'

'Have you tried to call her?'

'Her mobile just goes straight to voicemail and the office to answerphone.'

'Weird. What about Conor?'

'He said he'd arranged to meet her here. He didn't seem that bothered, but you know they haven't exactly been getting on lately so I didn't know if they were really talking.'

'Hmm,' mused Bella. 'Did Conor say when he was getting here?'

With that, the doorbell buzzed. 'Conor?' said Isla, going out to the hallway. 'I'll get it!' she called in the direction of the living room. She returned to the kitchen with Conor in tow.

'Is something wrong?' asked Conor, looking from one sister to the other.

'Esme's still not here,' said Isla. 'We haven't heard from her and she's not answering her phone.'

'I've come straight from work,' explained Conor. 'We didn't make a particular arrangement, just said we'd meet up here. I assumed she'd come when the kids were out of school. She said something about closing early.'

The ping of a text message broke through the conversation. 'That's probably her now.' Conor took his phone from his pocket and looked at the screen. 'Yep. Here we go ... Going to be late. Got caught up with something. See you as soon as possible.' Conor turned the phone to show Isla and Bella.

'Text her back and ask if she's OK,' instructed Bella.

'I'm sure it's not necessary,' Conor began.

'Text her,' said Bella again, with more insistence in her voice. 'Please.'

Conor eyed her for a moment before turning his phone back and tapping in a message. 'You OK? Call me. Urgent ... There, how's that?'

'Send it.' Bella exchanged a look with Isla.

'I'm sure she's fine,' continued Conor as he pressed the send button. 'Happy?'

'Has it been delivered?' Bella wasn't satisfied. She had an uneasy feeling that wasn't going away. If anything, it was increasing by the second.

Conor frowned at his phone. 'It's gone through as a text message rather than an iMessage.'

'Which means?' prompted Bella.

'That her phone is off,' supplied Isla and then, sounding

CHAPTER 27

rather more anxious, asked, 'Why would her phone be off when she's just messaged us? Esme never lets her phone run out of charge. She never switches it off. She always puts it on silent if she's in a meeting.'

'Isla's right. There's something wrong,' said Bella.

'Is there something you're not telling me?' asked Conor. 'Has she gone off on one of her mad private-investigator capers? I warned her about this.'

'Tell him,' said Isla.

'Yes. Tell me.' Conor squared his shoulders. 'I thought she was coming straight here from work. Let me try calling her.' He hit the call button but Esme's phone went straight to voicemail.

'See, that's what keeps happening,' said Isla. Her voice reflected the fear that was apparent on her face and made Bella think back to when Isla was little and used to get scared about things – it was her mouse voice. They used to tease her about it. The higher the anxiety levels got, the squeakier and quieter the mouse voice became.

'Can you track her iPhone?' asked Bella.

'I don't think it will work without her phone being on,' replied Conor.

Bella watched as he nonetheless tried to see where Esme was. He shook his head. 'No, it's not working. Where might she be going? Either of you got any ideas?'

Bella and Isla exchanged another look. 'I don't know,' said Isla.

'Now's not the time for sister solidarity and secrets,' said Conor. 'If she's on some fact-finding hunt and has got herself into trouble, I need at least some idea of where to start looking for her.'

'We genuinely don't know,' said Bella. 'But we were talking about Keith Bonham before we left the funeral parlour.'

'Bonham? What's he got to do with it?'

'It's a long story ...' began Bella.

'Just cut to the chase,' said Conor.

'That video footage I found; we think it was Keith Bonham who was creeping into the back of the schoolhouse.'

'Bonham? Why?'

'The pen he dropped — I saw him using the exact same pen when I was at the vicarage this morning,' revealed Bella. 'I went and told Esme, and she said we needed more proof than that.'

'For Christ's sake!' Conor ran a hand across his chin. 'And she went to see him?'

'I don't know. She didn't say what she was doing.' Bella looked over at her sister.

'She didn't say anything to me about it either,' said Isla.

Conor took another look at his phone and Bella could see he was scrolling through photos. He glanced up at her. 'Just checking the photo stream. We share the iCloud so we can see each other's photos. You never know, she might have taken some pictures before her phone went off.' Bella was glad Esme had married a police detective — she would never have thought to check the camera roll.

'Please let her have taken some photos,' squeaked Isla, crossing her fingers.

'Aha! Here we go.' Conor's frown deepened. 'Christ! It's Keith Bonham in his garden. There's an incinerator. She must've taken these earlier this afternoon. There are more.' Conor turned the phone so Bella and Isla could see. The last picture was of Esme herself, apparently crouched down somewhere as if hiding.

'It looks like the side of a shed,' said Bella, taking the phone. 'Wait, there's a video.' She pressed play and the three of them watched as, with shaky camerawork, the screen first settled on the wooden structure and then panned up to reveal a scene filmed through the window. 'That's Keith.'

'He's smashing something up.' Isla peered closer. 'It looks like a mobile phone.'

After a few seconds the video ended. 'I'm going over to the Bonhams,' said Conor. 'This doesn't look good at all. I could bloody kill your sister sometimes. The lot of you have been driving me mad with your sleuthing around and now look what's happened!'

Bella bristled at her brother-in-law's harsh words, partly because there was a certain amount of truth in them but she also felt offended by the lack of credit they were being shown for what they'd discovered so far. 'Now's not the time to give us a lecture,' she said. 'Besides, if the police had done their job properly in the first place, we wouldn't have had to resort to this sleuthing.' She emphasised the last word to underline her contempt for the description.

'Point taken,' replied Conor. 'But now's also not the time to blame the police.'

'Let's stop this point scoring and go and look for her.' It was Isla. Bella and Conor turned to look at the youngest Fairfax sister.

Bella raised her eyebrows. 'Since when did you become the shouty one? That's my job.'

Isla poked her tongue out at Bella and the usual order of hierarchy was resumed.

Conor by now had left the kitchen and Bella could hear him

talking to her parents. 'I've got a call in from work. Can't stop. Nice to see you, Frank, we'll catch up soon. See you later, Marion.'

Bella met him at the door. 'I'm coming with you,' she said.

'Me too.' Isla joined her sister.

'I haven't got time to argue with you both about all the reasons why you shouldn't, only for you to ignore me,' said Conor. 'Just let your mum and dad know you're leaving. I don't want them stressing out about where you are.'

It was Bella's turn to pop her head around the door. 'Sorry, Mum, Dad – I'm just popping out to the shop with Isla. Can you keep an eye on the kids? Great. See you in a bit.'

'Bye!' called Isla as she followed Bella out the front door.

They jumped into Conor's car, Bella in the passenger seat and Isla in the back. The interior smelt of leather upholstery and white-linen air freshener. 'Do you need to call for back-up?' asked Bella, fastening her seat belt.

Conor gave her a sceptical look. 'I hope not. In fact, I suspect this is all a bit of an overreaction. I'll call for back-up if I think it's needed.' With that, Conor started the car engine and sped out of the driveway and onto Lantern Road, heading into the centre of the village. He didn't waste any time in whizzing down the High Street, turning onto the Great Midham road and after he'd taken the sharp left turn onto the main road, which went over the new bridge towards Appleside, he accelerated hard. Bella's stomach gave a little flip as they hurtled over the hump of the bridge. Despite Conor's calm exterior, the speed of his driving was surely a more accurate gauge of his anxiety level.

His wheels cut into the gravel parking space at the back of number 1 Orchard Cottages and he leapt out of the car. 'Esme!'

CHAPTER 27

he shouted as he ran into the garden, and Bella noticed him clocking the incinerator as he raced up to the back door. Bella and Isla followed in his wake, coming to standstill behind him as he hammered on the back door for a third time, calling out to Esme, Keith, Maureen and Pippa.

'There's no one here,' said Bella.

'We've got to find her,' said Isla, sounding frantic.

Conor was already stalking back down the garden path. He gestured towards the incinerator as he passed it. 'Forensics will have a good look through that,' he said, before heading for the summer house. 'Empty,' he declared and turned his attention to the garage. He stopped short at the door. 'What the …?'

Bella looked at the door frame. 'Oh, God! Is that blood?'

'Looks like it. Wait there.' Taking a deep breath, he opened the door and peered inside the garage.

Bella wanted to push him out of the way and rush in there. What if Esme was lying on the floor injured and needing medical attention? She forced herself to let Conor do his thing. He was, after all, a police officer who was trained to deal with situations just like this.

'Is she there?' Bella called out after what felt like several minutes.

Conor came out shaking his head. 'No. But there's blood on the floor. Whoever was in there sustained some sort of injury and my guess is they touched the wound and then the door frame on the way out, hence the blood on there.'

'She's been injured? What if she's concussed and doesn't know where she is or what she's doing?' Bella's heart rate was off the scale and she struggled to catch her breath. 'We've got to find her.'

'I'm calling for back-up now,' said Conor. 'One second ...'

Bella put her arm around Isla, as much to reassure herself as her sister. 'Don't worry, Isla. We're going to find her. We've got to.'

'They're sending two cars over from Great Midham,' said Conor as he finished his call. 'They're going to be at least twenty to twenty-five minutes. They're also checking the hospital in case someone's found her and taken her in.'

'What are we going to do?' asked Isla.

'We're going to bloody well find her,' replied Bella. 'Come on.'

'Get in the car; it will be easier to look,' said Conor. 'I don't think she's gone back into the village – we would've seen her, or someone else would've and then rung me or your dad. We'll head out on the Appleside road.'

Chapter 28

ESME

No Time For the Faint of Heart

The first thing Esme became aware of was something cold and hard pressing against her face. The next thing was the shooting pain in her head. She went to move and realised she was lying on a cold, hard surface. Gingerly she opened her eyes and squinted as she tried to focus on her surroundings. It was dark, but not night-time dark. She closed her eyes and opened them again, staring into the murkiness as the shapes and shadows around her began to form recognisable shapes.

'Oh, good, glad you've woken up,' came a voice Esme recognised but couldn't place.

It took her a moment to register that it belonged to Pippa Bonham. Esme's fingers sought out the pain in her head and she flinched as she touched something wet and sticky in her hair. 'I'm bleeding,' she croaked.

'Yeah. Sorry about that, but you didn't leave me with much choice,' said Pippa. 'Please don't try to do that again or I might have to hit you a bit harder next time. Besides, I need you to be able to walk.'

Esme pushed herself to her hands and knees, the pain in her head making her wince with the movement. She felt groggy and a little confused. She couldn't quite remember what had happened. 'Why am I here?'

Pippa laughed. 'Do you really think I'm going to fall for that one – a convenient loss of memory?'

By now Esme was in a kneeling position and as her eyes adjusted to dim light, she could see Pippa sitting on a fold-out garden chair. She had something in her hand that just caught the light coming under the side door. Esme's breath snagged in her throat. It was a Stanley knife.

The memory of what had brought her here assaulted her with such clarity that she lost her balance and had to grab on to the edge of a nearby cardboard box.

'Ah, I think you've had a rather rapid recollection of events,' observed Pippa. 'Jolly good. It saves me having to go through it all.' She got up from her seat. 'Now, I want you to stand up very slowly.'

Esme didn't have any choice; speed was not something she could muster right now – not with her head pounding the way that it was. 'What now?' she asked once she was on her feet.

'We're going for a little walk.'

'You know Conor will be here any minute now, probably with back-up,' said Esme, hoping to stall for time. She bloody well hoped she was right about her husband.

'I don't think so,' said Pippa with a faux apologetic smile. 'It's handy you have Touch ID on your phone – I used your fingerprint while you were out cold and texted him to say you were going to be late. I've also switched your phone off so he can't work out where you are from the GPS.'

Esme swayed on her feet. That was not the reply she wanted to hear. 'Pippa, I don't know what's happened but you can still back out of this,' she began, with a vague recollection she'd already said this before. Her head was pounding and it was hard to think clearly. 'Don't try to cover up for your dad. He's not here. You don't have to do this. You don't have to be like him.'

Pippa laughed. 'Oh, shut up, Esme. You've no idea what you're talking about. Now, turn around and clasp your hands together behind your head.' Esme could hear Pippa opening the garage door and the space was flooded with the early-evening sun. 'Right, slowly walk backwards out of the garage towards me,' instructed Pippa, who was now holding a length of timber she'd picked up from a pile of offcuts in the garage.

Esme did as she was told, staggering slightly as she backed out of the garage. She paused and held on to the door frame to steady herself. 'Where are we going?' she asked.

'Don't ask questions. Now, keep moving. That's it, and stop there.' Without shifting her gaze from Esme, Pippa closed the door to the garage. 'We're going to walk along side by side as if we're the best of friends. I'm going to link arms with you, like this ...' She slipped her arm through the crook of her elbow, still holding the length of wood. '... and then, with this hand, I'm going to hold the knife right by your side. Don't even think about trying to escape – I'm not scared to use it.' With that, she dug the tip of the blade into Esme's arm and nicked the skin.

Esme screamed and tried to pull away but was surprised by how strong Pippa was. 'You've cut me!'

'Mm, I know. That's just to show you I'm prepared to use

the knife. And don't worry, it's just a scratch. You're not going to bleed to death.' Then she laughed. 'No, definitely not *bleed*.'

Esme was frantic. Pippa sounded so callous and removed from what she was doing. Esme could hardly believe it was the same Pippa who worked in the café, all meek and mild; the same Pippa who had been friends with Isla since school. Talk about still waters running deep. By now Pippa was forcing her past the side of the house and out through the front gate onto the river path. She turned right and headed away from the village.

'Where are we going?' Esme asked again.

'Please stop asking questions,' said Pippa. 'It's tedious. "Where are we going? Pippa, where are we going?"' she said, mimicking Esme's voice.

'Why are you protecting your dad?' asked Esme. If she could just tap into Pippa's psyche, she might be able to save herself – for she was certain Pippa didn't have a happy ending planned.

'Boring question, Esme!'

Esme looked over her shoulder. There was no one about. They were now out of the village and the Applemere road on the other side of the river had turned away from the water's edge as it wound its way to the next village. She needed to get Pippa talking. She tried again. 'Why did your dad kill Max? Did he find out about the two of you?'

'Now, that's not quite such a boring question,' replied Pippa. 'Only you're way off.'

'Your mother?' ventured Esme. She knew it had to be one of them.

'Try again.'

Esme swallowed hard as she considered the only remaining option. 'You? You killed Max?'

CHAPTER 28

'Well done, you got there in the end.'

They were now approaching the old toll bridge that gave Toll Farm its link to the main road, across the river. The farm was very run-down, as Ted Hammond was in his nineties and unable to work the farm like he used to, instead renting it out to younger farmers. Esme knew there was no one up here other than Ted – and he wouldn't be able to help her, even if she could get to his house somehow.

The bridge itself was only just wide enough to get a tractor over and the metal handrail – more like a scaffold pole – was bent out of shape where some of the larger farm vehicles had misjudged the dimensions and caught it over the years. Esme shivered as they stepped onto the bridge. It was desolate and isolated out here at Toll Bridge. Apart from those of the farm, the only building around was the World-War-Two pillbox sited next to the bridge, on the riverbank. When they were kids, they were told the pillbox was haunted by a soldier of the Home Guard who had fallen asleep on duty and got himself locked in; he hadn't been found for nearly a week and by that time had died. The village kids used to dare each other to go up to Toll Bridge and spend the night in the old pillbox. Normally Esme would dismiss any talk of ghosts but today, despite the warmth of the sun still lingering in the dusk air, she felt cold with fear on the inside, the notion of a nasty death happening suddenly seeming very real. If Pippa had killed Max, the man she claimed to love, then Esme had no doubt that she wouldn't hesitate to kill again.

'I thought you loved Max,' she began, stalling for more time in the hope that Conor would come and find her. 'How did it all go so wrong? What happened?'

Pippa paused before pushing Esme against the railing. 'You

really want to know?'

'Yes. I do.' Esme gave her what she hoped was a compassionate look. 'It must have been awful, whatever it was.'

Pippa eyed her with suspicion. 'It won't make any difference, you know. If I tell you, it won't stop me doing what I have to do.'

Esme swallowed hard and took a deep breath to try to remain calm. 'I am genuinely interested.'

Pippa shrugged. 'OK, but I want you on the other side of the railings.' She gestured with the Stanley knife.

Esme looked down at the tidal river below. If she ended up in the water she would be in serious danger. The underwater currents would drag her down and sweep her out to sea in a matter of minutes, especially now that the river looked to be heading towards Applemere, which meant the tide was on its way out. She looked back at Pippa, who thrust the blade towards her, slicing Esme's blouse.

'OK, OK, I'm doing it!' Esme dipped under the railing and, holding on to the metal pole, tried not to look at her feet, which were now on a ledge no more than fifty centimetres wide. 'Tell me about Max,' she said quickly.

'I loved Max and he loved me,' began Pippa. 'That is something you need to understand. We never meant to fall in love, it just happened. You can't choose things like that.'

'No, you can't,' replied Esme. 'Not matters of the heart. How did it begin?'

'I offered to help out at the staff Christmas party. I helped with the catering and it meant I got to spend time with Max, sorting out the arrangements,' said Pippa. For the first time that evening there was a softer tone to her voice. 'We didn't mean to fall in love. It just happened.'

CHAPTER 28

'And you felt you had to keep it a secret?'

There was a slight drop in Pippa's shoulders. 'Yeah. We didn't tell anyone because we knew it would complicate things. We were going to leave after Max retired. We were going to live in Spain. He's got – had – an apartment there. We were going to be so happy, just the two of us.' There was a wistful look in Pippa's eyes for a moment but it was soon replaced with something harder. 'I knew my parents would freak if they found out. I didn't tell them, but my mum got suspicious. She was talking about Max leaving and how he'd have to clear everything out of the Old School House and I made a stupid comment about how he was wondering what to do with all his photos. I tried to cover it up but it didn't get past Mum. She didn't say anything at the time, but she started spying on him and me.'

'Spying on you? Oh, that's awful,' said Esme, trying to sound sympathetic.

'I know, right! She saw me going in there one night. I didn't even know she was there and I was always really careful. She then told my dad, and that's when it all started to go wrong.'

There was genuine pain on Pippa's face and in any other circumstances Esme might have felt sorry for her. 'What happened?' she coaxed, keeping her voice soft.

'Dad went mad. He'd been friends with Max since they were kids. He said it was sick. He called Max all sorts of things. He made our relationship sound dirty and sordid. It was *never* any of those things. Never!' Pippa's fists balled and her knuckles went white as they gripped the Stanley knife. 'Dad said he was going to see Max. When I told Max, he said not to worry, that it would be OK and he wasn't frightened of Dad.'

'It's good that he stood by you,' said Esme.

'But he didn't!' hissed Pippa. 'That's just it. He didn't stand by me.' A sob escaped and she swiped the tears away with the cuff of her sleeve. 'I went to see him and he told me it was all over. That we had no future. It was all over. Just like that.'

'Oh no, I'm so sorry.'

'I pleaded with him. I begged him but he wouldn't change his mind. He said it had been a silly fling. He said it wasn't Dad who'd made him change his mind, but I think it was. I think Dad bribed him.'

'Why? Did Max say that?' Esme looked away from Pippa, casting her eyes back along the river towards Applemere. There was not a soul about, not even a car passing on the main road. Where the hell was Conor? She felt they were coming to the end of what had happened and then Pippa's attention would be back on what to do with her.

'No. But I heard Mum and Dad arguing about money. They thought I was out, but I was in the summer house and they were in the garden. Mum was saying they couldn't spare any more money. She said six thousand pounds was way too much and they only had four thousand left in their savings. Dad was adamant he was going to pay Max.' Pippa kicked the upright of the railing. 'Bastard! He'd paid Max off, and Max was accepting it and wanted more. Can you believe that? They all betrayed me. I was furious. I went to the schoolhouse.'

'I guess he was surprised when you knocked on the door,' said Esme, trying to work out why Pippa hadn't been seen on CCTV.

'Well, that's just it. I did surprise him but that's because I let myself in with the spare key Mum has.'

'Why did you do that?'

Pippa shrugged. 'I was angry. Basically, taking money from

my parents was like putting a price on me. How could he do that if he really loved me? So, I thought I'd get that money back. I felt sorry for Mum. She didn't deserve to lose all her savings just because dad agreed to pay Max off.'

'Were you going to steal the money, then? Is that why you crept into the house?'

'Pretty much. I thought Max would be out at the Round Table meeting he goes to every month. But he was there and we ended up arguing about why he finished our relationship. It was a bad argument.' Pippa began crying but she let the tears fall unchecked. 'He was speaking to me like I was a child or an annoying parent. I was so upset but he didn't care. And then, I just got angry. Like, really mad.'

'You poor thing.' Esme scanned the road and footpath. Still no sign of anyone.

'I asked him how he could be so cruel. And you know what he said?' Pippa wasn't looking at Esme now. Her arms rested on the railing and her head was bowed.

'What did he say?' Esme took the opportunity to take just a couple of steps sideways, a little away from Pippa.

Pippa looked up, her face contorting with pain. 'He said he hadn't really loved me. He was just flattered and now he was bored. He was going to find someone his own age.' Pippa drew in a deep breath, the tears drying up. 'I flipped. I couldn't cope with that. He'd left the cricket bat on the desk and I just grabbed it. The next thing I remember is seeing Max on the floor covered in blood. He was … dead. I'd killed him.'

'Oh, Pippa. You've carried that with you all this time.' Esme wasn't sure what to say, but she just wanted to keep Pippa talking in the hope that help would arrive in time.

'I phoned my mum. I didn't know what to do. Her and Dad

came over and said they'd sort it all out.'

'That's what parents do,' remarked Esme, wondering how far she'd go to protect her own children.

'I hate them,' announced Pippa. 'If they hadn't interfered in the first place, I know Max wouldn't have finished with me. The more I think about it, the more I wish I had just been patient. I'm sure he was just going along with it and then, once he had the money, he was going to come for me.'

Esme doubted that but she was wise enough not to challenge Pippa on this precious point. 'Do you think it might be good to speak to a professional about all this? They might be able to help you. And if you tell the police what happened, they would see that it wasn't cold-blooded murder. There will be so many people who want to help you.'

Pippa stood up and shook her head. 'No. No one can know. Mum and Dad will get in trouble for aiding and abetting. No one will understand, anyway. Whatever happens, I'll still be charged with murder or, at the very least, manslaughter. It was quite handy your dad going to see Max that night. My dad was able to cut the CCTV footage so I didn't appear on it.'

'Wait, what about the pen and the note about blackmailing Max – was that all to do with you?'

'Actually, the note was my mum's idea, to put the police off. She left it there hoping they'd find it, or someone else would. Dad had been back to look for the money. He was furious it had been found but, of course, couldn't say it was his. He blamed Mum for not telling him about the money being there but, you see, she didn't care about that. She said leaving the money in the secret drawer made the blackmail story more authentic. Dad was livid.'

'Honestly, Pippa, I don't think it will be as bad as you think.

CHAPTER 28

You just need to tell the police. If you tell them everything, they'll tell the judge and your sentence will be more lenient.'

'My mum won't be able to cope if she goes to prison,' said Pippa. 'You might think I'm cold-hearted, but my mum is the innocent one. She was only trying to protect her family. I can't let anything happen to her. I'm really sorry, but that means I can't let you go home.' She picked up the length of wood she'd brought with her. 'I'll make it as painless as possible. When they find your body, they'll think you struck your head on the way down.'

'But no one will believe it was an accident. I mean, why would I be up here in the first place?' Esme could hear the wobble in her own voice and she had to adjust her grip on the railing as the sweat in her palms was making it hard to hold on.

'Because you can't face the shame of what's happening to your father. You're married to a police officer – how can you hold your head up high if your father is a convicted murderer? It will be too much for you.'

Pippa raised the piece of wood, holding it with two hands as if she was waiting for the pitcher to throw the ball in a baseball game.

'Don't do this! Pippa! Please!' Esme cried out. She let out a scream as Pippa swung the wood at her. Esme ducked and managed to avoid the first blow. The wood smashed onto the railing, sending a fierce vibration through the metal.

Pippa raised the weapon again and took another lunge at Esme. This time it caught Esme on the shoulder.

Esme screamed as the impact forced her to let go with one hand. She turned just in time to see Pippa aim at the fingers of her other hand. Her instincts kicked in and she let go. For a moment she teetered on the edge of the plinth, in that perfectly balanced defying-gravity position where the whole world freezes.

And then she was falling, rushing towards the dark, cold water.

Somewhere in the background she was aware of an engine and shouting voices but before she had time to give them another thought, her body plummeted into the river. She went under, squeezing closed her eyes and mouth. She could feel the drag of the water pulling her down. Esme fought against the undercurrent. Her feet hit something solid and she used it to push away, sending her body towards the surface of the water.

And then someone was in the water beside her. She grabbed onto them, spluttering as she surfaced, taking in gasps of air.

'Grab hold of this!' It was Conor's voice. 'Esme! Grab hold of the life ring!'

Somehow her body responded to the instructions and she grasped the orange life ring, hooking her arm over the side of it.

'That's it. Don't let go.' She could feel Conor's hand on her shoulder and she looked up to see Bella and Isla pulling the other end of the rope, dragging her to the safety of the riverbank.

Esme clambered out of the river, crawling on her hands and knees, coughing and spluttering. She fell into the arms of Conor, who was panting hard from the exertion. 'Oh, thank God!' gasped Esme. She became aware of a flurry of activity up on the bridge. Blue lights flashed all around her. 'Pippa?'

'The police have got her,' said Conor. 'It's all over.' He hugged her close and Esme had never been so grateful to feel the strong arms of her husband.

Chapter 29

ESME

The End and The Beginning

'So, how are my three favourite ladies?' said Conor, joining Esme and her sisters in the garden of his in-laws.

'Hey, I hope I'm your favourite of favourites,' said Esme.

'Of course, but it's a brave man who disrespects the Fairfax sisters. I'm just covering all bases.' He gave Esme a peck on the cheek.

'Ah, still true love after all these years,' said Bella.

They were gathered in Frank and Marion's back garden for a barbecue to celebrate Conor's birthday. Frank was busy with the grill, turning sausages and flipping burgers, while Marion was in the kitchen and was insisting they all leave her alone while she put the finishing touches to her pièce de résistance: strawberry-meringue layer cake.

In the months since the Bonhams' arrest and subsequent trial and conviction of offences ranging from murder, attempted murder, kidnap and perverting the course of justice,

Marion had made a steady recovery back to her more confident self, much to the relief of the whole family.

'Speaking of true love,' said Conor with a mischievous glint in his eye, 'where's Ned?' Esme nudged him in the ribs. 'What? I was only saying.'

Bella scowled at her sister. 'As you well know, Conor, Ned and I have been friends for years – practically all our lives – and that's all. And you shouldn't listen to tittle-tattle from your wife.'

'Tittle-tattle!' Esme gave her best offended face. 'I never tittle-tattle, I merely discuss.'

'Tittle-tattle,' confirmed Isla. 'Anyway, there's nothing wrong with Ned. At least Bella has good taste.'

Esme gave her sister a sympathetic smile. Isla still wasn't quite over Dan Starling. 'Don't worry, your Prince Charming will come,' she said.

'Sometimes, they're right there in front of you,' said Isla. 'You just don't know it.'

Bella threw her hands up the air. 'Ned and I are just good friends!'

'That's what they all say,' replied Esme.

The sound of Conor's phone ringing broke up the debate. 'Murphy here,' said Conor. Esme rested her head on her husband's shoulder. She was so glad things between them were back on an even footing. She felt Conor's body tense as he listened to the call. 'OK. I'll be right there.' He finished his call and got to his feet. 'I'm really sorry. It's work.'

'But it's your birthday,' said Esme, disappointed that he had to rush off.

'It's serious. I'm the nearest.'

'What is it that's so serious you have to go now?' asked Esme, thinking of the cake her mum was so excited about having made as a surprise for Conor.

'About as serious as it gets,' he said.

'A murder?' Bella sat forwards.

'Where? Here in Applewick?' asked Isla, putting her drink down on the table.

'Oh, God, it is a murder, isn't it?' said Bella.

Conor held his hands up in surrender. 'A death, that's all,' he said in exasperation.

'But a suspicious one,' said Esme.

'I won't know until I get there.'

'And where is *there*?' asked Isla.

'Honestly, do I ever get any peace from you Fairfax women?' Conor let out a sigh. 'In Applemere. Now, you three' – he pointed his finger from one sister to the other – 'are not to get involved. None of this Applewick Village Mystery Club business. Do you understand?'

Esme nodded earnestly. 'Of course.'

'Hmm. I mean it.' He bent down and kissed his wife. 'No. Getting. Involved. Any of you.' He gave them another stern look before offering a quick explanation to his in-laws and then leaving.

Esme turned to her sisters. 'So, we shouldn't get involved, then.'

'No, we shouldn't,' agreed Bella.

'Not at all,' added Isla, sitting back and gazing out across the lawn.

There was a small silence before Esme spoke again. 'Technically, I didn't make any promises.'

'Neither did I,' said Bella, feigning nonchalance.

'That makes three of us,' said Isla.

They looked at each other and grinned.

Esme raised her glass. 'I declare the Applewick Village Mystery Club open for business,' she announced as the three sisters clinked glasses.

Acknowledgements

Dear Reader

I do hope you enjoyed meeting the Fairfax sisters and joining them on their first murder mystery. If you want to keep up with their sleuthing adventures, check out the next in the series.

DEATH AT APPLEWICK MANOR
Book 2 of the Applewick Village Mystery series

I always love hearing from and keeping in touch with readers, if you'd like to join my newsletter group, and be the first to get exclusive content, sneak previews, early news of books, special offers, competitions and giveaways, please head over to my website (suefortin.com) or ebook readers click the link below.

SUE FORTIN NEWSLETTER SIGN UP

***

The Applewick series has been in my head and heart for a long time. I had always wanted to write more of a cosy mystery series, being a big fan of suspense and mystery books, films and shows, the genre always finds its way into whatever I write. The same could be said for writing about families and it felt natural to revolve the series around three sisters.

It wasn't until 2020 that I had the chance to start the first book and I'm grateful for all the encouragement and enthusiasm my idea was greeted with by friends and family. They have been amazing in their unwavering support.

I'd also like to say a big thank you for my editor, Katharine Walkden, who has helped me shape and polish this book. I'm sure I wouldn't be at this stage without her. Also, much gratitude, to my wonderful ARC team who have read an early copy of this book and given such great feedback.

Thank you for visiting Applewick and if you enjoyed your virtual stay, I'd love it if you were able to leave a review as it really does help readers discover my books.

In the meantime, I hope you pay the village another visit and discover the secrets of Applewick Manor!

Best wishes
   Sue

About the Author

I write mystery, suspense and romance and am a USA Today bestseller and Amazon UK #1 and Amazon US #3 bestseller. I have sold over a million copies of my books and been translated into multiple languages.

I also write historical fiction as Suzanne Fortin, where those stories are predominantly dual timeline and set in France. My books feature courageous women in extraordinary circumstances with love and family at the heart. My book "All That We Have Lost" won the Romantic Novelists' Association's Jackie Collins Romantic Thriller Award in 2022.

You can connect with me on:
- https://suefortin.com
- https://twitter.com/suefortin1
- https://www.facebook.com/suefortinauthor

Subscribe to my newsletter:
✉ https://mailchi.mp/3ccb0e8d2d98/newsletter-sign-up

Printed in Great Britain
by Amazon